HEALING FOR MY SOUL

A HENDERSON FAMILY NOVEL

MONICA WALTERS

INTRODUCTION

Hello, readers!

Thank you for purchasing and/or downloading this book. This work of art contains *explicit language, talk of rape, moments of grief,* and *lewd sex scenes*. It also contains moments of *depression and anxiety* due to the death of a loved one. This book is an insta-love story, as most of my books tend to be. If any of the previously mentioned offend you or serve as triggers for unpleasant times, please do NOT read.

    This is a Henderson family novel, and most of the sub characters in this book have their own novels as well. There are some issues that are spoken of in this book that happened in previous books, mainly in *Let Me Ride, Better the Second Time Around, A Country Hood Christmas with the Hendersons,* and *Where Is The Love*, that I don't go into great detail about. It's in your best interest to read them in this order though. Here's the list:

<u>The Country Hood Love Stories</u>
8 Seconds to Love- Legend and Harper
Breaking Barriers to Your Heart- Red and Shana
Training My Heart to Love You- Zayson and Kortlynn

INTRODUCTION

<u>*The Hendersons*</u>
Blindsided by Love- Storm and Aspen
Ignite My Soul- Jasper and Chasity
Come and Get Me- Tiffany and Ryder
In Way Too Deep- Kenny and Keisha
You Belong to Me- Shylou and Cass
Found Love in A Rider- Malachi and Danica
Let Me Ride- Aston and Vida
Better the Second Time Around- Chrissy and LaKeith
I Wish I Could Be The One- Jenahra and Carter
I Wish I Could Be The One 2- WJ and Olivia
Put That on Everything: A Henderson Family Novella- all the Hendersons and spouses
What's It Gonna Be?- Marcus and Synthia
Someone Like You- Nesha and Lennox
A Country Hood Christmas with the Hendersons- all the Hendersons feat. Nate Guillory
Where Is The Love- Jessica and Brixton
Don't Walk Away- Decaurey and Tyeis

Also, please remember that your reality isn't everyone's reality. What may seem unrealistic to you could be very real for someone else. But also keep in mind that, despite the previous statement, this is a fictional story.

If you are okay with the previously mentioned warnings, I hope that you enjoy the story of Jakari Bolton (Henderson) and Yendi Odom.

Monica

Dedication…

Divine,

I am so happy I was able to make your wish come true! I want you to know that I didn't slut you out by page twelve, but y'all were on your way. I think it happened by page thirty. LOL!

Thank you so much for everything you do for us independent authors, by sharing your reads on TikTok. It's people like you that get our names and work out there for others to enjoy.

Thank you for allowing me to use your photos for promotion with those nasty ass quotes. LOL! The Hendersons love them some BBWs, so when I was tagged in your video by one of my readers, I knew you would be perfect for Jakari.

I hope I met your expectations from my statement about 'slutting you out respectfully' in my comment on your TikTok post. Yendi was a joy to write, although she was dealing with some extremely heavy issues in this book.

Readers, please go and follow @adivinefemme on TikTok for her endless book recommendations, to be thoroughly entertained, to be put in your place (LOL!), and to learn interesting things about her and her outlook on life itself. Since she is pleasing to the eye, it will be easy. Jakari loved those lips in the story! LOL! There is also a Linktree in her profile to access her initiatives.

Again, Divine, thank you so much for serving as the character inspiration for Yendi Odom, and I hope you feel I did you justice after reading. Much love!

Monica Walters

Henderson Family and Friends Family Chart
Wesley and Joan Henderson (Patriarch and Matriarch)

Wesley Jr. & Olivia
Nesha (WJ's daughter w/ Evette)
Shakayla & Chenetra
(WJ's daughters w/ ex-wife, Sharon)
Decaurey (Olivia's son)

Jenahra & Carter
Jessica & Jacob (Joseph's kids)
Carter Jr. (CJ)

Chrissy & LaKeith
Jakari, Christian, Rylan
(Avery's sons)
Janessa & LaKeith Jr. (LJ)
(LaKeith's kids w/ Nancy)

Kenny & Keisha
Kendrall Jr. (KJ)
Karima
Kendrick (Kenny's deceased son w/Tasha)
King
Kane

Jasper & Chasity
Ashanni
Royal
Crew

Tiffany & Ryder
Milana (Lani)
Ryder Jr. (Ryder J or RJ)

Storm & Aspen
Bali & Noni (twins)
Maui
Seven Jr. (SS)
Remington (Remy)

Marcus (Wesley's son) & Synthia
Ace (Marcus's son w/ Heaven)
Malia (Marcus's daughter w/Mali)
Seneda (daughter w/ Syn)

Malachi & Danica
(cousin of the Hendersons)
Malachi Jr. (MJ)
Deshon
Niara

Kema & Philly
(Tiffany's friend and Ryder's brother)
Philly Jr. & Philema (twins)
Kiana

Shylou & Cass
(Friends of Kenny and Keisha)
Shaydon
Shymir

Vida & Aston
(Friends of the Family)
Synthia (Marcus's wife)
(Vida's daughter with Jerome)

Nesha (WJ's daughter) & Lennox
Baylor

Jessica (Jen's daughter) & Brixton
Pregnant (girl)

Decaurey (WJ's stepson) & Tyeis
Angel (Tyeis's daughter w/ bitch ass Kelvin) LOL
Ellison & Essence (twins)

Jakari (Chrissy's son) & Yendi

PROLOGUE
JAKARI

TEN YEARS AGO...

She slow whined on my dick as I sat in VIP, trying to see what I could see as "Wishing" by DJ Drama and Chris Brown blared through the speakers. I swore, she wanted to get dicked down right here in front of everybody. I glanced over at my brother, Christian, as he danced on some woman that I was sure he would be getting a piece of later. Bringing my attention back to the woman on my lap, I gripped her hips and watched her hair sway across her back.

She looked back at me and bit her bottom lip then bent over, showing me the part of her I admired the most. Her ass was fat as hell, and the way it was bouncing and twerking on my dick told me she was ready for those cheeks to be spread. It had been a few months since I'd engaged in extracurricular activities like this, but I was willing to break my sabbatical for her ass.

I slid my hands over her ass then squeezed her cheeks. After I slapped each one, she stood, turned around, and straddled me, showing me her skills as she dry-fucked me. I bit my bottom lip as I slumped in my seat and let her work my shit out. When she leaned over to kiss me, I frowned. "Naw, baby. Just because I wanna fuck you, don't mean I wanna kiss. That shit is reserved for a woman I at least know. That ain't the vibe we creating right now."

She frowned slightly, but she didn't dare get up. She saw the attention Christian and I were getting. If she got up, I would have another woman in her place instantly, holding no memory of who she was. Sliding her hand up my neck, she said, "Okay."

I grabbed my cigar from the tray next to me and took a puff, blowing the smoke in her face as she gripped her nipples through the fabric of the short ass dress she wore. It was extremely noticeable that she wasn't wearing a bra, and judging by how hot her pussy was against me, she wasn't wearing underwear either. If she was, that shit wasn't catching a damn thing. The moisture on my pants was saying so.

"What's your name?" she asked as she leaned over to my ear.

"Jakari. What's yours?"

"Hmm. That's interesting. My name is Shakari."

"Interesting indeed. You wanna see what kind of magic we can make? Seems like we supposed to be right here at this very moment. Plus…" I said as I gripped her pussy from the back. "This fat shit calling me."

She pulled away from me for a moment then slid her pussy up and down my erection. Leaning over to my ear again, she said, "Take my number, and we can hook up another time. I'm not ready to leave just yet."

She glanced over at Christian who'd sat next to us. He gulped his drink and looked like he'd had enough of this scene. "A'ight. I'll get at you soon," I said, knowing that I probably wouldn't.

I was a spur of the moment type of nigga. I'd been that way ever since I had to deal with being forcefully pushed into being the "man of the house". It would be that way until my youngest brother graduated from college. He was only a senior in high school. Ever since my biological father had been arrested and charged on crimes involving minors almost two years ago, taking care of my mama and brothers had been my focus.

When I found out he'd been molesting and raping young girls, I disowned him. Finding out that he'd raped Nesha had made it even worse. Out of all my cousins, she and Jessica were the ones around my age. Although both were a little older than me, Nesha a year and a half and Jess a couple of months, I still looked at myself as their protector, especially at school. Jess and I were in the same grade, and Nesha was a year ahead.

I could remember instances where Nesha would be extremely quiet or not wanting to be bothered. I just figured it was a girl thing and thought nothing further of it. My own father had stolen three of my cousins' innocence, Nesha and both of her younger sisters, Shakayla and Chenetra. I felt like he targeted them because Uncle WJ was having issues and couldn't give them the attention he should have been.

I still blamed myself for not noticing something was wrong. Unbeknownst to Nesha, I watched her all the time now. She had graduated college already and was fucking around with some woman. She didn't think anybody knew, but I knew everything she tried to hide. I had to make sure she was okay. She was so timid, not nearly as aggressive as Jess. Jessica could hold her own. I truly believed she would fuck a nigga up if it came down to it. She was in Houston though, which made it a little harder to keep tabs on her.

After all that bullshit, Avery Bolton had might as well been given the death penalty. He was dead to me, and there was no coming back from that shit. His calls went unanswered, and his email address was blocked. There was no excuse he could give me that would be good enough to justify his actions. He was a grown ass man that knew he had a problem. When he had a desire to touch my Aunt Syn when she was four years old, he should have gotten help.

I patted Shakari's thighs, signaling for her to get her ass up. She slid next to me, and I pulled my phone out to put her number in it. I almost gave it to her for her to do it herself, but I didn't need her calling herself and getting my number. Nothing about her said that I would want anything more than a fuck with her. The attraction was only physical. My heart was off limits anyway. Once I saved it, I lifted my head to tell her bye, and she softly kissed my lips.

She caught me off guard with that shit, but her lips were so fucking soft, I had to go against my rule about kissing and feel them again. I pulled her back astride my lap and pulled her face to mine by gripping her neck. I kissed her and before I knew it, my tongue was ravishing her mouth like it was in search of something. I gripped her ass with my other hand as I separated our kiss and moved to her neck.

The taste of her sweat slowed me down, thankfully. I gave her a head nod as she smiled. When she stood, I turned to Christian to see he was staring at me. "Let's roll, man."

He stood from his seat as I gulped the last of my drink. After standing as well, Shakari approached me. I leaned over and hugged her. She was a good foot shorter than me. I got that all the time though since I was six four. All the Henderson men were tall. It didn't help that Avery Bolton was over six feet as well. I hated comparing myself to him though because he was the last person I wanted to be like now. It irritated me that I looked just like him, had his dark complexion and every other feature of his.

When I pulled away from her, she slid her hand over my cheek and winked. *Hmm. I may call her after all.*

I walked out, and Christian followed behind me. Normally, Nesha kicked it with us, along with Jess when she was in town, but they were both busy. Uncle WJ's soon-to-be stepson was tryna chill with us from time to time too, but he was still reeling from the death of his sugar mama. Nigga was dating his mama's best friend. That was some fuck shit. I mean... if my mama had a fine friend, I'd probably try to hit, but it would definitely be subtle. However, it would never go any further than that.

Vida was fine as fuck, and I'd fantasized about her ass a few times, but when she hooked up with Aston and I found out she was Aunt Syn's biological mother, those thoughts went right out the window. Me being subtle though caused me to miss my opportunity. She liked young niggas, since Aston was only a few years older than me.

When we got to my new whip, Christian said, "I don't think I'll ever get used to you driving this Escalade. This shit nice. Working for the family business is that lucrative, huh?"

"Hell yeah. You should come over. You could maintain the A/C and shit since that's what you went to school for. I know you work for LaKeith, but maybe y'all can do our shit on the side. Besides, Henderson Farms and Ranches is only going to get bigger. I have so many ideas to get us to the next level."

"Well, we already maintain everyone's businesses anyway. We'll see though. What I wanna know is how the fuck you let that girl kiss you?"

I chuckled. "Shit, she snuck that shit on me. I told her I didn't go there with women I didn't really know. After she did that though and I felt how soft those muthafuckas were, I had to feel 'em again."

He laughed as he slowly shook his head. "You gon' call her?"

"Mm hmm. Probably not till next weekend though. I got a lot of shit to do this week at work. Plus, I gotta run through Lena's Tuesday night."

"Lena? Zayson's cousin in China?"

"Hell yeah. My dick ain't been the same since she sucked my shit up. Had a nigga blasting off in two point two seconds."

He chuckled and shook his head. "Well, shorty you was with tonight is fine as hell."

"Mm hmm."

"You gon' have to let me know how that shit turn out."

"Yep. I have a feeling she got a super soaker too. She was worth my time tonight."

"Chick I was dancing with got a man. I ain't tryna get caught up in no shit."

"That's why you were ready to leave?"

"Yeah. Fucked my night up."

I shook my head at his sensitive ass. I would have just moved on to the next one in line. He was gonna be just like our uncles, moving fast as hell and falling in love at first sight and shit. Not this nigga. She was gonna have to be sent straight from heaven to catch me slipping… a whole ass angel.

"Rylan gon' go to the fucking pros if he keep playing like a beast. I swear my nephew remind me of how I used to ball," Uncle Storm said, causing everybody to roll their eyes simultaneously.

We were about to walk in the gym to see my brother get down. One thing Uncle Storm was right about was Rylan's skills. If he chose to focus completely on basketball, he could make it. I wasn't sure if that was what he wanted though. He mentioned working for the family once he graduated from college. He would use his basketball skills to pay for his education.

He was smart as hell. The business could benefit from him being a part of it if Grandpa would loosen up on the reins a bit. The man didn't want to take chances. Taking risks was usually a part of everyone's success story. Whatever Rylan chose to do, I would be ten toes down for him. That was my baby brother, and I would forever have his and Christian's backs.

I was just happy that I was in a financial position to handle it now. When Avery first got locked up, we struggled for a few months. Although he was splitting his income with another family, he was contributing quite a bit to the household. If it weren't for our family stepping up to help us, we wouldn't have made it.

As we walked toward the gym entrance, Uncle Jasper said, "Storm, the only thing you remembered for around here is bringing that fucking gun to school. You were nowhere near close to being a baller like Rylan."

My mama chuckled as I slid my arm around her. Chrissy Henderson was the sweetest woman in Nome. People knew that if they needed a listening ear, she was the Henderson to go to first. If she thought you were bullshitting, then there was no hope for you. She looked up at me then tiptoed and kissed my cheek. I leaned over and kissed her head. She was my first love and the blueprint as far as I was concerned. If a woman didn't exhibit characteristics like my mama's, I didn't want her.

Once we walked inside, the band was already on one. I rolled my eyes. Hardin Jefferson's band was full of shit. It was majority white, and you couldn't tell them they weren't jamming. "I should have smoked before we left so I could deal with all these white folks," Jasper said, voicing my sentiments exactly.

"Hell yeah, Unc," I responded. "When they play a real nigga school, they be scared as hell. Silsbee and West Orange fuck up their focus every time."

Uncle Storm chuckled. "I love my people, man. They intimidated by our greatness."

"As they should be," Aunt Tiff added.

Those three were always ready to address shit. They were more like older siblings than my uncles and aunt. Uncle Kenny always stayed pretty quiet, but I knew he could be just as rowdy. I heard all the bullshit that went down between him and Aunt Keisha a few years ago, I remembered Uncle Jasper laughing about how Uncle Kenny fucked that cop, Reggie, up.

Once we were all seated, we took up a whole section, per usual. There was no mistaking when a Henderson was involved in shit, because the entire family showed up. My grandparents were here, along with our cousin Malachi and his family. We always wanted our kids to feel and see the support they had in place, especially for home games. Everybody couldn't make time to travel for away games, but we all damn sure made the games in our backyard.

As we were seated, they began introducing the starting lineup. They would be playing Hampshire Fannett, a school not too far from ours and one of our biggest rivals. We usually ran over them in basketball... hell, in every sport. Their cheerleaders lined up, and my eyes widened. *I know the fuck not.*

My eyes stayed glued to one of the cheerleaders as she back flipped all the way to our side of the gym. When she lifted her hands in the air, her eyes met mine. *Shakari.* I immediately got sick to my stomach. My brother turned to me, his eyes wide. How in the fuck did she get in the club if she was a fucking teenager? That club was twenty-one and up. *What the fuck?*

I stood from my seat and slowly walked out toward the bathroom. I didn't want to move too fast and have everybody in my fucking business. Her eyes followed me until I was no longer in her line of vision. The minute I knew my family could no longer see me, I powerwalked to the restroom and threw the fuck up. I'd touched every part of her body and enjoyed every minute of it. I said some inappropriate shit in her ear. Had Avery Bolton's way infiltrated me anyway?

Hell fucking no. She looked like a grown ass woman, and she was in a club for grown ass people. Was this shit my fault? I felt like it was. I should have asked her age. I just fucking assumed she was at least twenty-one. She looked like she'd shitted on herself when she saw me. I was glad I hadn't called her ass. I'd planned to, though. Thankfully, it was only Thursday, and the next weekend hadn't rolled around yet.

"You okay, bruh?"

I turned around to see Christian. "Naw. Fuck naw."

"You had no way of knowing, man. Don't be hard on yourself."

"Man, what if I had fucked her? I wouldn't have been no better than Avery. I'm not a fucking pedophile, but I was physically attracted to that lil girl. What that shit say about me?"

"You ain't him, J. You far from being him. She built like a grown ass woman. Nothing about her said teenager Saturday night, not even her face. I would have guessed that she was around twenty-three or so."

"You can't tell nobody about this shit."

"You don't have to worry about that. It will be between the three of us," he said as I washed my hands then my mouth.

I didn't know how I would get through the game with her hopping around, cutting flips and shit. Christian clapped my back as we left the restroom, and said, "I got'chu, bruh."

I nodded and made my way back to the bleachers. Uncle Storm was giving me the side-eye, and I knew he had something slick to say, as usual. "I told that lil girl to keep it pushing because you damn near thirty."

I rolled my eyes. "Nigga, I'm twenty-three."

"Whatever. Same thing. Either way, her sixteen-year-old ass need to be looking at Rylan or Jacob, not you."

"Right."

I knew he would notice. Nothing got by his ass. Uncle Jasper slid down to the bleacher I was seated on, and said, "We'll smoke when we leave here. You look like you need it. She duped your ass. I'll let you tell me how later."

I lowered my head. Uncle Jasper was someone I didn't mind talking to. I knew it would stay between us, but I still wasn't sure if I was comfortable telling him this. As I stared across the way, my anger started to consume me as I watched her with her pom poms. Her eyes met mine, and she quickly looked away, doing her best to avoid my gaze. She didn't have shit to be worried about. I would walk right by her like her ass was invisible.

The problem now was that I knew I would be way too careful, going overboard to assure this wouldn't happen again. No fucking body was going to catch me slipping, making me feel like I was just a chip off the old fucked-up block. She taught me a valuable lesson. If they weren't family, they couldn't be trusted.

CHAPTER 1

JAKARI

THE PRESENT...

"And the new mayor of Big City Nome, Texas is Seven Storm Henderson!" Uncle WJ exclaimed, like Uncle Storm had won some kind of prize.

That fool put on his Stetson and tipped his hat to the people in the diner who had come to the celebration, mostly family and a few friends. "There's a new sheriff in town. Get ready, because I refuse to hold back and spare anybody's pitiful feelings."

"Storm, when have you *ever* spared anybody's feelings? You've always been on some 'fuck yo' feelings' type shit," Uncle Jasper said, causing everyone in attendance to laugh.

"First of all, you will address me as Mr. Mayor or Brother Mayor. Secondly, I spare yo' feelings every day when I don't say shit about some of the shit you be wearing. Thirdly, I ain't neva been on the type of time I'm about to be on. We gotta whip Nome into shape and make it great again," he said with a smirk.

"Aww shit. Let me find out you the black version of Donald Trump. These people will overthrow yo' ass, and I will help them," Uncle Kenny said.

Everybody laughed loudly as Uncle Storm frowned. After a moment or two, his smile finally came through. He shook his head then cleared his throat. "On some real shit though, this win is for Mama. She was already proud, but I know this moment would have made her even prouder."

Everyone clapped in agreement. It was always implied that the Hendersons ran all of Nome because of the businesses and Henderson Village, but that shit was a reality now. Uncle Storm and Uncle Marcus would be officially running shit. I was proud and worried at the same fucking time. These people didn't know what was in store, but I could only imagine.

Thankfully, only family and our closest friends were here for this celebration. The city council would be celebrating him tomorrow. Abney never got in the race, so he was a shoo-in. When we all voted and he was the only one listed on the ballot, we knew what the end result would be. We'd been turning up all day. We were at the family barn earlier. J. Paul had rolled through, and we all got good and lit… well, except Nesha, Tyeis, and Jess.

They were all pregnant. Nesha was due in another month or so and Tyeis was due not long after her. I didn't know what we would do with all these newborns. There would be four of them since Ty and Decaurey were having twins. Jess was the only one that didn't know the sex of her baby yet. So far, two boys and a girl would be gracing the Henderson family. I was pretty sure at least one of these lucky babies would have me as a godfather.

"Mama Henderson was definitely proud of all her babies," Aunt Liv, Decaurey's mom, said as everyone nodded in agreement.

Grandma had only been gone for a couple of months, but it felt like longer already. I missed her something fierce, as did everyone else. She was often in the business office, acting a damn fool with Aunt Tiff and Aunt Chas. One time, I'd literally walked in on her watching porn. She turned her phone to me and asked how that woman got her shit to "shoot out" like that. I was done. There was no way I was about to talk to my grandmother about women squirting or anything else related to having sex.

HEALING FOR MY SOUL

Philly sat next to me as Uncle Storm continued talking like he was giving a damn acceptance speech. None of us here gave a fuck so we'd started engaging in our own conversations. I looked over at Philly to see what he had to say. We worked together nearly all day every day. We'd gotten closer over the past few years. "What you got going tomorrow?"

"I have to go have a meeting with the trucking company about transporting our goods. Being that we're our own distributors, we need to get a better rate. There's no middleman. They are extremely proud of their business with the prices they charging us. Our business is probably keeping them afloat. Either they can go down on those prices or lose us altogether."

"Damn. Who are you going to get if they don't fall for the bluff?"

"I'm not bluffing. Uncle Jasper and Uncle Kenny are partnering with Uncle Kenny's friend, Price Daniels. He already owns a trucking company. He would need more trucks, but because he's already licensed, it would be seamless. There's also F.A.N. Transport, owned by Ford Noel. He's venturing into more avenues. He primarily does hazardous materials but is trying to get into transporting food grade and dry goods."

"Well shit. Sounds like you got it all figured out."

"Naw. Once I get numbers, I'm coming to you. After you put your expertise on it, *then* it will all be figured out."

He nodded with a slight smile. "So, Seneca from Watchful Eyes called earlier."

My eyebrows lifted. "He had an update?"

"Yep. Tyrese is in Beaumont. A guy named Ali is on him now."

"Ali is the owner of the company. A'ight. I'll make a call. Matter of fact, we ought to go by there tomorrow."

"Sounds like a plan to me. Will it be early or late?"

"Probably early, before my meeting. I'll let you know after I contact him."

"A'ight."

I tuned back in to Uncle Storm's rambling to hear him say, "I will be dropping by all businesses to make sure they are catering to the needs of Nome."

"Nigga, shut the fuck up, and sit yo' ass down!" Uncle Jasper said.

Even Uncle Storm had to laugh at Unc's outburst, then he took off his hat and had a seat as Aunt Jen set a bowl of banana pudding in front of him. "Congratulations, baby boy. I'm proud of you."

She kissed his cheek, and he turned red. It was something about Aunt Jen and my mama that made him sensitive. "Thanks, Jen. After tomorrow, the diner will be the official caterers for city meetings and gatherings. They don't like it, they can kiss my ass."

"You have to put it to a vote, baby. Make it fair."

"This ain't gon' be a democracy, sis. This gon' be an all-out dictatorship. They didn't include our black asses in a thing. Well, it's our turn now."

Aunt Jen slowly shook her head as Jess and Nesha approached him. Since Philly and I were sitting at the table right next to him, we could hear the conversations. "Uncle Mayor, we already knew you had the seat months ago."

"Thanks, Jess."

"Jess don't be putting all that helium in that nigga. His big ass head gon' float away in a minute," Philly said as Uncle Storm frowned.

He pointed his fork at him. "That's yo' ass when I finish this pudding."

I slowly shook my head. This family was a handful, but I wouldn't trade them for the world.

"I KNOW YOU'RE PROBABLY BUSY, BUT ASHANNI AND MAUI HAD TO stay after school for some project they're doing with the librarian, and the twins left them," Aunt Chas explained.

"I don't know why they insist on riding with their asses. They all have cars. Ashanni and Maui should have ridden together," I said as I grabbed my keys.

I'd just gotten back from getting the price decrease we wanted from the trucking company. They just didn't know… As soon as the trucking contracts were cool with Price, we would be getting rid of their asses anyway. One of the deliveries was late, and they couldn't give me a legitimate excuse. Ali with Watchful Eyes was out of pocket today, but he agreed to try to meet up with us before the week was out. In the meantime, he would keep us updated on Tyrese's whereabouts.

That nigga had better chill if he knew what was good for his ass. His teeth would be buried right next to his uncle's. Reggie was a bitch ass nigga that needed handling a long time ago… long before Tyrese was of age to even know what was going on. My uncles dragging their feet about that shit caused other problems.

"I'll go get them, Aunt Chas. I'm on my way."

"Okay. You may have to go in to get them. You know their signals are full of shit when they're at school. They called me from the school landline."

"A'ight."

"Thank you, Jakari. I owe you."

"Uh huh. Long as Unc has my ganja Friday, we're straight."

She chuckled. "Well, you already know his ass have that."

I chuckled too. Uncle Jasper was never short on smoke. After ending the call, I got in my blacked out Suburban and headed to the high school. I'd be sure to let them know that they needed to drive their own vehicles when they had to stay late. The terror twins were worse than Uncle Storm's ass. He would have at least gone back and got them. Their asses refused to go back to the school.

When I got there, I parked in the driveway against the curb in front of the school. The library was right in front, so I wouldn't have to traipse too far through the school. As I entered the second set of doors, my nieces appeared in the hallway with a voluptuous sistah that immediately grabbed my attention. She was bad as fuck. She reminded me of Aunt Aspen. She had to be about five nine, and I could clearly see her dimples as she smiled at my nieces. *Fuck!*

Her curves took me on a journey all over her body until I got to those pretty ass toes. That was definitely a fetish of mine. Those feet couldn't be busted, or I was done. My eyes slid back up her body, over her fat ass to her massive titties. I loved fucking with BBWs. All of 'em had juicy pussies, and I couldn't help but wonder if she did too.

As I approached, Maui said, "Jakari! Hey! What are you doing here?"

I lifted my eyebrows and held my hands out like, *duh*. "Umm, don't y'all need a ride?"

Ashanni giggled. "Jakari, this is our librarian, Ms. Odom. Ms. Odom, this is our cousin, Jakari," Ashanni said, glancing from me to her.

Our eyes held one another's gaze. When her cheeks reddened slightly, I knew I had her fine ass. Those lashes were doing their fucking job, batting at me, pulling me closer to her. I extended my hand, and she placed hers in mine. "Nice to meet you, Ms. Odom."

"Call me Yendi. Nice to meet you as well, Jakari."

Her smile was everything. The wider she smiled, the deeper those dimples got. Her cheekbones were high and forced her eyes to practically close when she smiled. Yendi Odom was beautiful. The crazy part was that my entire body heated up when I grabbed her hand... the hand that I was still holding in mine.

She cleared her throat and pulled it away, bringing her attention back to the girls. "Thank you for helping me, girls. Let me know when you'll be able to stay late again."

"Whenever you want us to, Ms. Odom," Maui said. "I can stay tomorrow. We don't practice with Aunt Tiff until Friday this week."

"Sounds like a plan. See y'all tomorrow. Thanks, Jakari, for coming to get them, but I had no issue with getting them home."

"What type of project are y'all working on?" I asked, mainly to have more time in her presence.

I didn't give a damn about their little project. The only project I needed to find out about was the one standing in front of me. I'd work on that shit every day if her pussy was as good as she looked. Yendi smiled big again. "They are helping me develop programs to get more students reading, coming up with incentives to make them *want* to read. We are trying to reach the masses and not just the bookworm. We want to attract new readers."

I nodded repeatedly. "Sounds interesting."

"You should come tomorrow and help us," she said.

I frowned as Maui and Ashanni laughed. "Jakari, we have to go back inside the library to get our things."

Perfect. "A'ight." When they walked away, I turned to Yendi. "The only thing I wanna help you with is achieving the most powerful orgasm of your life." Her eyebrows lifted, and before she could respond, I continued. "I'm as forward as they come, Yendi. I don't beat around the bush, wasting people's time." I pulled my wallet from my pocket and gave her a business card. "If you on the same wave I'm on, hit me up."

She hesitantly took the card. While she tried to act like she was offended, I knew her pussy was leaping for joy. She didn't say another word, but I could see how her skin had started to glisten. "Yendi, look at me, baby." When she did, I said, "You fine as fuck. Where you come from?"

She cleared her throat. "I moved here from D.C., but I'm an army brat. Been all over the world. We settled in D.C. once my dad retired nearly twenty years ago. I wanted to get away from the city life though. When I saw a position open for a librarian here when I was researching Texas, I jumped on it."

I have plenty you can jump on. She seemed sweet. If she didn't come back at me with nothing smart to say, then my assumption had to be correct. "Well, I'm glad you chose here to work. I wouldn't have gotten to see perfection. I hope you call so I can see just how perfect you really are."

"Jakari, I would really like to get to know you a bit. I don't have sex with strangers. I don't know what type of women you've been dealing with, but I'm not one of them."

"I beg to differ. You may not be one of them, but you *are* intrigued for sure. I can see how your body is responding to me, about to sweat and shit. Secondly, you're still engaging in conversation with me instead of telling me to get the fuck on. But check it. Call me, and maybe we can go to dinner or something. I'll meet you halfway with your demands."

She nodded. "We'll see," she said as the girls rejoined us.

I gave her a one-sided smile. She was going to call. I didn't know why she was playing games. The girls told her goodbye, and we headed to my Suburban. Once inside and I'd driven away, Maui said, "You like her, huh?"

I frowned slightly as I looked at her in my rearview mirror. "You don't have to admit it, cuz. We can see it. She likes you too," Ashanni added.

"I'm starting to think this was a setup."

They giggled, indicating that was exactly what it was. "I told my mama to send you to pick us up. I think y'all would make a cute couple."

"Ashanni, you and Maui a trip. I never expected y'all to be on this level of foolery. We gon' see though. I gave her my business card."

"Aye!" they both yelled and high-fived each other.

I slowly shook my head but couldn't stop the slight smile from forming on my lips. Yendi Odom was gon' get the business. Relationships were still off limits though. She would have to be a fucking saint and a devil at the same time to get me to go there. I wasn't writing that off as impossible, but it would definitely be a challenge if she was up for it. Those thick, plump lips were glossed to perfection, and I could imagine her leaving that gloss all over my dick.

I hadn't had a girlfriend since my second year of college so the simple thought of thinking she could have my ass on lock was something serious. Maybe I was more like my uncles than I thought. At first sight, I was wondering if she would be the one to pull a nigga like Jakari Bolton. She didn't know who she was fucking with yet, but I would surely make that shit known when she called. Honestly, I was anticipating it.

CHAPTER 2
YENDI

Had that fine nigga approached me anywhere else other than my job, he would have gotten a mouthful. My pussy had enlarged herself to receive him, despite me trying to act offended. He read me perfectly. Most men assumed I was a nerd because I was a librarian and avid reader. The glasses I wore and my work attire definitely fit the stereotype. Jakari saw right though that shit. *Whew!*

I couldn't move until I no longer saw him. That nigga came out and told me what he wanted then walked off without so much as a glance back. His last name was Bolton, but I knew he was a Henderson as well, because the girls' last names were Henderson. Plus, his business card indicated that he worked for Henderson Farms. I'd heard how they practically owned Nome. Maui's father was just elected mayor of the town. She was excited to tell me when she got to school.

For the family to practically own the town and be as prosperous as they were, there had to be some confidence and aggressiveness about them. Jakari exhibited those qualities. Just from our minute-long conversation, I wanted to spread my legs for him, and I didn't even know his ass. I loved a man that took charge and didn't play games. *Say what you mean and mean what you say. Stand by that shit.*

I hated putting on a front, but I didn't have a choice. Most times, I was quiet and slightly reserved, but there was no way a nigga would have gotten away with what he said scot-free. He would have gotten one of two reactions. Either I would have handed his ass to him when I cursed him the hell out, or I would have come back with something just as nasty, challenging him to back up everything he said. I was *ready* to feel the most powerful orgasm of my life.

Just staring at his chocolate complexion, slanted eyes, the slight scowl on his face, and the way he towered over my five-feet-nine-inch frame had me ready to release right in my panties. They were wet as hell when I sat back at my desk to gather my things. It was like I could still feel his touch. His hands were strong. Although they were somewhat soft, I could tell that they were working hands. There was one callus right beneath his fingers.

He was a country boy, and I always fantasized about being with a country man, but they were never as hood as the man that stood before me today. He had diamond earrings in his ears, a gold chain with a diamond cross hanging from it, tattoos on his arms and I assumed his chest, because they were peeking out above the rim of his shirt, but wore cowboy boots, jeans, a belt with a rodeo buckle, and a graphic tee. He was so fucking fine, but I had a feeling he was dangerous.

While I would love for him to slut me out, I was also ready for something meaningful. I was lonely, and I'd had a difficult few months before I moved here a month ago. My father got sick, and my mama lost her fucking mind, leaving my three siblings and me in disbelief. When he passed away, it was like we lost both parents, although it felt like we lost her well before he left this earth. It caught us off guard.

My mother was always there for my dad. He'd been dealing with illnesses for a while. You named it, he had it. The list was long, but congestive heart failure, high blood pressure, fluid retention, and diabetes were at the top of the list. He'd had many hospital stays, and she was there for him each time, taking off work and keeping us in the loop of what was going on. We couldn't all be there all the time. As his wife, it was her job to be there. We all had to work, and my two sisters had families to take care of.

HEALING FOR MY SOUL

This time, she wasn't there for him and was making decisions that were the total opposite of what he would want and what we had discussed as a family if he were ever critical. It left us all feeling weird about the whole situation. What made it worse was when we questioned her actions, she snapped and started lying to people about us.

Hearing my dad's emotional turmoil about how she was treating him made my heart cold. I no longer wanted anything to do with her. I knew I did whatever I could for my dad. It was no secret to anyone how close we were. I talked to him every day. Right under God, he was the one. He was an amazing father, and I had no regrets. However, to know he died from a broken heart kills me. He couldn't understand why she was throwing forty-five years of marriage to the wayside and acting like he no longer meant the world to her.

He didn't spare any details. He was only at home with her for two weeks before he died. I'd seen him the day before, and I could tell he was emotionally upset. Since his nurse was there, he couldn't tell me what was going on. He didn't have to tell me. I knew she was on bullshit. She'd been on bullshit since he'd ended up intubated and unresponsive in ICU almost two months prior.

I hadn't spoken to her since his memorial service, and I made it clear that I didn't want to hear shit from her unless she was ready to address her behavior and make some changes. Apparently, that time hadn't come, and in my heart, I knew it would never come. The day she admitted she was a compulsive liar would be the day Jesus returned. Her actions only made me assume the worst about her. In my heart, I felt like she let my dad die. Like she stood there and watched him drift off and didn't call the ambulance until he was gone.

I couldn't publicly make accusations, because I had no proof. Her cold and heartless attitude toward him said she wanted him to die. The more time passed by, the harder it would be for her to rectify this. I didn't think she wanted to rectify it though. She was content with creating drama, and I refused to be a part of it. I told my siblings that they could sweep it under the rug and move on with her in their lives if they wanted to, but that was a no-go for me.

That admission made me feel so alone. I was still grieving my father's death, because it was filled with so much turmoil and drama I couldn't grieve properly. I didn't truly grieve until I moved here, out in the middle of nowhere with nothing to do but sit with my thoughts. I still spoke to my siblings and a couple of my dad's siblings, but that was it. Grief had been a monster to overcome, but I could finally think about my dad and smile at times.

Now that I was at peace again, I could entertain the flirtatious glares I received. They were usually given by white men because that was the majority at the school. However, Jakari let me know that Nome was where it was at. The girls had told me that their aunts had a diner out there that served soul food through the week and a little bit of everything on the weekends. I would definitely have to take a trip to see what I could see, Friday.

As I headed to my condo in Sour Lake, my thoughts drifted back to Jakari. I was going to make his ass sweat. While I wanted to see what hung between his slightly bowed legs, I didn't want to seem too thirsty. He seemed like a fuckboy. I needed to get my mind right for that. I had needs, but because I was so thirsty for affection, I was afraid that I would confuse what I felt from him as that instead of what he said it was.

There was something about him that intrigued the fuck out of me. Besides his audacity to approach me the way he did, I could tell there was more to him that he kept hidden. The eyes often led to the soul, and I could see that while he tried to play the role of a player, that wasn't who he truly was. I didn't even know how I saw all that in his gaze, but I did. When the girls mentioned that their cousin was coming to get them, I didn't think anything of it, but the minute they left us alone, I could see that they'd set this whole thing up.

The two of them were my brightest students. They loved to read, and I almost found myself sharing one of my reads with them. They were so mature for their ages I'd almost forgotten they were kids. While I was pretty sure they were reading books they had no business reading, I couldn't be the one recommending them. I'd gotten into reading a lot of black independent authors and chose to review the reads I enjoyed on TikTok. I'd gained a little over two thousand followers and more people were following me every day.

Reading and doing TikTok reviews kept me busy to where I didn't have too much time to fall down a rabbit hole, thinking about my dad and family drama. Maui had somehow found my page and shared it with Ashanni, so I supposed I was recommending books to them indirectly. They'd been trying to get their cousin, Milana, involved with our project, but she wasn't an avid reader. She was more concerned with her budding rodeo career.

Once I got inside and got situated, I warmed some pork ribs I'd baked yesterday along with some rice dressing, green beans, and baked beans. After adding a scoop of potato salad from the fridge, I went to sit at the table. This was a Sunday dinner I'd cooked on a big Tuesday, but once I started, I couldn't stop adding shit to my meal. The green beans were the last edition because I realized I didn't have a vegetable.

After my first forkful of potato salad, my phone started ringing. I rolled my eyes, knowing it was probably someone I didn't want to talk to. I didn't have many friends because I lowkey didn't like people like that. When I picked it up and saw my baby sister's number, I smiled. We hadn't talked in a couple of days, and I was always glad to hear from her. "Hello?"

"Hey, Yendi! How are you?"

"Hey! How are you, Janay?"

"I'm good. How was your day?"

"It was pretty good. I actually just got home not long ago. A couple of my students have agreed to help me with my initiative to get more teens to read. We were making plans, and I'm excited about some of their ideas. How are you and JaCory?"

JaCory was her eight year-old son. I didn't ask about her husband, because she'd left him only a couple of weeks before Daddy died. Our mother had the bright idea to go visit him after my sister and her son moved out. She stayed there for two whole hours... just him and her in the house. My sister had to witness that shit from her doorbell camera app. That was another story though.

"We're good. I called to tell you about your mama."

I rolled my eyes. "What has she done now?"

"She called Terrence and told him she's been trying to call us, because she's selling the house."

Terrence was Janay's ex-husband. Although they weren't legally divorced, that was what he was now referred to as. "She hasn't called me. And furthermore, I don't give a damn. She can do what she wants. That's what she's been doing anyway."

She literally planned my dad's service without any of our input and told people we didn't show up to help her. Of course, that was a lie. I'd shown up and she either wasn't home or had refused to answer the door. Janay called her and she said she was at her brother's house, because when I called her, it went straight to voicemail like she'd blocked me. We literally had to find out from someone else when the memorial service would be. I was so done with her foolishness.

Janay laughed. "Me either. I told him that she hasn't called me either and that she's lying. Of course, his ass believes everything she says. I don't care about anything she does at this point. I just wanted you to know, especially since he said Marie knows."

Marie was my older sister. She and my brother were still trying to entertain my mother simply because of that 'we only have one mother' bullshit. If my only mother was putting me through bullshit, I refused to stick around.

"It doesn't make sense for her to sell the house just to go rent somewhere else. The house is paid for. She's going to pay at least a thousand dollars a month wherever she goes. That's dumb to me, but whatever."

"Right. Whatever she's going to be paying in rent, she can save to pay the taxes and homeowners insurance."

"Right!"

I rolled my eyes. "In other news, I got propositioned by a fine ass country man today."

"What! What did he look like? What did he say?"

"Girl, he came to pick up his lil cousins from school. They were helping me in the library. I asked him if he wanted to come tomorrow and help us and that nigga told me the only thing he wanted to help me with was experiencing the most powerful orgasm of my life."

"No he didn't! Did you shut him down? I can't believe he said that his first time meeting you."

"I didn't shut him down, per say. I was in shock that he actually said that. He's chocolate like we like them, and he has to be every bit of six feet three. He looks to be about Pete's height, maybe a little taller."

Pete was our older brother. He was the oldest and thought he was always right. Couldn't tell him shit. I continued. "It's something about him that won't let me ignore him. He was so damn confident and had the right amount of aggression. If anything, it turned me on."

"You slut!" she yelled then laughed. "So are you going to call him?"

"Probably this weekend. I told him I didn't fuck strangers. I need to get to know him a little bit first."

"Good. I don't want to have to put an APB out on you way out there in Texas. I miss you, Yendi."

"I miss you too, sis. You'll have to come visit. Who knows, you may find a country man out here that will put Terrence's pitiful ass to shame."

"Well, that won't take much."

We laughed at her comment. "I'm going to a neighboring town where he's from Friday. His family is extremely prominent and practically runs the town. From what his cousins have said, they have a large family. The diner I'm going to eat at is owned by a couple of their family members. I'm almost sure he'll be there."

"Okay! I see how you playing it. You trying to force him to see more than sex when he looks at you."

"Yeah, but honestly, I think he already does. The way he stared at me said more than fucking."

"Well, you'll find out soon enough."

"Mamaaaa!" her son yelled.

"And that's your cue to go. Kiss my nephew for me."

"I will. I love you."

"Love you too."

I ended the call and finished my dinner, my mind going back to my mother. She thrived on attention. It was driving her crazy that she wasn't getting it. I could be the cutoff queen at times. I hated drama. I just hated that I had to cut my own mother off. She had always been a liar. That was nothing new. Knowing how she was treating my daddy for his final days was the nail in the coffin. He told me everything, and I begged him to live with me. Had he moved in with me, I felt like he would still be alive.

I hated talking about her, because it always put me in a funk. I stood from the table and scratched my food in the trash then went to run my bath water. After coming back to the kitchen to clean my mess and put the leftover food away, I grabbed the bottle of Stella Black from the fridge and made my way to my bedroom. I was done for the night.

CHAPTER 3
JAKARI

It had been two days, and I was sure I would have heard from Yendi Odom by now. I supposed I was too forward for her. My gut never usually steered me wrong, and it told me that she liked that aggressive shit. There was no way I was losing touch. I was about to head to the diner for lunch. Philly and I were going to meet with Ali of Watchful Eyes when we left from there. As I grabbed my keys, my phone started ringing.

Hopefully it wasn't business. Nothing would deter me from my mama's smothered pork chops. Every Friday, everybody found their way to the diner. I ate there almost every day. It was the same food I grew up on. Mama and Aunt Jen always made sure we ate good growing up. I looked at the caller ID to see it was Nate.

"What's up, bruh?"

"J! How you been, man?"

"Good. Same ol', same ol'."

"I got tickets for you. Box seats. If you got a lady friend, y'all should come out. It's for the game next month."

I briefly thought about Yendi, and I didn't even know why. I slowly shook my head. "A'ight. Sounds like a plan. I can't wait to hang."

"Me either. How long has it been? About five months?"

"Something like that. Since Noah's video shoot."

"We gotta change that."

"Absolutely. You know I'm game for whatever you have in mind. Since all of my cousins in our crew are pregnant, Friday nights been filled with me getting high with my uncle or hanging with my younger brothers. They be on some different shit, especially Rylan. He ain't but twenty-seven. I'm not even trying to be a part of their crew."

He chuckled. "I got'chu! You already knew this though, so I don't know why you been suffering in silence."

I laughed as I got in my ride and headed to the diner. "Shiiiid, I know, nigga."

"How's Jess, man?"

"She's good. She's about eighteen weeks along."

"That should have been my baby, but I'm glad that she's happy."

"You gon' have to move on, my nigga."

"I know. Noah keeps telling me the same thing. He said he's been there and done that and that shit wasn't healthy for nobody involved. I'ma get over her. It ain't even been a year since I met her. Only about six months since we were last together intimately. Give me time."

"You right. It just seems like longer," I said as I parked in the lot at the diner. "Let me hit you back though. I just got to the diner for lunch."

"A'ight, man. No hurry. I can holla at'chu whenever you have time."

"A'ight, bruh."

I ended the call and slowly shook my head. That man was so in love with Jessica he couldn't fucking function. Ever since they met at Nesha's wedding, he'd been pining after her ass. I got out of my ride and made my way inside, only to see a thickums at the counter, ordering food. I glanced down at her ass then glanced over at my family to see they were looking right at me.

"Hey, baby! You want your usual?" my mama asked.

"Yeah, Ma. Thank you."

The woman at the counter turned to see who was talking, and I couldn't help but give her a smirk. It was Yendi Odom. She smiled slightly. "Hey, Jakari."

"What's up?" I asked as I bit my bottom lip while staring at her.

I swore I wanted to live between those big ass titties. I walked closer to her as Aunt Jen smiled at me. "Hey, Aunt Jen."

"Hey, baby."

She rang up Yendi's food, and I surprised myself by saying, "I got it."

She smiled at me then grabbed her container and walked away. When I turned back to the counter, my mama was standing there with her eyebrows lifted. "How do y'all know each other?"

"She's the librarian at the school. I picked up a couple of your nieces from school Wednesday, and they were playing matchmaker."

She chuckled. "Well, she's a beautiful woman."

"She is, but don't go getting no ideas. I don't even know her like that."

She dramatically poked her lip out as I slowly shook my head. She'd been expressing her need for grandbabies. Now that Aunt Jenn and Uncle WJ had grandbabies on the way, I supposed she felt left out. She handed me my container of smothered pork chops, rice, yams, and cabbage. I ate almost the same thing every Friday, so there was no guesswork involved.

"Thank you, Mama."

"You're welcome."

I gave my card to Aunt Jenn to pay for Yendi's food, and she quickly handed it back to me. "I just wrote it off. Enjoy your lunch, baby."

"Thanks, Auntie."

I made my way to my family first as they watched me. "What's up, y'all?"

"You tell us," Uncle Storm said as he glanced at Yendi.

She was watching me hard, probably trying to figure out why I didn't sit with her. I needed to talk to my people first. "Uncle Storm—"

"Hol' it right there. You need to take a lesson from Jess and Tyeis's book. Uncle Mayor to you. Even Decaurey has gotten with the program."

I slapped his hand as I rolled my eyes. "I'm not calling you that shit. Does Uncle Jasper call you Brother Mayor?"

"No, but I'm already having sanctions imposed on his lil liquor store."

He could barely get that shit out before he started laughing at Uncle Jasper's facial expression. "Storm, I will fuck you up like I used to do when we were kids."

Those two were always going back and forth and didn't care who heard them. I could see Yendi smile at their banter. "Well, actually, Unc, I wanted to see how things were going with Price Daniels. Where are we on the contract to partner with him?"

Uncle Jasper tuned his attention to me. "Nesha is drawing up the contract as we speak."

"That's what's up. Philly and I are also going to Watchful Eyes today, since the nephew is in Beaumont. We want to discuss a plan of action."

They all nodded as I glanced over at Yendi. "Uncle Storm and Uncle Jasper, will y'all come over here with me for a minute?"

I stood from the table and headed to Yendi. Her eyes widened slightly when she saw my uncles behind me. "Yendi, this is my uncle, Jasper Henderson, Ashanni's dad, and this is Uncle Mayor Storm Henderson, Maui's dad," I said, smirking at how I introduced Uncle Storm.

She stood from her seat and shook both their hands with a smile. Uncle Storm frowned as he always did. I could see that made her uneasy by the stiffness in her shoulders. Finally, he said, "Are you related to any St. Andrews?"

"Not that I know of. Do I look like them?"

"You somewhat resemble my wife. That's her maiden name."

"Oh, well I know that's a compliment. Thank you, Mayor Henderson," she said, then winked.

Oh, she was full of shit. How did she know to kiss up to his ass?

He loved that kind of carrying on. Uncle Jasper chuckled as Uncle Storm smiled. "Yeah, 'cause my wife fire. It was nice meeting you."

"Same. Maui is a wonderful student."

"She is, thanks to her mama."

"I'm surprised you admitted that," I added.

"If I didn't, I'm more than sure one of you would have," he said, then fake coughed out, "Jasper."

I chuckled as Uncle Jasper pushed him out of the way and shook Yendi's hand again. "It's nice to meet you, and Ashanni gets every good thing from her father. Her mother is a smart, fine ass hellraiser."

I slowly shook my head as Yendi laughed. "Nice meeting you as well, Mr. Henderson."

Once she sat, I did so as well, as my uncles walked away, going back to their seats. "This is a nice diner. Thanks for lunch."

"Mm hmm. You knew I would be here, didn't you?"

"Not for sure. So how are you related to the Hendersons?"

"My mother is one of their older sisters and part owner of the diner."

"The one who fixed your food, right?"

"Yeah. You smart as hell. I see what you did here. Versus getting the side of me you saw the other day, you wanted to see what I was like around my family."

"Actually, no. I didn't know this diner belonged to anyone you were related to."

I twisted my lips to the side as she chuckled. I discreetly watched her titties slightly bounce as she did. "Our family owns nearly every business in town. I believe you already knew that."

She tilted her head to the side as she rested her fork. "What makes you think so?"

"You been around Maui and Ashanni for an extended amount of time. I'm more than sure they've told you quite a bit about our family."

She chuckled. "They did, but they didn't tell me that the owners of this place were your mom and aunt, just family. I was actually hoping to see you."

"Well, baby, all you had to do was call and you would have seen as much of me as you wanted to see."

She blushed as I opened my container and dug into my cabbage. "Oh, that looks delicious."

I glanced over at her plate to see she had Aunt Jen's stuffed chicken, red beans and rice, and greens. "It is. What is the chicken stuffed with today?"

"Mac and cheese. She stuffs it with other things?"

"Yep. Aunt Jen can stuff it with almost anything you can think of. She's done greens, mashed potatoes, yams, you name it."

"Wow. That's amazing."

"Mm hmm. Why are you off already? School ain't out."

"I'm the librarian. Fridays are half a day unless I want to stay. Had Maui and Ashanni wanted to stay late, I wouldn't be here."

I nodded as I stuffed my face with pork chops and rice. She went back to her food as well while I watched her not so discreetly. After she swallowed, she asked, "Can I ask you about yourself?"

I nodded, hoping this shit didn't get too deep where I would have to shut her ass down. This was already deeper than I originally thought it would be. I ate more food as she stared at me. "How old are you?"

I put my hand over my mouth as I chewed my food, and said, "Thirty-three. You?"

"Thirty-three. I figured you were about my age or a little older. I noticed a couple of gray hairs."

I stared at her without cracking a smile. I had a few gray hairs, but I supposed I took that from Aunt Jenahra. She had a headful. Uncle WJ had quite a few in his beard as well, ever since he was in his late twenties. Yendi cleared her throat and asked, "Did you go to college? Or did you just go straight into the family business?"

"I went to Lamar. A business degree or something related to business, like marketing, is required, even for family, unless they are just maintaining the rice or hay fields or the grass farms. Office jobs definitely require a degree or extreme expertise."

I added that part because I knew Philly didn't have a business degree. That nigga had the expertise needed though. He ran our numbers like *his* money was at stake. He was smart as hell and had to be if he was once a kingpin. It was time for a question of my own though. "How did you find Hardin Jefferson? I know they don't pay a lot, because they cheap and can't afford to anyway."

She looked away for a moment. "It wasn't about the money. It was about peace. I was actually looking at Beaumont first, but I wanted something even smaller than their district. So, I looked up surrounding districts. In D.C., I was the director of all the libraries in the district. That came with a lot of pressure and stress."

"So what you running from to where you had to come way out here to find peace?"

"Just... personal issues with my family."

She tilted her head again, and I immediately wished I wouldn't have asked that question, because now the tables had turned on me. "I don't think that's uncommon though. I feel like you have issues too that you are trying your best to deal with. That's why you're so forward. You can't handle holding anything else back, because what you're holding is heavy enough."

"So you diagnosing me? You have some therapy you wanna offer me? I'll cancel the rest of my day for that shit."

"You don't have to cancel your day, but maybe we can meet up later."

She looked away from me, but I reached across the table and grabbed her chin, turning her face back to me. I pulled off her glasses then slid my finger over her juicy ass lips. "Now say what you mean, Yendi."

She bit her bottom lip as I watched the goosebumps appear on her skin. "I want to feel the orgasm you spoke of a couple of days ago. Is that direct enough for you?"

I removed my hand from her chin and began eating my food again without giving her a response. I could see her from my peripheral, watching me. She cleared her throat and went back to her food, sliding her glasses in the pocket of her V-neck top.

After eating a good amount of food in silence, I reached across the table to grab her hand. When her eyes met mine, I said, "I'll be glad to come through and give that pussy what it needs. Send me your address."

She blushed at my words as I felt my dick stiffening. Images of her naked body flashing through my mind had caused that reaction. When she nodded in agreement, I released her hand. I closed my container, knowing if I ate any more food, I would only be good for a nap. I watched her devour her yams. She literally closed her eyes and everything as she chewed. I could relate. My mama's yams were the fucking truth.

When she opened her eyes, she met my gaze. "That's that good shit, huh?"

Her face reddened again, but before she could respond, Nesha appeared next to me. "Hey, J." She then looked over at Yendi and said, "Hello. I'm Nesha, his cousin."

"I'm Yendi. Nice to meet you."

Nesha nodded politely then turned her attention back to me. "The contract is done. I emailed it to Mr. Daniels, and he's already signed and emailed it back. Uncle Kenny and my dad are going to go preliminary truck shopping this weekend. They aren't going to purchase any until they have a meeting to get input from everyone else about the ones they selected as potential buys."

"Damn. That went quicker than I thought it would."

"First of all, that Henderson name carries weight. Mr. Daniels and Uncle Kenny have been friends for a while. He knows we're good people and on top of our shit. It's a win-win for everyone involved. These trucks will run specifically for us, but his name will be on them."

"You damn right. We don't fuck around. How you feeling though?"

She brought her hand to her belly and rubbed it in circles. "Pretty good. I can't wait to meet our baby boy. Lennox and I agreed that his name will be Baylor Grant Guilman."

"Okay. That's a nice name. I'm glad all is well. How did you come up with Baylor?"

"On Huggies dot com. Baylor means one who tends to horses. I thought it would be fitting. My baby is gonna know everything I know. Ooh! Feel right here!"

I brought my hand to her belly and felt my little cousin moving around like crazy. It was one of the most amazing feelings. I knew if it felt that great and he was just my cousin, it would be overwhelming to feel my own seed having a fit like that. "That's that Henderson in him got him moving around like that. You know the Hendersons don't mind fighting. He getting ready."

She laughed then hugged me. "Are we going out to dinner tonight? I miss y'all on Friday nights."

I glanced at Yendi, then asked, "What time?"

"I don't know. Around eight or so? That'll give everyone time to get home and get situated. Ty is finally feeling okay today. I couldn't imagine carrying twins."

"Okay. I'll hit y'all up later to find out where we're going."

She glanced at Yendi and said, "Okay. See you later."

She knew better than to put me on the spot and ask if I would be bringing her along. When Nesha left, I turned to Yendi, and she smiled. "So, sometime between five and seven?" she asked.

"I have a meeting in an hour. It should only last an hour or so. I should be home by three to take a shower."

She nodded. "Well, I look forward to it. I just texted you."

I pulled my phone from my pocket and saw the message. As I was about to check it, it started to ring. She sat back in her seat and allowed me time to answer. "Henderson Farms. This is Jakari Bolton. How can I help you?"

"Hey, son. I called from someone else's phone. I just needed to hear your voice. Your mother said you were doing well. I just wanted you to know that I love you, and I'm proud of you."

I slowly pulled the phone from my ear and ended the call. I immediately blocked the number, then looked up at Yendi. My face was hot as hell, and I couldn't stop the frown from forming. "I gotta go. I'll hit you up in a lil while."

I stood from my seat and got the fuck out of there.

CHAPTER 4
YENDI

I wasn't sure what Jakari's phone call was about, but it clearly bothered him. He was dark complexioned, but the red hue was as visible as the flames of hell. The frown that followed made me shiver. He looked like he was about to fuck the diner up. When he stormed out, a couple of the men seated followed him out, as well as his mother. A couple of members of his family looked over at me like they thought I'd done something. I simply shrugged my shoulders, indicating I didn't have a clue as to what happened.

I stood from my seat and was heading to the door when a young man who looked a lot like Jakari came inside. He walked right up to me and said, "J told me to apologize for the way he left."

I gave him a soft smile and a nod as he smiled. He was definitely a cutie. He seemed like the flirtatious type. I could tell by the way he scanned my body. I walked past him and out the door to my car. I was surprised that he cared enough to apologize. I supposed he was right about him being different around his family. He was softer, but that BDE was still at the forefront. Had that man told me to suck his dick at the table I would have probably seriously considered that shit.

I was literally hanging on his every word and what I thought he was thinking. When he told me to say what I meant and I did, I thought

I'd fucked up when he didn't respond right away. Then I realized he was playing with me, just like he thought I was playing with him. While he had a ton of people to have his back, I had no one. I was out here in these country sticks all by myself. I wasn't playing with him. I was trying to be cautious, despite what my body was wanting to do.

When he slid his finger over my lips, I almost pulled it into my mouth to suck. Had I done that, he would have canceled his day for sure. So to say I was anticipating his arrival this afternoon was an understatement. Despite all that, I was still worried about how he was feeling. Clearly, nothing had happened with his family, because most of them seemed to be in attendance, besides the kids.

I wanted to call and check on him, but I felt like he would shut me out. He didn't seem very forthcoming with his personal information. While we really didn't even get past our ages and educational background as far as getting to know one another, I could tell by the way he diverted the conversation to sex. I understood that I was basically a stranger to him, but I got the feeling he was like that with everyone. I just happened to "pull a fast one" on him by going to the diner today.

I knew it was owned by his family, but I was only hoping that he would come through today. Just because it was family, that didn't mean he had to eat there. When he spoke to his mother, I knew it was him. I could never forget his smooth ass voice. His voice wasn't deep, but it wasn't high pitched either. It was that of the typical male, but it was so smooth, almost like he was about to sing or something. It had remained calm and laidback until he said he had to go before he bolted.

After parking in the lot, I grabbed my purse and my satchel and headed inside my condo. Once I dropped everything on the kitchen countertop, I poured a glass of wine. While the day hadn't been long, my nerves were on edge about what I was about to do. I seemed so confident in what I wanted earlier, but I knew that man was going to slut me the fuck out and have me all in my feelings.

I put my food in the fridge then headed to my bathroom to start the shower. As I stepped into my room, it seemed it hit me all at once. *My daddy is gone.* I burst into tears and couldn't stop them from falling even if I tried. I wasn't trying. I missed him so much. If my phone was dry all day, I could count on it to ring at least once in the evening with a call from him. If he didn't call me, I surely called him.

Now, a huge part of my life was missing, and I didn't know what to do to fill the void. Not only did I lose him, but it felt like I'd lost my mother and most of her family too. None of my aunts and uncles called my siblings or me to offer condolences when he passed, and strangely, out of the two months he was in the hospital, none of them came to see about him. Out of my hundreds of cousins on my mom's side, only a couple of them checked on him when he was alive, and a handful checked on us after he passed.

My dad's family wasn't nearly as big, and we weren't as close to them. I checked on my aunt and one of my uncles and they checked on me. That was it. Since my mom had spread so many lies about not only us, but my dad also, it felt like we were ostracized by our own family. She'd even gone as far as to say my dad had a newborn. My exact reaction when I heard it was, *what the fuck?*

When I told my dad that, he asked, *how?* We laughed about it, but I knew he was hurt by the things she was saying about all of us. The tears continued streaming down my face. Setting my wine glass on the vanity, I disrobed and got in the shower, hoping that by the time I got out, the tears would be gone as well.

THE KNOCK AT THE DOOR CAUGHT ME OFF GUARD. WHILE I KNEW IT could only be one person, I was expecting him to call or text to let me know he was on his way. It was only three o'clock, so I was glad that I had taken a shower as soon as I got home. I was somewhat tipsy, because I had drunk that entire bottle of wine, trying to drown out my sorrows.

After peeking through the peephole, I opened the door for Jakari. His eyes were filled with emotion. I couldn't tell what exact emotion it was, but there was something dark about his gaze. I stepped aside and let him in. Once I locked the door, I turned around to find him standing there watching me. "Would you like something to drink?"

"Yeah. You have anything strong? Or did you drink it all?"

I rolled my eyes and chuckled as I almost lost my balance. "I drank a bottle of wine. I do have some Henny if you want that."

"That's fine. You drank the whole bottle?"

"Yeah."

"Why?"

"Why did you bolt out of the diner?"

He looked away from me and a deep frown appeared on his face. "That's not your business."

"Neither is why I drank an entire bottle of wine."

He remained quiet as I poured him a glass of Hennessey. I put the bottle back in the cabinet as I asked, "You want Coke with it?"

"Naw. I'll take it straight."

I turned and handed it to him as he allowed his eyes to rake over my body. I'd worn shorts and a tank top with a silk robe. There was no point in getting all dressed up when I planned to take it all off in a matter of minutes. One thing I was never ashamed of was flaunting all this body God blessed me with. The ones who were meant to like it and admire it, would. Everyone else could shut the hell up. I knew I was a BBW baddie, and there wasn't a thing a bitch could tell me about my size twenty-four frame.

Jakari gulped the alcohol then walked past me and went over to my couch and sat. I followed suit and grabbed the remote to start my music. When "Soon As You Get Home" by Rose Gold came through the speakers, I closed my eyes. That was my shit. I could listen to that song all day every day. That was how much I loved it.

While my eyes were closed, I could still feel Jakari's presence. I felt it get closer to me. Within seconds, I felt his fingertips gliding down my arm. I opened my eyes just in time to watch his fingertips graze over my hard nipple through my tank. I licked my lips as my body heated beyond what I'd ever known. I needed his touch right now. I needed him to make me *feel* needed. For some reason, I felt like he needed the same.

I sat up slightly and allowed the robe to fall from my shoulders. Jakari stared at me for a moment then sat up and pulled his shirt over his head. His slightly defined, tatted chest called out to me. I ran my hand over it, stroking the silky layer of hair on his chest. His hand slid up my arm to my face, and he pulled me to him. I thought he would kiss me, but he leaned in and went to my neck. I would take that.

"You smell good, Yendi."

"So do you."

I slid my fingers through the curly hair atop his head then gripped it as his tongue graced my spot. A soft moan left my lips, voicing my satisfaction with what he was doing to me. His hair was soft as hell. When he pulled away, I opened my eyes to stare at him. He stood from the couch and extended his hand to me.

I stood and led him to my bedroom. I had clothes everywhere earlier, but I scooped all that shit up and threw it in the closet. I was a diva at times and had to find the perfect outfit to wear. Most times I'd end up wearing the first thing I took out of the closet. He looked around my room as I pulled my tank over my head.

"Take that off too."

I frowned. "Take what off?"

"The wig."

"Why?"

"Because I'm not worried about all that superficial shit. I want the real you, from head to toe. The only part of you I'm gon' judge is that pussy. I feel like that shit finna suck me in though. It's gon' be everything I'm expecting it to be."

My body shivered as he stepped closer to me. The way he licked his lips as he stared at my nipples had my pussy on ten! She'd gotten started without him and would probably finish without him if he took too long. He slid his palms over my nipples then slid them to my waist and inside the elastic waistband of my shorts. "Yendi…"

"Huh?" I practically moaned out.

"You gon' take that wig off or not?"

I closed my eyes and took it off. He'd better be glad it was glueless. Had it not been, he would have had to deal with it. I pulled the cap off my braided hair as he stared at me. He brought his hand to my cheek and gently stroked my face. When he leaned in again, I tilted my head back, preparing for him to go back to my neck. Instead, he softly kissed my lips. My entire body heated up and when he pulled away, I knew he'd felt the fucking fireworks as I had.

He quickly pulled my shorts off and grabbed my ass, lifting me to the bed. My eyebrows had risen. Before I could even address it, he said, "I don't fuck nobody I can't handle, Yendi. Now spread them legs for me. Let me see your prized possession."

I did as he said, still in shock that he picked me up like that. That almost killed my tipsy state. I slid my hand to my pussy as he took off his pants. His eyes stayed on what I was doing. Flicking my fingers over my clit for a moment, I then brought my fingers to my lips. I wanted him to see that I enjoyed my taste. If I enjoyed it, he could rest assure that he would enjoy it too. He licked his lips as he watched in silence for a few seconds longer.

He came to me and slid between my legs, his lips meeting my lower ones. I was surprised that he was actually going to eat my pussy. While I was trying to coax him into doing it, I didn't think he would. I closed my eyes as he lifted my legs and dove all the way in.

"Oooh fuck!" I voiced as his mouth slurped up my clit and repeatedly tugged on it.

When his other hand found my nipple, I knew this wouldn't take long. He was stimulating me in every way. Although he was barely making a sound, my mind was working overtime trying to figure him out. Our sexual chemistry and attraction to one another was through the roof. I grabbed a handful of his hair and slightly lifted my hips, pushing my shit in his face.

He lifted his head and said, "Quit being reserved and shove that shit in my face if you want to. I didn't have time to condition my beard anyway."

He was giving me free reign over his face? This nigga didn't know what the fuck he had just unleashed. I immediately lifted my hips and rolled them, sliding my pussy all over his face. Somehow, he held onto my clit in the process. Within seconds, I detonated, squirting all over him and my bed. I could feel the warmth between my legs.

Jakari stood and stared at my pussy. That muthafucka took both of his hands and started massaging my juices into his beard like it was some damn beard oil. My eyes fluttered as I stared at him, and my pussy squirted a little more.

"This shit turn you on, Yendi?" he asked in a low voice.

I nodded, barely able to speak. When he finished, he reached into his pocket and pulled out two condoms, then dropped his jeans. Seeing his erection through his boxer briefs caused me to sit up slightly, propping myself up with my elbows. That shit was a sight to see. However, when he pulled his underwear off, it nearly took my breath away. It was long, dark, and thick. I needed every inch of his shit too.

He stroked it a couple of times then covered it with a condom. I thought I would be sucking his dick or that he would at least want me to. When he got to the bed though, he went to his knees next to me and dropped that shit on my lips. I was shocked that he wrapped up for this. I slid my tongue over it and realized it was mint flavored. I could deal with that, because I hated the taste of latex.

However, what I did notice was that he didn't seem to care about eating my pussy. Then it dawned on me... He was protecting me from him, not necessarily him from me. That realization only made my heart softer. I supposed he hadn't been tested recently and wanted to be sure of things before he exposed himself to me, although any infection could possibly travel through his saliva. *Damn.* Whoever met a sensitive and protective fuckboy? My thoughts about this only being a cover up to protect the real him were probably spot on.

I rolled over on all fours and took him into my mouth slowly, sucking him while he stared down at me. There wasn't a visible emotional expression on his face, so I began working harder. I could tell he wasn't for the teasing. As I applied more suction, a frown appeared on his brow. When he put his hand to the back of my head, I prepared to die.

If this nigga was gonna fuck my mouth, he would surely kill me. Totally opposite of what I thought, he began a slow rhythm, feeding me his dick a little at a time. I sucked in my jaws even more. They were practically tingling as I showed him how majestic his shit was.

"Mm, yeah, Yendi. Show this dick what you made of, girl."

I stared up at him as he gave me more, grazing the back of my throat. He tucked his lips into his mouth as his pace quickened some, but his moans made my throat enlarge herself to receive him. He held my gaze, but not for long. His eyes rolled shut, and he slowly began ravaging my mouth. The crazy part was that I was enjoying every minute of it.

"Fuck! I'm about to nut!

Shit, I was about to cum too. I'd never sucked dick like this to where it caused me to orgasm. Pleasing him, for some reason, meant something. Just the fact that I thought I even had something to prove was different for me, especially since this was supposed to just be casual sex. His oversized candy cane seemed to enlarge with excitement as he chased his nut down. That shit stopped running, turned around, and grabbed him by the balls though.

"Oh fuuuck!" he yelled.

I kept sucking, trying to milk him of every drop while my orgasm ripped through me. Although, I wasn't getting his flavors, I wanted him to be completely satisfied, as was I. I supposed his satisfaction had extremely turned me on, and my body couldn't help but to express its excitement. His large hand palmed the back of my head as he said, "You tryna make this a waterbed, baby?"

He pulled me off him as the foamy saliva fell from my lips, and I saw how wet the bed was in front of me. I must have squirted and didn't feel it. I definitely came though. I felt *that* shit. I nearly bit his dick off trying to contain myself.

"You so fucking sexy, Yendi."

He gently pushed me, causing me to lay on my back then he lay next to me, staring into my eyes. *What is he doing?* He was fucking with my emotions now. He rubbed my cheek with his thumb as he continued to stare then pulled my face to his. His soft lips met mine, and he kissed me passionately, like he was receiving something from the connection. His tongue slipped inside so I reciprocated his actions.

I moaned against his lips as the kiss deepened. He eased his body on top of mine without breaking our kiss and began grinding against me. Pulling away from me slightly, he sucked my bottom lip. When he released it, he said, "I've been wanting to suck your lips since I first saw you."

I slid my fingers through his beard. It was somewhat sticky. "Do wanna go wash your conditioner out?"

"Not until the job is done, baby. That would be like taking a shower and immediately getting dirty all over again. I'm not done tasting that sweet shit."

I bit my bottom lip. "Are you trying to make me a fiend?"

"I'm trying to show you what you should have *always* been getting."

He lowered his head and began teasing my nipples with his tongue, swirling it around them, then gently sucking them as his hands went on an excursion over my body. It was like he was trying to learn every part of me, and I didn't know how to take that. I didn't want my emotions to take over. Remaining detached was part of the plan but that shit was falling apart right before my eyes. "Jakari… yeeeeeesss."

I wrapped my legs around him as he continued to please me. Turning his head, he began licking my leg, sucking it in various spots before gripping it and lifting it. He went up on his knees and softly kissed behind my knee, sending shock waves through my body. He stayed there for a while, licking and sucking, until I orgasmed once again. My body was spent, and I hadn't even had his dick stroking my walls yet.

I'd had three orgasms, but I knew even more were in my future. After kissing a trail down my leg to my ankle, he stopped for a moment and stared at my toes. "You have pretty ass feet."

When he licked my big toe, my eyes rolled to the back of my head. Just from the foreplay alone, I wanted to be his. If he was this thorough every time, I could only imagine what it would be like if he loved me. *Damn.* I wanted to get used to this. He pulled it into his mouth and began sucking it like he was making love to it, and I swore I was about to squirt on him full force like he was on fire.

"Give it to me, beautiful flower."

My eyes misted over simply because I knew he took the time to look my name up. The African meaning of Yendi was just that… beautiful flower. It took me no time after that. I squirted the hardest I ever had. "Oh shit!" I yelled.

My screams were uncontained at this point. Jakari had my emotions all over the fucking place. He pulled away from me and pulled the first condom off, setting it on the nightstand, then sheathed himself with the other. When he rejoined me, he turned me over and slid his body on top of mine, kissing my shoulders and back as he rubbed my ass. As his kisses got lower, a shiver went up my spine.

He shifted lower and pushed my ass cheeks up, spreading them, then licked from my vaginal entry to my asshole. He stayed there for a while, licking and kissing it. I was so overwhelmed with pleasure I didn't know how else to express it. Turning me to my side, he lifted my leg and slowly slid his dick inside of me, pushing the tears right out of me. I knew he would fuck me up, but I wasn't expecting it to be like this.

He leaned over and softly kissed my cheek and the bridge of my nose where they were falling. "I hope these tears aren't a bad thing."

I shook my head as he fed me more of his dick. His shit was so big I nearly felt like a virgin all over again. Apparently, he was used to that. I supposed that was why he was taking things slow. The man was experienced and considerate, not just wanting the best time possible for himself but for me too.

He pushed more inside of me and moaned in my ear. "Yendi, fuck. You have some good pussy, just like I thought you would. Let me vibe in this shit for a while."

He bit my lobe then sucked it gently and pushed even more of his dick inside of me. "Mmmm, good girl."

My eyelids fluttered, and I came all over him. This thing between us was more than sexual, and he wouldn't be able to convince me otherwise. Him calling me a good girl was a weakness of mine. He stroked me faster as I continued to orgasm. "You like being called a good girl, beautiful? You got a praise kink? I do too. So tell me what this dick doing to you."

"I... can barely... form words, Jakari. Oh my God! You feel... so goooood!"

He thrusted into me as my pussy blossomed for him, giving him the space he needed. "Mm. Yeah, baby. You feel good too," he responded. "I'm balls deep in your shit now. That's rare that I can do that."

I turned my head to stare at him only to find that his eyes were closed. I knew that he felt me turn to him, but he refused to open his eyes right away. When he did open them, he turned me to my back and ground his dick into me while staring into my eyes. My tears started falling again, and he gently swiped them away. It felt like he was making love to all my fucking feelings. He lowered his head to my nipples and made love to me for a good ten minutes, making sure every nerve my pussy possessed had been touched. Overwhelmed wasn't even an accurate enough word to describe what I was feeling.

However, the tender moment was coming to an end as his strokes became more forceful. My moans became louder as I took him, trying to drain him of everything he had to offer. I tightened my muscles around him, putting those Kegel exercises to use. "Jakari, oh my God! I'm about to cum again!"

"Sink this muthafucka then."

Within seconds, I screamed out my orgasm, promising to do just what he demanded. As well-endowed as Jakari was, I could barely feel him anymore. That was just how wet I was. Showing his experience with that matter, Jakari pulled out of me and began slurping up my juices once more. He said he wasn't done and got dammit was he right. Either my shit was extremely sensitive or he was holding back with me earlier.

His tongue exposed and exfoliated every fucking nerve on my clit, getting those dead cells out of there and exposing the new ones. "Jakariiii!"

I knew there was no way I could take anymore. I'd orgasmed so much I'd lost count. He kept licking and sucking until I gave up the fucking ghost. After I came, he stood from the bed, seemingly admiring his work, then left the room. I was trying my hardest to catch my breath, but shit, I was tired.

He came back with a bottle of water. "Drink this, Yendi. You ain't finna tap out on me yet."

The last thing I wanted to do was sit up, but I accomplished the feat. He opened the bottle of water and handed it to me. Surprisingly, I gulped that shit like I hadn't had water in years. I heard him chuckle, but when I looked at him, he had a serious expression on his face.

"Is it okay if I get a towel from your bathroom?"

"Yeah," I said softly.

He came back and cleaned between my legs then threw the towel to the floor and rejoined me in bed, slowly sliding his dick up and down my slit. When he shoved it inside of me, he knocked the fucking wind out of me. I refused to be defeated though. I wrapped my arms around his neck and let him destroy me in the most pleasing way.

He pulled away from me and roughly rolled me to my stomach then pulled me by my hips to him. "Yendi, I hope you have more sheets, because these are going to be all fucked up when I finish with you. Those nails are about to rip them to shreds."

When he reentered me, I clawed at the sheets trying to grip them and literally snagged them. He was right. I would need new sheets.

CHAPTER 5
JAKARI

I could kick my own ass for going to Yendi's place. I was feeling all sensitive and shit after listening to Avery, and then my mama and Uncle WJ. She got parts of me I vowed no woman would ever get. I didn't even know her yet. I knew the shit was going to be intense when I kissed her. That was a huge no-no.

The crazy part was that I couldn't stop myself if I tried. It was like she pulled everything good out of me. I could tell her feelings had gotten involved just that quickly. After I nutted in her sweet pussy, I had the fucking audacity to take a shower with her. Who the fuck was I? If I would have brought another condom, I would have fucked her again.

After I got dressed, I got out of there. I could see that she was wanting to cuddle and shit. I couldn't do that. Women were already emotional beings, but after the shit I gave her, her emotions were going haywire. I'd never seen a woman cry during sex. That shit fucked me up and had me even more sensitive than what I had been already.

When I got home, I changed and met my crew at Floyd's in Beaumont. I almost asked Yendi if she wanted to go. That was how I knew I needed to get the fuck out of there. Truth was, I was afraid of relationships. I was afraid of being hurt and let down, like a fucking female.

HEALING FOR MY SOUL

Seeing how Avery fucked my mama and all of us up by the horrible secrets he was keeping, not to mention that lil teenage girl that thought she was slick years ago, made me swear off relationships all together.

That shit had me being careful as hell. I refused to fuck with women I met in a club or somewhere minors could be. If I didn't have a way of verifying their age, I avoided them like the fucking plague. Being that Yendi was the librarian at a high school, I knew she was of age. There was no further verification needed. The other woman I had been fucking around with worked for a bank and had a daughter.

Maybe I needed to dip back to someone else I had already fucked to get Yendi out of my system and off my mind. I couldn't fuck her again. The worst part was that she knew how to find me. I didn't think she would be shy about popping up either. I slid my hand over my face as Decaurey said, "Nigga, you a'ight? You been quiet as fuck and fidgeting."

I looked up at everyone to find all eyes on me. Nesha was sitting across from me, holding Lennox's hand, and Decaurey and Tyeis were sitting next to them so they could see my face clearly. Jess and Brix were seated next to me so they hadn't seen a thing. "J, you good?" Jess asked as she grabbed my hand.

"Yeah, I'm good. Chill out, Bestie Jessie."

She shoved me and went back to her appetizer. However, Nesha's gaze didn't waver. I was more than sure she knew I had "talked" to Avery. I hadn't said a word to him, but I listened longer than I should have. She reached across the table, her hand palm up. I put my hand in hers, and she gave me a slight smile. I lifted her hand and kissed it. While Jess and I were close, I was even closer to Nesha. I just stopped looking out for her when she and Lennox got serious. I knew he had her from there, especially being that he was a detective.

When I released her hand, I excused myself from the table and went outside to get some air. As soon as I walked out the door, my mama called. "Hello?"

"Hey, baby. I just wanted to check on you."

"I'm okay, Ma."

"Jakari, I no longer need protecting, baby. It's time that you tend to yourself. You've suppressed so much over the years for the sake of your brothers, your aunt Syn, Nesha, and me. We have all moved on to healthier relationships and have put the trauma of what Avery did behind us. It's time for you to do the same, baby."

I closed my eyes and took a deep breath. While I knew she was right, I didn't even know how to begin doing that. I'd been dealing with this shit the best way I knew how for over twelve years, fucking women to distract myself from my issues. Yendi had read me perfectly, and maybe that was another reason why I was running from her. It was like she could see my soul.

"I know, Mama. I will."

"You know Serita will be happy to counsel you. There's no harm in talking to someone, son. Christian had a couple of sessions with her and so did Rylan. They both said she helped them tremendously. I know Avery is your father, and you inherited all the good parts of him... his good looks, his business sense, and his charm. However, you are not him."

"Yes, ma'am. Let me call you back, Ma. I'm at dinner with the crew."

"Oh, I'm sorry, baby. Call me back. I love you."

"I love you too."

I ended the call and blew out a hard breath of irritation and exhaustion. I was tired of feeling like I was the one that had fucked up. While I accepted some responsibility of what happened to Nesha, I knew that Avery was the guilty party. I slid my phone into my pocket, knowing that Yendi was a big part of why I was feeling the way that I was. I'd gotten thoughts of Avery out of my head, but they were replaced with all the shit I did with Yendi.

After sliding my hand over my face and willing myself into a better mood, I headed back inside. When I sat, everyone stared at me. "Damn. I mean that much to y'all? I'm good."

Nesha smiled and ate a fry from her plate. My food was waiting for me, and I could only hope that it hadn't been here long enough to get cold. I grabbed a fried shrimp and found it to still be warm. *Thank goodness.* There was nothing worse than eating cold fried food. As I ate, Jess shoulder bumped me. "You know if you wanna talk, I'm always available."

I gave her a one-cheeked smile, waiting for the bullshit. She was just as bad as Uncle Storm sometimes. "Although, I heard you had a badass BBW with you at the diner earlier."

I rolled my eyes. "She wasn't with me. She was there before I even got there. I just happened to have met her at the school when I was picking up Maui and Ashanni."

"Why were you picking them up when they both have cars?" Nesha asked.

"Because they were dipping their noses in my business, thinking I needed to be hooked up with Yendi's fine ass."

She giggled, and I couldn't help but chuckle too. "I wouldn't expect that out of the two of them," Tyeis added.

"First of all, just because they're sweet, they still have parts of their fathers. Uncle Storm is always meddling in somebody's business. Uncle Jasper does too, but he isn't as blatant about it as the mayor. So they get it honest," Jess said with a shrug of her shoulders.

"Well however y'all met, it looks like y'all would make a cute couple," Tyeis said.

Everyone at the table agreed. "A'ight, so when is the baby shower again, Nesha?"

They all laughed again as I tried to direct the conversation to something else. "I'm gon' let'chu make it with that because I know you private when it comes to that. Everyone is just buying pampers and wipes. I already have a closet full of clothes, because I just couldn't help myself," Nesha said.

"Man, this woman was shopping as soon as we found out the baby was a boy," Lennox added with a chuckle.

They were so happy. It was crazy, because I wanted what they had, but at the same time, I didn't trust that the person I chose would be loyal. I was all kinds of fucked up.

"Well, fuck that. I want y'all to pull out all the stops for my baby shower," Jess added. "No expense spared, because guess why?"

Everyone just stared at her waiting for her to continue. "We're having a divaaaaa!"

The women started screaming as I frowned up, and Decaurey put his finger to his ear. Lennox glanced around the restaurant, nodding at people, assuring them all was well. I slowly shook my head. Jess was already loud, but ever since Tyeis had joined us, she'd gotten even louder, because she had somebody to get loud with her.

"Congratulations, Jess! Our baby girl will have a playmate, just like our baby boy!" Tyeis said excitedly.

"After that shit, we gon' have to drop them home and head to Uncle Jasper's," Decaurey said.

"Hell yeah. But you know Lennox ain't coming. He like the James Carter of the family. He don't participate, but he knows what goes on," I said with a smirk.

"Hell yeah. It'll kill Aunt Boosie if I have to bust y'all asses," Lennox said, causing another outburst of laughter.

"Y'all gon' get our asses kicked out of here," Nesha said.

We used to wear *Rush Hour* out! We were little when it came out, but we laughed like we knew everything they were talking about. We couldn't fully appreciate the comedy until we got older. However, we knew every line of that shit. So Lennox quoting that line almost took Nesha, Jess, and me out.

"Tyeis, is Aunt Liv doing a shower for you?" I asked, realizing I'd unintentionally left her out after Jessica's outburst.

"Actually, yes. She said she would be handing out invites to everyone tomorrow. It's gonna be in three weeks, and it's co-ed... mainly a big family gathering at the barn. Plus, the article Aunt Aspen asked me to help with will be available for all your reading pleasure that day."

"That's what's up, Ty," I responded.

"That's my best fren! That's my best fren!" Jess said while wiggling in her seat.

Then she and Tyeis made L's out of their fingers on both hands and started doing a lil jig with them. They burst into laughter, and I was confused as hell. I looked around the table and everyone else seemed just as confused as me. Brix had shaken his head like he'd seen them do it before.

"Nesha, we gon' have to show you the TikTok video, so you can be with us whenever we do it," Jess said.

"Yeah, because I feel real left out right now," she said and pouted.

"I'ma need that blunt soona than right now, nigga," Decaurey said.

"Agreed."

We continued talking for a little while longer then left, heading back to Nome. Since we all lived in Nome now, it was easy to carpool. Decaurey and Tyeis had ridden with Brix and Jess. So Brix and D got in the vehicle with me and let the two sillies ride together.

"Jessica's video with Noah premiers next month," Brix said as we drove.

"Oh cool! I can't wait to see that shit," Decaurey said.

"Yeah, I can't wait to see it either," I added.

"I can. I don't wanna see Noah grabbing my cake."

We laughed, and he chuckled. I knew he wasn't serious, but I also knew he was extremely possessive when it came to Jess. Nigga could barely function if he was missing her. He was somewhat like that in high school, and they weren't even a couple. However, him bringing that up reminded me that I hadn't called Nate back. I would have to do that tomorrow.

"THANKS FOR MEETING WITH US ON THE WEEKEND, ALI," I SAID AS I extended my hand.

Yesterday was a bust after I talked to Avery. I had to get my mind right. He told me that he didn't have anything to do today, so Philly and I could come by the office. "That's no problem. I'm honored to be in partnership with the Hendersons. Real shit," Ali said.

"Well, we're honored too, because now, we don't have to get our hands dirty. We can focus on business, and not have to worry about bullshit like this," I said as Philly continued to stare at him.

Ali noticed, and he cracked a smile. "Yeah, I used to run," Ali said to him. "Who don't know Philly "trigger happy" Semien?"

Philly grinned as Ali continued. "I ran for the Pattersons in Houston back in the day. By the time I ended up in Beaumont, you were out the game."

"Damn. Okay. I remember the Pattersons, and I knew I remembered seeing you somewhere."

"Yep. Jungle Patterson works with us. He dismantled all that shit. He said he was tired of that shit."

"Damn. I can relate to that. Sounds like you have a good set up here though."

"I do. It's backed by my best friend, Attorney Shyrón Berotte."

"That's what's up," Philly said as he nodded and looked around.

"So what's up with Tyrese?" I asked, getting us back on track.

"He went back to Houston, so Jungle and Seneca have picked him up again. That nigga don't even seem like a threat. I think he just bumping his gums. He ain't got so much as a speeding ticket. The only record of arrest he has is when he fucked with your people. I'm gon' keep digging though. If he's hiding something, I'm gon' find that shit," Ali said.

I nodded again. I was glad to have his crew on board. Watchful Eyes could be extremely beneficial to our family. As he and Philly talked a little more, my phone chimed with a text message. It was from a number that wasn't saved in my phone, but I recognized it immediately as Yendi's. I opened it to see what she had to say. *Hey. I hope you're having a good weekend.*

I closed out of her message without responding. I would respond later when I got home. Ghosting her had crossed my mind, and I honestly thought that may have been best, but after yesterday, I knew that shit would be hard to do. However, I refused to save her number. That would seem more permanent in my mind.

I tuned back into the conversation to hear Philly say, "Well, I guess you have it under control. If you need anything from us, just let me or Jakari know."

"Most likely, Philly will be your point person since y'all are familiar," I added.

I could see Philly's interest in their business, and I could actually see him working with them sometimes. His eyes were wide with curiosity the more Ali talked. I could see how Ali's work as a PI and security could be lucrative. Some people probably found him intimidating as hell with all the tattoos. They covered his skin completely. The only place he didn't have them was in his face.

"Okay. Whatever y'all decide is fine. Just let me know. Next time we meet up, maybe y'all will get to meet Shy, Jungle, Seneca, Chad, Rondo, and Jericho. I have other employees, but they are my main go-to's, and they're my brothers. My cousin, Dinalee, works with us as well, but she hates when I include her as one of the fellas."

I nodded. "Yeah, just let us know when. We'll try to make time for that."

I shook his hand and so did Philly. We made our way to the Suburban. The minute we got inside, I turned to him. "I can see your wheels turning. That trigger finger itching, ain't it?"

"Shiiid, it's been itching for a while, but I think I may have found a way to scratch it. I mean not full time, but maybe part time."

"I don't have an issue with it, but you know who you would have to talk to about that. I think you would be good to be their point person though."

"I think so too. Now that I know who he is and who he's associated with, I think we'll get along just fine. I know how to function with street niggas. While they aren't in the streets anymore, the streets are still in them. I can see it, because they will always make up who I am."

"I get it, bruh."

We rode in quietness for a while. When he opened his mouth again, I wished it would have remained quiet. "So what's up with you and the chick at the diner?"

"Nothing. I met her at HJ Wednesday. Two of your nieces were trying to play matchmaker."

He chuckled. Although Philly wasn't related, my uncles looked at him like a brother. So to everyone's kids, he was Uncle Philly. Nesha,

Jess, and I even called him that from time to time. His brother was our uncle since he married Aunt Tiff.

"You gon' try to get to know her?"

"I don't know yet," I said, leaving the conversation just like that.

He caught the hint and started talking about his racecar. Philly was a smart dude and could easily peep shit. There was never much I had to explain to him. He could read my mannerisms and somehow knew exactly how to respond or approach me. I was grateful for that because I wasn't the most expressive person in the world.

Once we got to Nome, I dropped Philly at the office so he could get his car, then headed home. When I got there, I pulled up Yendi's message again. I responded, *Hey. It has started off good. I hope you're enjoying your weekend so far.*

I got out and carried my things from the office inside. Work was never done when it came to the family business. We were always trying to evolve with the times and how frequently they changed. Because of that, I was always running statistics and reports, detailing our sales and marketing successes. The reports helped us know how to proceed.

My phone chimed again so after unlocking the door and setting my things on the table, I checked it to see Yendi's response. *I am. I'm at a massage parlor in Beaumont. I had this nigga over yesterday that was bending me all kinds of ways. Almost every muscle in my body is sore.*

I chuckled. *That nigga must be the real fucking deal if he got'chu sore. He worked that ass out, huh?*

Hell yeah. I didn't get out of the bed until it was time to come here. Can I hit you back when I get home?

Yeah, that's cool. Talk to you then.

I smiled slightly as she sent a kissy face emoji. I cleared my throat, trying to shake myself of the haze she had me in. I slid my hand over my face and began going over the reports from the many stores that carried our rice, roux, and rice dressing mix. Once I tallied up the demand, I could decide if our production numbers were compatible. Empty shelves at the grocery store weren't putting more money in our pockets. We needed to make sure the supply matched the demand.

I also planned to visit a couple more stores by next weekend. One in San Antonio and another in Mesquite, not far from Dallas. Aunt Tiff and Malachi had participated in rodeos out there. I enjoyed selling our products. It made me proud to be a Henderson. Sometimes, I wished I would have changed my last name to Henderson. I supposed it wasn't too late.

Rylan had adopted my stepfather's last name. He was Rylan Douglas by the time he graduated from high school. Christian had changed his last name to Henderson. I didn't know why I hadn't done it yet. It was the one thing in my life I didn't follow through on. At first, I was hoping the mess with my father was all a big nightmare. I would wake up from it, and he and my mom would still be married and happy.

I wasn't so fortunate. I looked up to him. We had a fairly decent relationship up until that point. He taught me how to be a man. How could he teach me to be someone that he wasn't? There was no excuse for what he did to my cousins, aunt, and that other little girl. As a grown man, he knew that wasn't right. He knew he had a problem. It was up to him to seek help instead of hurting innocent girls.

I supposed I took what he did super hard… harder than my brothers. As the oldest, I tried to be like him. He broke my heart and now it wasn't fit for anybody. At this moment, I knew I needed to make a decision to get the help I needed instead of being like him and ignoring the signs, thinking I could handle it myself. At least I knew not to get seriously involved with anyone. I had issues that needed to be dealt with and refused to bring anyone into my turmoil.

That meant I surely needed to back away from Yendi. With the state my mind and heart were in, I wouldn't be able to handle everything she had to offer me. I didn't deserve her love. I would only hurt her. I went to Serita Gardner's website and made an appointment for next week. It was time to get on track with who I knew I was supposed to be.

CHAPTER 6
YENDI

I was dragging this morning. This week couldn't be over fast enough, and it was only Tuesday. Sleep had been evading me, and I knew it had everything to do with Jakari Bolton. When I called him Saturday evening, he didn't answer, and he never called back. I sent him a text on Sunday to let him know that I'd called and left a message and was also asking if he was okay. Still nothing. My mind was filled with possibilities of what could have happened. Surely, he wouldn't ghost me after what we shared.

I let my feelings get involved, but it was like I didn't have a choice. While he said he just wanted to fuck, his actions were showing something totally different. After only one sex session, I was sprung. That shit had me angry with myself and fucking depressed. I wasn't even mad at him. He didn't owe me a thing, not even an explanation. However, I needed him to know that I was here for him… whenever he needed me. I didn't regret anything. *I'm fucking pathetic.*

I wouldn't bother him to death, but I would visit the diner for just a glimpse. I needed to see him at least. It felt like something was off with him. It was almost like I could feel him. Maybe it was just that I wanted to make an excuse to justify why I hadn't heard from him. He was responding to my text messages Saturday, so something had to have happened to make him not answer my call.

As I sat at my desk looking over Maui and Ashanni's proposal about a game we could play to get kids involved, I lifted my eyebrows. These girls were promising a brand new iPhone to the winner of a 'bomb' book report. I didn't know who they took me for, but there was no way I was giving away a twelve-hundred-dollar iPhone. I would have to burst their bubble after school today.

The stipulations and requirements were great though. The book had to at least be a ninth-grade level chapter book, it had to be a book checked out of our library that they've never read before, and the report had to be detailed and at least two pages long. The most creative and accurate report would win.

I went on to look at another contest. It promised a pizza party for the top readers before the Christmas break. I could possibly fund that since I still had some of my dad's insurance money. It was like he knew my mama would act a fool. He had separate policies. She was the beneficiary of one of them and my siblings and I were the recipients of the other. She got a five-hundred-thousand-dollar policy, and we split two hundred thousand. That gave each of us fifty grand.

That was much more than what I expected, because I wasn't expecting a dime. We weren't the ones depending on his income to live. So rightfully, it should have gone to his spouse. The money I received helped me though. Like Jakari had pointed out, HJISD didn't pay shit. After paying my bills from my salary, I didn't have a dime left. I was using the money from my dad to buy groceries and anything else I may have needed.

I knew that money wouldn't last forever, but it would hold me over until I got a better paying job. I had only had to use five hundred dollars so far. This job definitely taught me to be frugal. I never had to pinch pennies with my last job. I made more than twice what I was making now. I'd saved some money as well, but I had put most of it in a traditional IRA account to supplement my retirement later. My dad had told me that retirement money wouldn't be enough for me to live comfortably with the direction the country was headed. So I took his advice and started investing money.

I began thinking of things I could possibly do to supplement my income. I didn't really have a talent that could make me extra money. Any part-time job I could obtain in the area, without a specific expertise, were businesses owned by members of Jakari's family or fast-food places. I refused to work fast food. I would be eating the entire time I was there, especially at Sonic. Sour Lake only had Sonic, Dairy Queen, Subway, and a pizza place called Goodfella's Pizzeria.

They also had a grocery store, but I didn't get good vibes in there the last time I went. They were expensive as hell, and they stared at me like I didn't belong there. I simply stared right back like I had a whole army behind me. I never let people intimidate me. They put their pants on the same way I did.

As I surfed Amazon on my computer, a class of students came in. I smiled politely and nodded at them as they spoke. Most of the kids here were friendly, and they learned my name quickly. By my second day, a lot of them were calling me by name, speaking to me like I'd been here for years. Maui Henderson was one of them. Ashanni was somewhat quiet at first, but she always smiled.

When Maui walked in, she smiled and came straight to my desk. "Hey, Ms. Odom!"

"Hey, boo. How are you?"

"I'm good. Umm... For my birthday, I asked my daddy if we could have a cookout at the family barndominium, and he said yes. So, I was wondering if you would come."

I briefly thought about Jakari, knowing that I would probably see him. "Yeah, of course. When is it?"

"It's a month away, but I wanted to tell you about it early in case you had something else to do."

She was so sweet and obviously, one of my favorite students. I smiled at her as she handed me an invite. I glanced at it to see it had a country theme: hay bales, cowboy boots, and wagon wheels all over it. I looked back up at her. "I'll be there. Sounds like it will be a good time. What do you like to do besides read?"

"I'm into rodeoing and anything to do with horses. I like music too."

"Okay. I'll have to think of something. I have time."

She smiled and clapped in excitement as I chuckled. I was happy that she took a liking to me, but I knew this had to do with Jakari. They were playing matchmaker. I didn't mind it since it was subtle. Their family was chill and seemed fun to be around, especially the mayor and the brother that introduced themselves to me at the diner.

When Maui walked away to go look for a book, I turned my attention to my phone to see I had a message on Facebook. I frowned slightly because I rarely got those. When I opened it, I saw it was one of my mama's old friends, asking me to call her and listed her number. I rolled my eyes, not because of the message but because I knew my mom was probably ignoring her calls.

She only wanted to talk to people who would believe her lies or that she could manipulate. If something she said was questioned or if someone called her out on her bullshit, she was done with them. She knew Ms. May would question things. I hadn't talked to Ms. May verbally in years, but she always engaged whenever I made a post on Facebook. I put my phone down, making a mental note to call her later, then stood to begin helping students check out the books they'd chosen.

"Hey, baby. How are you doing?"

"Hi, Ms. May. I'm doing okay. How are you?"

"I'm good. I'm retired now, so I'm doing my best to enjoy life."

"That's great."

"Listen, I was calling to check on your mom. I've tried calling, and I went by there and left a note for her in the mailbox. How is she?"

"Honestly, I don't know. I haven't spoken to her since my dad's funeral."

"Aww no. She's grieving hard and secluding herself from people?"

"No. She's talking to who she wants to talk to."

The line went quiet for a moment, then Ms. May asked, "She's not talking to y'all?"

"Not really. She talks to Marie, but that's about it."

"Oh my goodness. Well, did she allow your dad's other daughter to attend the funeral?"

I rolled my eyes hard, and I could feel myself getting angry. I hadn't even gotten in the house yet when I called her. This shit was back again. Now I would have to relive this shit all over again, because I refused to allow her to keep smearing shit on my daddy's name. "What daughter?"

"Umm… your mom said he had an outside kid with a woman at Antioch. She ought to be around eighteen years old now."

"She's a liar."

"What?"

"My daddy didn't have any outside kids. She's a liar. If it were true, she would have been sure to tell us, because she couldn't stand that we were closer to him than her."

"Oh my God. Why would she lie about that?"

"She lies about everything. Anyone that can lie about having cancer is a sick individual."

"Who had cancer? She told me your dad had cancer, but he overcame."

"He did. He had colon cancer, but they did a partial colectomy, removing lymph nodes as well. He did a round of chemo, but his heart couldn't take it. However, he was cleared of cancer because they caught it early. She was telling people that *she* had cancer and was going through chemo. She lied about that twice."

"My friend needs help."

I was totally surprised that she was actually listening to me. After I started spilling tea, most people were in a hurry to get off the phone. Either she sincerely cared, or she was being messy. I didn't care. I refused to stifle my voice when it came to my mama. I was sick of her lies. "She really does, Ms. May, but she has to admit that she has a problem in order to get help."

"You're right about that."

"People always say, 'you only got one mama', but guess what? She only has one Yendi. If she's destroying my peace, then I have to distance myself. I told her not to call me unless she was ready to have an honest conversation of her accepting responsibility for all the drama she started. That was before Dad died."

"Wow. I'm just shocked. This is unbelievable."

"We were shocked by her behavior as well."

"Baby, I'm so sorry. Lock my number in. I'm saving yours now. I'm going to be praying for her, that she can get herself together."

"Yes, ma'am. Me too."

"You take care of yourself, and I'll be checking on you."

"Okay. Love you."

"Love you too, baby. And I'm so sorry about your daddy."

"Thank you."

I ended the call and sat in my car in my thoughts. I slowly shook my head, knowing that I would have to eventually confront her ass. She used to always talk about God and raised us in church, making us memorize scriptures. But now, she hadn't been to church in years, and had turned into the devil himself. Maybe she'd been the devil all along. The devil went to church too and knew the scripture as well. She'd convinced people that she was an innocent lamb, but she was definitely a wolf in sheep's clothing.

I made my way inside and immediately dropped all my shit on the floor. My mood was fucked. I went to the kitchen and grabbed the bottle of Hennessy and poured a glass. Rehashing this shit was getting old. I wanted to let it go, but my mind wouldn't seem to allow me to. People always said to just let people spew negativity and lies about you. That you didn't have to tell your side. That shit was easier said than done.

I wasn't volunteering my side of what happened, which was the truth, but when people asked questions, I always gave them the real. Just hearing my mother's name or just hearing people ask how she was doing, put a bad taste in my mouth. Knowing that my *own* mother was spewing lies about me and had been doing some extremely hateful things to my siblings and me was hard to just accept and let go.

I was filled with malice and hatred for her. Hating her wouldn't do a thing for me, but yet here I was, in this space… a space I'd never been in before. While it had only been a few months, I needed these feelings to leave me. They were tearing me down and making me more sensitive with people I shouldn't be that way with. My feelings were always on my sleeve, and the ones that were still inside, Jakari had pulled them out of me.

Jesus. I didn't even know how my thoughts about my mother led to him, but it seemed that was the way it had been since I met him. My every thought ended up finding its way to him. I didn't even know him well enough to miss him, yet I missed him like crazy. Maybe I missed what I thought could have been. After the other night, I thought we could possibly have something special. *Wishful thinking.*

I grabbed my glass of Hennessy, choosing not to add anything to it and just gulped that shit. I tried not to drink the hard stuff during the week, but there was no way a glass of wine would suffice. Dropping the glass in the sink, I went back toward the door and picked up my stuff and headed to my bedroom. Once inside, I dropped my things to the floor again and went to start a bath.

As my water ran, I checked my email to see one from Maui. I took a deep breath and opened it to see what she needed.

Hi, Ms. Odom. Did you forget that Ashanni and I were coming today? I could tell you seemed a little distracted today. Although I'm only fifteen, I'm a good listener if you want to talk. Maybe we can stay after school Thursday. We practice on Wednesdays.

I huffed loudly. "Fuck!" I said aloud.

I completely forgot the girls would be coming after school today. After hitting reply to her email, I typed out, *I'm so sorry, Maui. I completely forgot. I am a little distracted, and I appreciate you offering a listening ear. I can handle it though. I'll see you and Ashanni on Thursday. We need to discuss the prizes and exactly who's supposed to pay for them. LOL*

I hit send and smiled slightly. There was no way I would catch myself telling all my business to a fifteen-year-old. I didn't want to tell most *adults* my business let alone a kid. No matter how mature she seemed, this tea was nowhere near appropriate to share with a kid.

After getting a night gown, I made my way back to the bathroom and disrobed. I stepped in the tub, and just as I was about to sink in the hot water, there was a knock at my door. I frowned. It could only be one person. I hadn't made friends here yet… at least not any that would pop up at my place. I quickly grabbed my robe from the hook on the door, leaving wet footprints all over the floor.

When I reached the door and looked through the peephole, I nearly came on myself. Jakari was standing there. He wasn't looking straight forward. All I could see was his diamond stud in his ear and the waves and curls in his naturally gorgeous hair and beard. I took a deep breath then unlocked the door and opened it.

When his eyes met mine, I felt a shiver go up my spine. His eyes dipped to what I was wearing, which was practically nothing. "Umm… come in."

I stepped to the side as he walked through the door. Him being here had me soft as hell. I could see in his eyes that something was wrong. After closing the door, I turned to see he had sat on the couch, so I made my way to him.

"I'm sorry for interrupting your evening. I won't be long."

"You aren't interrupting much of anything. I was just about to soak and then go to bed early."

I was dying to tell him how much I missed him. Since he was here, I was hoping he would offer some sort of explanation about what was going on with him. Once I sat, he turned to me and said, "I can't see you anymore."

That shit felt like a bullet to the chest. I nodded quietly, then asked, "Why? I mean, I thought this was just casual."

He could have just continued to ghost me. I would have eventually gotten the hint, but him coming here to tell me just solidified his position. "I have a lot of shit going on right now. I'm way too sensitive with you. I don't want to lead you on in any way. I'm not ready for anything more than fucking, and honestly, I probably can't even handle that shit right now. Not with you. I don't know what it is, but being with you exposes all my nerves... fuckups... insecurities."

I grabbed his hand and felt the heat between us. "Jakari, you feel that? I don't want to let it go. I know you said we were just fucking, but you made love to me. I can't shake that shit. You being here to tell me that you can't see me anymore proves that you feel the same way I do. Otherwise, you wouldn't have felt the need to explain anything to me. Let me be here for you... whatever it is you're going through."

"Why though? You don't even know me."

"I don't know. I can't explain why I feel the way I do, but in my spirit, I feel like you need me as much as I need you. Don't push me away."

I kissed his hand as he stared at me. I could see the torment in his saddened eyes. He pulled his hand away from mine and stood from the couch, heading to the door. I quickly stood and practically ran after him. "Jakari, wait—"

He spun around and crashed his lips into mine, kissing me like it would be the last time. He tried to pull away, but I slid my arms around him, keeping him close. He didn't fight against me. Instead, he untied my robe, revealing my nakedness beneath it then lifted me and walked to my bedroom.

I stared into his eyes the entire time and surprisingly his gaze didn't waver. He lowered me to my bed and spread my legs. "Jakari, I haven't bathed since last night. I was about to take—"

All talking ceased when he practically dove in my pussy tongue first. My eyes rolled to the back of my head, but my mind was screaming. *Is this a goodbye or the start of something special?* I wanted to just be able to go with the flow and enjoy the moment, but the voice in my head wouldn't rest. As if sensing my inner voice, he lifted his head, my juices damn near dripping from his beard.

"I don't know what this is between us. You said you would be here... That's not fair to you. I got some deep issues I need to get a handle on. You telling me you would be okay with a piece of my love whenever I decided to give it? You good with giving me that much power over you?"

"Jakari, it's not you having power over me, but it's about me putting power back into you. There's a tinge of insecurity in you. I need you to know that you are enough. You're more than enough, and you're worthy of everything I have to offer, especially my patience. You're chosen for beautiful things, even in your brokenness. I got caught up the first time I saw you. Your desires I'm here to fulfill. This level of submission is new to me. I'm not asking for you to force anything with me, but I *am* asking for you to allow me to be around. You're more than a dream come true, Jakari."

He groaned as he nearly sucked my pussy right off my body. His fingertips dug into my flesh as he devoured every part of me. My heart was wide open, and I didn't know why. Was it because he put that demon dick on me? I didn't have a clue, but time would definitely tell. My words had moved him. The way his tongue began slowly stroking me, lapping up as much of my goodness as he could, I could only relax in what I felt was right.

What was right? Being his rock, his peace, his confidant. I wanted to be whatever he needed me to be. It was like God used those girls to bring us together. I wasn't sure what His purpose was for us, but I could only hope Him bringing us together would be permanent.

He lifted his head again and stared into my eyes. "You're so beautiful, Yendi. Inside and out. I want you to be mine, but I know I'm not ready. If you're telling me you want to be here anyway, waiting for me to get my shit together, then I'll let you be. I just hope I can handle that though. I don't want to feel like I'm using you."

I sat up and pulled him to me by placing my hands on each side of his face. "Use me. Just don't discard me. I want to be with you. Although you're in turmoil, I feel a sense of peace when I'm around you. It could be that I'm just lonely. In that case, I suppose we'd be using each other."

I kissed his lips, and he began slowly sucking my bottom one. When he pulled away, he said, "I didn't bring any condoms. It wasn't my intent to be with you like this. So let me please you, baby. Let me finish sucking the fuck out this sweet pussy."

I gushed at his words and slowly leaned back to lie in bed. "See, you got me wasting my dinner, baby. I almost wanna suck these sheets to get what you wasted. He flattened his tongue and licked my pussy from back to front, landing on my clit. He sucked slowly, taking me to ecstasy instantly. My legs trembled, and my entire body heated up and christened him, offering him my loyalty and devotion, although he warned me he couldn't do the same.

What in the fuck was I doing?

CHAPTER 7
JAKARI

I got out of my pickup truck to check on Jacob. He was in the rice field on a combine, harvesting the last crop of rice for the year. That nigga was in that shit jamming. I could see his head bobbing and his arm in the air while his body bounced. I slowly shook my head as he noticed I was watching him. He smiled big and hit the switch to stop the header from cutting.

When he hopped out, I chuckled. He had on shorts and cowboy boots along with his diamond earrings, a chain with a gold cross hanging from it, and a Stetson. This boy looked all kinds of confused. "What's up, cuz?" he yelled over the engine of the combine as he approached.

"Ain't shit, Jake. I just came to check on you to see how it was going."

He slapped my hand when he got close. "Everything cool. I had a little hiccup with the header, but I got it fixed. Those days of working with Uncle Storm and Uncle WJ paid off. I can fix almost anything now."

"That's good, man. You on track to becoming the next family mechanic then. We could always use more. We have a lot of equipment. As soon as you get licensed, let me know. Your pay will go up."

"That's what's up. This is my last semester. I should have my certification next month."

"Good. Well, I'll talk to Uncle WJ about it and get the ball rolling then."

"Thanks, man. You ought to go out with me, Christian, Rylan, and KJ tonight. The Park on Calder is supposed to be fire tonight."

"Hmm. I'll let y'all know."

"A'ight then."

We slapped hands again, and he made his way back to the combine as I turned and headed to my truck. As I did, my phone chimed with a text message. I pulled it from my pocket to see it was from Yendi. *Hey. I hope you're having an amazing day.*

I smiled slightly then got in my truck. What happened with her the other day was *not* planned. My plan was to let her down easy. I was really feeling her, but I knew I couldn't be the man she needed and deserved right now. However, she wasn't taking no for an answer. Just the fact that I wanted to explain was a sign within itself that this was different. She'd read the fuck out of me, and I couldn't understand how.

After checking on KJ at the hay field and Rylan and Christian at the grass farm, I headed to the diner to get something to eat. It was Thursday, so I knew I would be eating Aunt Jen's chicken. I wondered what she'd stuffed it with this time. So far, I believed the mac and cheese was my favorite. The minute I walked in the door, I knew I would be here for a while. Uncle Storm was on the rampage.

"You seen this shit?" he asked Uncle Kenny.

"I saw the picture, but naw, I didn't see them in person."

"Me and Aspen gon' have a whole ass conversation when she gets back from Florida."

I walked to the counter with a frown on my face as my mama tried to suppress her smile. "Storm, they are growing up, baby. They're seventeen," she said as she fixed my food. "Hey, baby. How's your day going?"

"It's going okay, Ma. What's gotten up his ass?"

She bit her bottom lip then gave me her phone. There was a picture of Noni and Bali in what looked to be midriff shirts. Their belly buttons were showing. *So what.* Their faces were made up more than normal. He couldn't have been tripping over no damn makeup. I frowned slightly and she said, "Swipe to the next picture."

When I did, Bali was turned to the side. My eyebrows lifted. What looked to be a midriff shirt in the other picture looked like a damn handkerchief in this picture. Her entire back was out and part of her side. You could almost see where her breasts began from the side. Being that they had long hair, it somewhat covered it, but not nearly enough.

"Somebody gon' get fucked up. They growing up, but they ain't grown. That shit ain't acceptable. Aspen should have run that shit by me before she even bought that. I try to be cool about shit with the girls because they *are* growing up, but this? They crossed the fucking line, Chrissy, and you know it," Uncle Storm ranted.

I extended my hand to shake his as Aunt Syn walked in. He shook it and gave me a head nod. Oh yeah, he was pissed. He normally had some stupid shit to say to me. Not today. "Hey, Jakari," Aunt Syn said as she hugged me.

"Hey, Auntie. How you doing?"

"I'm good. Did I miss Marcus?"

"No, he hasn't gotten here yet," my mama responded as she handed me my food.

"Thank you. What's it stuffed with?"

"You'll find out when you bite into it," Aunt Jen said as she came from the back with another pan of chicken.

I gave her a smirk as I made my way to the table. After setting my food down, I went back to get something to drink. My eyes met Aunt Syn's, and she smiled then headed my way. She and I had a unique relationship. She was my aunt because she married Uncle Marcus, but she was also my aunt because she was my dad's adopted sister and the first little girl he molested. I'd known her for my entire life as my aunt.

I was the only family that knew how she got down back in the day.

While I didn't know my dad had been molesting her, I'd witnessed the real her on several occasions. One time she'd shown up at an Alpha party at Lamar and ended up sleeping with my frat brother the same day she met him. I actually walked in on it and was ready to throw hands.

That was when she had to tell me more about herself... things that no one else knew. She didn't divulge that my father was the one who introduced her to sex, but she'd insinuated that she'd been touched inappropriately as a kid. I was sworn to secrecy so I didn't dare betray her trust by telling anyone. At that point, she was grown so it didn't matter. We were close in age, and I considered her like more of a sister than my aunt. She used to insist that I called her aunt when we were little, so she could have a title to boss me around.

I chuckled at the memory. After finding out about my dad, just like I checked on Nesha and had her back when she didn't realize it, I did the same for Aunt Syn. I knew about her fucking around, so I would always text her when she went somewhere with a man or to someone's house. She would always respond that she was good and to live my life without worrying about her.

"So how have you been, nephew?" she asked when she got to the table.

"I've been okay," I said as I stood to help her in her seat.

She gave me a soft smile. "Thank you."

I nodded then reclaimed my seat. When I sat, she asked, "So, are you dating the young lady you were here with last week?"

"No. We're just cool."

"Nephew, look at me."

I looked up at her from my food and could see she was about to say something heavy. Her face was serious, not a hint of a smile in sight. "Don't be like me. Admit that there is a problem and get help. You were trying to be there for me, and I ran every chance I got, knowing that I could have used someone to talk to, someone who knew the real me. Talk to someone. I don't mind listening."

I bit my bottom lip and nodded then continued eating my food.

HEALING FOR MY SOUL

Before she could say anything else, Uncle Storm got cranked up all over again. "They didn't look like that when they left the house."

"How did you even get the pictures?" Uncle Jasper asked.

"One of their friend's parents that I'm friends with on Facebook posted pictures of her daughter and all her friends. I'm gon' charge her ass up too for posting pictures of my kids without my permission, especially wearing this shit."

Aunt Syn rolled her eyes playfully while I chuckled. Noni and Bali had fucked up this time. I was sure I would hear those cat five winds howling as soon as they got home from school. Poor Aunt Aspen was gon' get the business too. Hopefully, she didn't know about it either. I was almost sure she probably did though. I supposed as an overprotective big cousin, although Bali and Noni got on my last fucking nerve sometimes, I could see a problem with their attire. I didn't find it appropriate for a school-aged girl either. My experience with that underaged girl didn't help matters.

He and Uncle Jasper continued going back and forth as I remembered that Yendi had texted me. I pulled my phone from my pocket and messaged her back. *Hey, gorgeous. My day has been interesting. I hope yours has been good so far.*

I looked up to find Aunt Syn staring at me. I gave her a slight smile and went back to my food. She was wanting me to talk about my issues with Avery Bolton. That shit wasn't going to happen, especially not here in the diner with all these fools. Thankfully, Uncle Marcus walked in, and Aunt Syn's attention was totally redirected on her political thug. I bit my bottom lip to keep from smiling.

That nigga went from being a fucking stick-up kid to halfway running Nome. He kissed Aunt Syn, then said, "Storm, we're getting complaints about that game room they're running out of Nome Drive-In."

"What are they complaining about? Those people ain't bothering nobody. People are just haters. I don't give a shit about no fucking game room. I need to know why these fucking roads ain't getting fixed and why the county ain't digging out these ditches. A game room is the least of my worries."

"What you want me to tell them then?"

"Tell their asses we'll check into it. Fuck them people."

Everybody laughed. Uncle Storm had only been mayor for a little over a week, and he was already with the shits. Aunt Jen slowly shook her head as she fixed Mr. Tony's plate. As we ate, Uncle Ryder walked in with another nigga behind him. He looked familiar, but I wasn't sure where I knew him from. They went to the counter and ordered food as I shook Uncle Marcus's hand. Once they placed their orders, he introduced him as his new protégé, Darius Gilbert. He was working in his shop in Baytown, but he was from Nome. That was probably why he looked familiar.

When he made his way to me, he extended his hand. "What's up, Jakari?"

I frowned slightly as he chuckled. "I went to school with Rylan. I have a twin brother named Jarius. Dana is our mom."

"Oh shit. What's up, man?"

"Not much. Just trying to make an honest living."

"I feel that. How's your brother?"

"He's good. Just working."

"That's what's up. Well, you hooked up with the right nigga to elevate your game."

"That's what I know," he said with a smile.

Uncle Ryder came and shook my hand then they went back to the counter to get their food. While everyone was distracted, I closed my box of food and got the hell out of there. Aunt Syn wasn't about to catch me slipping and bring that bullshit up again. However, by the time I got to my truck, my mama came running out of the diner. I took a deep breath as she came to my truck.

"I wanted to talk to you before you left, baby. Umm… Avery is eligible for parole. He sees the board next week. It's very possible he could be getting out. I wanted to give you a heads up just in case they granted it. I would hate for you to see him somewhere and lose it."

I was damn near about to lose it now. "It doesn't seem like he's been there long enough. The time they sentenced him to didn't seem long enough. If I see him, I may be in jail next."

"In my opinion, he *hasn't* been there long enough, but there's nothing we can do about that, baby. I just wanted you to know."

I pulled her in my arms and hugged her tightly as I trembled in anger. "Thanks for telling me, Ma. Does Aunt Syn and Nesha know?"

"Syn knows, but I haven't talked to Nesha to see if she knows. The DA called Syn, so he probably called Nesha too."

"Okay. I'll check on her later."

I kissed her head and got in my truck. She took a step back, watching me closely. I started my engine, then pulled off. There was no way they could let that nigga out so soon. No one seemed as bothered as me though, and I didn't know what to think of that.

"So what's up? You gon' come to the game or what?"

"Yeah, I'll be there. I'm not sure if I'll have a date or not though."

"No pressure, man. I'm just happy that you will make it."

I was sitting on my couch talking to Nate. He had a game tonight so I knew we wouldn't be on the phone long. I'd been meaning to call him and had never gotten around to it. I didn't want to talk to Yendi until I cooled off, because she seemed to be able to sense when something was up with me. I wasn't too fond of that shit, mainly because it only made me more sensitive around her.

I'd come home after sitting at the office making phone calls for another two hours, scheduling meetings and shipments. I took a shower, ate the rest of my lunch, then called Nate. "Yo, you good, man?" he asked.

"Yeah, I'm cool. Why?"

"You just seem kind of quiet. You know the video premier is the day after the game. Well… the private viewing for Noah and Jess," he said quietly. "Damn, I wanna go to that shit."

"Have you talked to Jess?" I asked out of curiosity.

"Naw. I been wanting to though. I've listened to a voicemail she left me months ago repeatedly just to hear her voice."

This nigga had it bad as fuck. Jess must've put that fucking whip appeal on that nigga. "Damn, nigga."

"Shit, I know. Feel like she put voodoo on my ass. The crazy part is I ain't even fucked nobody since I've been with her. You know how long ago that shit was?"

"Hell yeah. Maybe that's the problem. You need to fuck somebody else."

I needed to take my own advice. It felt like Yendi had my nuts in a vice grip. After having her last week, I didn't wanna experience nobody else. Her pussy had me in a trance like I was fucking hypnotized. It was hard to resist her ass. Seeing her was like experiencing her all over again. I could feel her without even touching her. So I understood what he was going through, but to be going through it for so long, even after Jess was happy, in a new relationship and pregnant, was a trip.

"So, how are things between you and your mom?" I asked him.

"Man, about the same, I guess. We don't talk that often. During basketball season, it's pretty easy to avoid her since I'm always on the road. Whenever I look at her, I think about the relationship I missed out on with my father. I know that's one of the reasons I stay so close to Noah when I can. It's like I can get a piece of David and what he would have been like as a father by talking to him."

"Damn, man."

"Yeah. I know eventually I'll have to have a more in-depth conversation with her. I just don't know when that will be. There's still a tinge of anger inside of me. Noah said I needed counseling to help me through it or to at least talk to someone I trust. Sometimes you just wanna be... in all your toxicity, dysfunction, and hurt. I still just wanna be. When I feel like it's time, I'll talk to her again."

There was no need in me offering any words. I was having the same issues. I think his was a little more emotionally charged though. He missed out on an opportunity to know his father because his mother wouldn't tell him who he was. She didn't tell him until long after David had died. Almost immediately, he had his last name changed to

Guillory. His father was a professional basketball player as well, and he'd unknowingly followed in his father's footsteps.

As we continued to talk about some chick he met and how fine Noah's sister-in-law was, someone was beeping in. When I saw Yendi's number, I wanted to hang up with Nate immediately, but I didn't want to be so accessible either. It seemed I was a creature of habit, because although I wanted to talk to her, I was keeping myself from doing so. I'd call her when I got off the phone with Nate. She said she wanted to be here for me, so she would have to get all sides of me without apologies.

I was going to fuck this up with her. I should have stuck to my guns and just left her alone. Instead, I was in her sweet ass pussy face first. I ate that shit until I had fucking lockjaw, and she'd came three times. For reasons unknown to me, I actually gave a fuck about her feelings. I'd been seeking an explanation for that since I met her. It was like my ways of sticking and moving didn't apply to her.

"Well, I plan to talk to Noah's sister-in-law next time I see her. She's older than me, but shit if she ain't fine as fuck."

I was completely lost on what the fuck he was talking about. I'd zoned out, thinking about Yendi. "Good luck with that, bruh. Let me holla at you another time. I told Christian I would go out with them tonight."

I did? I rolled my eyes and slowly shook my head as Nate said, "Okay, bruh. I'll hit you back another time."

"Good luck tonight. Run it up on their asses."

"'Preciate that, bruh. Like my big brother says, *You know my name*."

I chuckled at him using Noah's signature statement. "A'ight, nigga."

I ended the call and stared at my phone, debating whether I would call Yendi back or not. I really needed to check on Nesha. While I knew she was done with the issue about Avery molesting her before he even got locked up, I still needed to know if she was okay. I clicked on her name icon, making the call. She answered on the first ring, giggling.

"Hey, J. Lennox… stop."

"You don't mean that," Lennox mumbled.

I rolled my eyes. "Call me back, Nesha."

I ended the call. I didn't need to hear them on the verge of fucking. That only propelled my finger to hit Yendi's icon to call her back. She answered happily. "Hey! How was your day? Did it remain interesting?"

She giggled, and I couldn't help but smile. "It was cool. Uncle Storm was pissed about an outfit the twins wore. His anger was warranted this time. I'm just waiting on the winds to pick up."

"What?" she asked while chuckling.

"Come on, Yendi. You gotta be quicker than that. His name is Storm. When he's angry, his winds howl. I'm sure he got in all the girls' shit when they got home from school."

"Oh! It didn't click." She laughed. "That shit is funny though."

There was a moment of silence, but we began speaking at the same time. She chuckled, and I said, "You go first."

"No, you can go."

"I was just gonna ask how your day was," I said softly… softer than I intended.

"It was good. Nothing exciting happened today. Just a normal day as a school librarian."

Sounded boring as hell to me. Choosing to keep that to myself, I asked, "So what were you about to say?"

"I umm… I…" she said, pausing like she was having trouble expressing herself.

"Spit that shit out, girl."

"I just wanted to see if you wanted to come by or if I could come to you."

Yendi had never been to my house. That wasn't because I didn't want her to know where I lived. It was mainly because I knew my family would be all in my fucking business. I lived in the village near my brothers and cousins: Nesha, Christian, Rylan, Jacob, KJ, Jess, and Decaurey. All of them had inherited the nosy ass Henderson trait.

Nesha's sisters were looking to purchase houses as well. Until I was in a committed relationship, I needed to maintain my privacy.

I looked at the time, and decided to give in. Standing, I went to my room and grabbed a handful of condoms. That had to be at least seven since I had big hands. My dick didn't get the chance to experience her last time, although she'd wanted to suck me off. I wouldn't allow her to do that, despite her begging. "I'm on my way, Yendi. Have that pussy waiting and purring for me."

CHAPTER 8
YENDI

When Jakari arrived, I knew something was eating at him. The minute he walked through the door, and I had locked it, he took me right against it. He lifted my ass and fucked me senseless. That nigga had strapped up in the small amount of time I was locking the door. I had never had no one to handle me the way he did. I knew I was heavy, so no one had attempted to pick me up. My size didn't stop or intimidate him. I loved that shit.

I loved it so much I nearly came before he even entered me. That first stroke took me out the game. The way he stared at me when I came only heightened my feelings. He was probably in shock that I came so quickly. It wasn't long before he was joining me in ecstasy.

When he lowered me to my feet, I grabbed his hand to lead him to my bedroom. However, he had other plans. He pushed me over the back of the couch and bent over to get another condom from the pants still around his ankles. After sheathing himself, he slapped my ass then entered me, promising to do damage. "Oh fuck!" I yelled as he grunted.

He'd been pretty quiet besides the grunts. This time was nothing like the other times. He seemed so disconnected. I knew this was what he was trying to protect me from, but I needed him… all parts of him. I wanted to be the one to cast out his demons and soothe his soul. The reasons why still eluded me, but I didn't even care why I felt this way about him. The point was that I felt something for him. Shit, I felt a lot of something for him.

As his pace slowed some, I said, "Talk to me, baby. Oh shit!" I yelled as my legs trembled. "Tell me what my pussy does to you."

I was hanging on by a thread, but I was trying to get him here in the moment and away from whatever was troubling him. "This shit has the power to make me forget my fucking name. Juicy ass shit. It takes my breath away every time I'm in it. Yendi, beautiful, delicate flower, your pussy might eventually lock a nigga down. That shit is saying a lot."

Suddenly, he pulled out of me. I frowned when I heard his belt buckle rattling. I turned to him to see him getting dressed. My eyes widened. "What happened? Did I do something?"

"Naw. I can't do this. I gotta leave."

"Jakari, please talk to me. Don't leave. We don't have to have sex. Just stay with me."

I slid my hands up his chest, wanting to erase the pain he was feeling. His eyes were emotionless, but the tremble I felt go through his body was saying a lot. He closed his eyes and took a deep breath.

When he reopened his eyes, he said, "I don't have a relationship with my father anymore, ever since he got locked up a little over twelve years ago. He's been trying to contact me despite me blocking him. The day at the diner when I bolted, he'd called me from someone's cell phone. Although I hung up on him, my mama informed me that he's eligible for parole. If the board approves him, he'll be out again."

My eyebrows had lifted. I was shocked he'd told me that. He'd never mentioned his father, and I never asked about him. If Jakari didn't volunteer personal information, I didn't ask. I'd picked up on just how private and closed off he was. However, my mind was racing, wanting to know what his dad was locked up for.

Instead, I grabbed his hand, leading him to the couch. "I'm sorry."

"What are you apologizing for?"

"That you are feeling the way you are... going through the issues you're going through. So you were twenty-one when he got locked up?"

"Twenty. He got locked up about three or four months before I turned twenty-two. My birthday is in two months."

"You're a Capricorn?"

"Mm hmm. That a problem?"

"Hell naw. Natural born hustlers."

He chuckled then turned serious once again and sat on my couch. I sat next to him and grabbed his hand again. "Him being out doesn't mean you have to be around him."

"No, but that doesn't mean he won't try. I want nothing to do with no parts of him."

"What did he do?" I asked, almost immediately regretting it when I saw the expression on his face turn dark.

"Deceived my mother, making her believe he was a good man and left me to take care of her and my brothers." He took a deep breath as I waited for him to explain. "He's a fucking pedophile and went in with two counts of rape of a minor and three other counts of inappropriate behavior with a minor or some shit like that. I don't even know why I told you that shit. Fuck!"

He stood and practically ran to the door as I ran to catch up with him, circling my arms around him and laying my head on his back. I was shocked. I didn't expect that. I thought he would say murder or street shit. I could now see why what his dad did fucked with him.

He turned in my arms and before he could say a word, I said, "I don't have a relationship with my mother. Whenever I would see her, I would get sick to my stomach. I feel like she's responsible for my father's death. That's why I moved. I needed to get away from her. I couldn't properly grieve around her and her bullshit."

His eyebrows lifted as mine had done. It seemed we both had serious issues going on. Maybe that was why I was so drawn to him and him to me. He lifted my head by my chin and softly kissed my lips, then led me to my bedroom. He disrobed again and helped me in bed. When he got in with me, he circled his arms around me. No words were spoken for a few minutes. I supposed we were both in our heads.

Finally breaking the silence, he asked, "You want to go to Nesha's baby shower this weekend?"

Without turning to face him, I said, "Yeah, sure. You gonna pick me up?"

"Yeah."

He kissed my shoulder repeatedly, causing me to turn to him. He kissed my lips, then said, "I'm sorry I dropped all that shit on you. I'm actually surprised I was able to tell you that. I've never repeated his offenses to anyone that didn't already know. Most of my friends are also family."

"Is that why you feel like you aren't ready for a relationship?"

As I waited for his reply, I was only met with silence. I didn't press him for an answer. I knew when he was ready to talk about it, he would. I wasn't expecting him to talk to me. I just wanted him to stay. His arms tightened around me as he took a deep breath.

"I don't want to be in a relationship because I don't wanna fuck it up or get hurt like he hurt my mama. Seeing her at her lowest was hard for me, Yendi. But you… you have a lot of her qualities. I always said that I wanted a woman that possessed the amazing qualities of my mother. I also said that the woman I committed to would have to be a whole ass angel. I feel like God was like, *Here she go. Now what?* I have so many hangups. I don't want to hurt you. Just the fact that you still wanna be here for me makes me uncomfortable. You gon' get hurt fucking with a nigga like me. Why you won't let me go?"

"Because I can't," I said, bringing my hand to his face. "I think about you all day. It's like I can barely focus on work and what I need to be doing. My spirit longs for you, Jakari. I feel like we are both in a spiritual turmoil and have been hurt by one of the people that should care the most — my mother and your father."

"I'm sorry about your dad, baby."

He said that shit so tenderly it practically ripped the tears from my sockets. I broke down in his arms, burying my face in his chest as he repeatedly kissed my head. After a moment, I did my best to contain myself and reel my emotions back in. I pulled away from him. "I'm sorry."

I stood from the bed and went to the bathroom. After I closed the door, I stared at myself in the mirror, feeling a lot like I knew Jakari was feeling. I didn't mean to break down in his presence. It was bad enough I was practically begging him to be in my life. I grabbed a towel and wet it with cold water then patted my face with it. I took a couple of deep breaths, exhaling them slowly, then opened the door to see Jakari was no longer in bed.

I glanced around the room then went to the front to see that he'd left. My eyes closed involuntarily as the tears fell. I wasted time composing myself because I was in shambles all over again.

I WAS IRRITATED BIG TIME. I DIDN'T KNOW WHY THEY EXPECTED ME TO stay the entire day today. It was Friday, and I normally worked half a day, but they thought I should stay to attend the pep rally like the rest of the staff. I couldn't give two fucks about going to a pep rally. They pumped football up entirely too much. If they focused on academics and reading as much as they did football, we would have a school full of A-honor-roll students.

Hardin Jefferson had a great curriculum and did hold their students to a high standard, but in my opinion, there was always room for growth, even if only one student in the entire school was failing. As I shut down my computer and prepared to head to the gym, I saw the twins. Seeing them only reminded me of how Jakari left me last night. To my surprise, I still wasn't angry about it. He'd tried to leave, and I made it difficult for him to do so.

When I went to the bathroom, he didn't let his window of opportunity pass him by. I texted him, apologizing for trying to force him to do something he didn't want to do. As much as it pained me, I also told him that I would wait for him to reach out to me and stop being so clingy. This wasn't like me one bit. I didn't chase no got damn body. I slowly shook my head as I thought about him. He told me he wasn't ready, but I wouldn't take no for an answer.

Maybe he'd gotten what he wanted from me. My mind constantly reiterated that to me, but my heart would immediately shut that shit down. I knew what I felt from him, and that was why it was so hard for me to let go. He needed me. The way he told me about his father last night, it seemed like he'd been dying to get that out. The crazy part was that *he* didn't even know why he felt so comfortable doing so.

Knowing his dad was a pedophile had to be a hard pill to swallow. I wondered if he knew any of his victims. A lot of predators usually went after people they knew. I felt like that was mainly because people would be at ease, not suspecting foul shit to happen. Just the fact that it had been twelve years since his father got locked up and he still had such a bad taste in his mouth about it, led me to believe his victims were probably people he was close to… possibly family.

As I continued to the gym, I did my best to put Jakari out of my mind. Hopefully this shit would go by fast so I could get home. When I walked inside the gym and saw a few familiar faces, I took a deep breath. Mayor Henderson was here along with a couple of his brothers, one of them being Ashanni's dad. My heart rate had quickened even more when I saw the guy Jakari worked with the most. If I was remembering correctly, his name was Philly. If they were all here, then Jakari was probably here too.

I quickly made my way to the restroom, hoping none of them noticed me, only to walk right into Jakari after going through the door. He reached out to steady me then just stared into my eyes. I could see the sadness in his, but I wondered if what I saw in his eyes were only a reflection of what was in my eyes. Although I blamed myself for what happened, I couldn't say that it didn't hurt.

I cleared my throat and said, "Please forgive me. I'm so sorry."

Before he could respond, I walked away on trembling legs, hoping they held up at least until I got to the restroom. When I walked inside, his cousin Nesha was washing her hands. She looked up and smiled. "Hi. Yendi, right?"

"Yes, ma'am. Hello. How are you?"

"I'm good. How are you?"

"Great. Thanks."

I made my way inside a stall before she could continue into a conversation. I was curious as to why they were all here though. It was definitely for business reasons, because I didn't think any of their kids were old enough to play varsity football. Jakari had told me that most of the boy cousins were either grown or barely in middle school. Most of the girls were in between.

When I made my way back to the gym, I saw a boy in a football jersey talking to the brother that was in a suit like the mayor. I could assume he was working with Mayor Henderson in some way. "Let's go, Ace!" he yelled as the boy ran back to the huddle of football players.

I tried to find a seat as quickly as possible without drawing attention, but I wasn't so lucky. The minute I sat and got situated, my eyes met Jakari's. I swallowed hard and closed my eyes. I lowered my head then opened them, proceeding to pick at my nails the entire time to avoid ogling him. Someone sat next to me, claiming my attention.

When I saw Ashanni's dad, my mouth went dry. "What's up, Yendi?"

"Hello, Mr. Henderson. How are you?"

"I'm good. How about you?"

"I'm okay. Thanks."

"You're lying and so is his ass. Both of you are doing your best to avoid each other, and I can tell it's killing the both of you."

"I'm only trying to honor his wishes. He said he didn't want to talk to me anymore, and I kept trying to hang on to him. That wasn't right. I made the situation worse by trying to force him to do something he didn't want to do."

He chuckled and that caused me to frown. "Let me tell you something about Jakari's cocky, prideful ass. Nobody can force that nigga to do anything he didn't already want to do. If he was still being around you, it was because he wanted to be."

I glanced over at him as he stared at the football players. When he turned to me, he gave me a slight smile. "That nigga feel like shit about last night. He came to my house afterward to ascend to the clouds then told me about what happened. Don't stop what you're doing. Whether you realize it or not, you're melting that ice he surrounded himself with years ago. He's just struggling with how to handle feeling so vulnerable now that he's losing the battle."

"What battle?"

"Resisting love and anything that resembles it. What his dad did, did a number on him. He told me that he told you. If he told you that shit, then trust, you the one, baby girl. He keep that shit locked away and hadn't mentioned his father to me in over ten years. Please catch up with him before we leave. He thinks you're better off without him."

He grabbed my hand and squeezed it as I nodded. The moment he got up, Maui sat right next to me. "Hey, Ms. Odom. What was Uncle Jasper yapping about?"

"Hey, baby. He was talking about your cousin. Who are they here to see? I didn't know you had a boy cousin your age."

"Uncle Marcus's son, Ace, just started going here last year. He used to live with his mom, but when he got older, she allowed him to live with his dad. That's her over there."

"Oh okay. How old is he?"

"Seventeen, I think. He's in the eleventh grade but plays like he's in college. He's awesome."

"Oh. That's great."

"Yeah. What's your weekend looking like?"

"Well, I was invited to the baby shower tomorrow, but I'm not sure where it is."

"Oh! Yay! It's on Highway 365. It's a barndominium on the left side. You can't miss it. 365 is the same highway this school is on. It's 326 here, but it changes names when you go through the traffic light in Nome."

"Oh okay. Do you know what time it starts?"

"I think three but let me text my dad. He knows everything."

I chuckled as I watched Mayor Henderson pull his phone from his pocket. He frowned then glanced around the gym. I supposed he was looking for Maui. When his gaze made it to our vicinity, she stood and waved. He smiled at her and went back to his phone. She showed me the text message that came through. *Tell Yendi I said what's up. It's at three.*

I smiled and said, "Tell him I said hello Mayor and thank you for donating the iPhone for the prize giveaway."

Maui slightly rolled her eyes, probably because I called him mayor but relayed the message perfectly. When he smiled, it made me smile as well. "He's so vain," she said as the band got cranked up.

When I averted my gaze to the football players, my eyes met Jakari's again. I couldn't look away. Shit, I couldn't even breathe until he turned away. Bringing my gaze to my nails, I found it best if I focused on them than anything else. I was going to show up at the baby shower. I knew I was taking a huge risk by doing that, but I wanted Jakari to know that I wasn't giving up on him. If he didn't want to talk to me then I wouldn't stay long. Just long enough to wish Nesha the best and give her the gift I still had yet to buy.

As the pep rally came to a close, I looked over where the Hendersons were in time to see Jakari leaving. I supposed he didn't even want to take a chance coming close to me again. I stood from my seat and Maui did as well. "See you tomorrow, Ms. Odom!"

"Okay, sweetness," I replied as she hugged me.

Once she walked away, I realized I didn't bother to ask if she was having a girl or boy. I supposed the most gender-neutral shit I could buy were diapers. She would never have enough of those. As I made my way down the bleachers, Jasper smiled and nodded at me. I did the same and left the gym, heading to my car.

Tomorrow could be either the best decision I'd ever made or the worst. I hoped Jasper wasn't gassing me up with helium instead of petroleum. I didn't want to see Jakari's bad side, but I *did* want to see him. I could only hope he wanted the same.

CHAPTER 9

JAKARI

"I went the fuck off as soon as they walked their narrow asses through the door. Everybody evacuated, trying to get away from the cat five force winds. Remy went his ass under the damn coffee table. Aspen claimed she didn't know. I believe her, because she wouldn't dare leave them out to dry if she did."

I rolled my eyes as Uncle Storm talked about how he got in the twins' shit about their outfits. We'd just finished setting up tables for the women to decorate for Nesha and Lennox's baby shower. If Nesha and I weren't as close as we were, I wouldn't have even come today. I just wanted to be alone. Seeing Yendi yesterday was hell. I felt so fucking guilty about bailing on her, but I felt like I was suffocating.

I went straight to Uncle Jasper's house, and he insisted that I was having an anxiety attack. He helped me calm down some then gave me a blunt to finish the job. I saw him talking to Yendi at the pep rally and that was why I got the hell out of there. I couldn't talk to her about what happened with all those people around. That woman had me tripping for real. Even with all my shit, she still wanted me.

When she bumped into me and I saw the sadness in her eyes, that shit paralyzed me. I wasn't expecting her to even be at the pep rally. She normally left early on Fridays. I wanted to scoop her up in my arms and kiss her until all her clothes melted away. I wanted to tell her how much I felt for her, but just like my body was paralyzed, so was my tongue.

I walked out of the barn and went to the pasture next to it. Whenever I really needed to think, I would find myself on a horse or putting out hay for the animals. It was somewhat chilly outside today, and I knew the grass would be dying sooner than later. Although I worked in the office now, I wasn't a stranger to the hard work of tending to the animals. I still did it from time to time. When I was little, I had a little pot belly pig as a pet. I loved farm animals.

By the time I got to the stable to saddle a horse, I could hear someone approaching. When I turned around and saw Uncle Jasper, I wasn't surprised. He paid the most attention to me. Out of my uncles, he knew me the best. He said we were a lot alike. I could see that. Just from some of the stories he told me about his past before Aunt Chas came along, how he withheld his love because he hadn't healed from his past, proved that.

"You finna ride?"

"Yeah. You gon' join me?"

"Might as well. Storm done started bossing niggas around so that was my cue to get out the way."

I chuckled as I saddled a horse. While he did the same, I noticed Aunt Syn watching us. *Aww shit.* I was already feeling sensitive and shit. She would only make it worse. As I stared back at her, she began making her way to us. I glanced at Uncle Jasper to see he noticed her too. He pulled a blunt from his shirt pocket and fired up. It was only ten in the morning, but he was right on the money as to what I needed. He took a pull then passed it to me.

I took the longest pull known to man and exhaled slowly. When Aunt Syn got to us, she took the blunt from Unc and took a long pull as well. Her tear-stained cheeks caught my attention. Once she passed the blunt back to him, I pulled her in my arms. "What's up, Auntie?"

"He's getting out. He fucked with me for fourteen years of my life, and what he did fucked with my mental even longer. He gets twelve years and gets to live back on the outside. How is that shit fair?"

"It's not," I said through clenched teeth. "That shit is fucked up."

Uncle Jasper joined us. "That nigga ain't coming nowhere near us. He knows that he didn't get what was coming to him. That beat down WJ gave his ass before the police showed up wasn't shit. But listen… I know the shit he did was hard to put behind you. Don't let this set you back. Syn, you've been doing well, baby girl. Your family needs you. You got this, baby. You strong, resilient, and smart enough to know if you need help. Serita will take you back in a heartbeat to assure you don't decline."

"I know. Thanks, Jasper," she said, lifting her head from my chest.

"Your husband is running this way," I said as I looked up at Uncle Marcus.

"Baby, what's wrong? I was looking for you. You good?" he asked when he got to us.

She went to his arms and hugged him tightly around his waist as Uncle Jasper put his arm around my shoulders. "Remember what we talked about ten years ago when that under-aged girl almost duped you?"

I nodded. "I'm not him. Until I could separate his illness from who he was to me I wouldn't heal. I guess I'm still broken, Unc. I didn't realize just how broken I was until Yendi showed up."

"Speaking of, she asked what time the baby shower was, so I assume she's coming. Quit running like I did. Although I still obtained Chas's heart, I played around for over a damn year. I'm just thankful she didn't run into another nigga that would have made her happy. Don't take that risk, nephew. She's a beautiful woman, and she seems just as beautiful on the inside. I swear she love you. I could see it in her eyes. Must've been love at first sight and shit. Y'all met, what? Two weeks ago?"

"Something like that. Almost three, I think."

"Y'all fucked already too. So that shit must've been all consuming."

"Unc… shit like I ain't never felt. It wasn't just physical. She snatched my fucking soul, and I don't know what to do about it."

"Let her have it then. If she could snatch it with as tightly as you were holding and guarding it and is willing to be here for you, then she gotta be the one. Stop fighting that shit based on the shit Avery did and that lil mishap with that girl. That wasn't your fault. I'm just glad it didn't go any further than what it did."

"Shit, me too. I'm gonna try to give in to her. She done resuscitated my heart, and it won't let go of her, no matter how strongly my mind is against it. She knows about Avery, but I need to tell her what happened with that lil girl. I get nauseated whenever I think about it for too long."

"Get it out yo' system then. You need to purge. Let that shit come up and cleanse your temple. Real shit."

I nodded repeatedly. Talking to Uncle Jasper always gave me clarity. Just as I was about to mount my horse, my phone chimed with a text message. I pulled it from my pocket to see a message from Nesha. *You okay? I heard the news from Aunt Syn. Does your mom know?*

Today was her day, and she was worried about everyone else. *I'm good. Uncle Jasper here with good sense and good smoke. How are you handling the news, baby? I haven't spoken to my mama yet, but I can imagine she isn't handling it too well since she hadn't told me yet.*

After sending her the message, I mounted my horse, then said to Unc, "Let me check on my mama right quick."

He nodded as I called her. "Hey, baby."

Her sad voice had me even softer than I was after seeing Aunt Syn's tears. "Mama, you okay?"

"I'm okay. I suppose you've heard already. I was trying to get myself together to tell the three of you at once. I just got off the phone with Rylan and was about to call Christian."

Rylan was at a rodeo with KJ and would be back before the baby shower was over, and Christian was on a call, repairing someone's heater. "If you want me to, I'll let them know."

"It's okay, baby. I'll talk to Christian before the shower and to Rylan whenever he gets here. It's not exactly a conversation I want to have by phone. That was why I hadn't talked to you yet."

"I understand, Mama. Aunt Syn is at the barn helping to decorate, and she told me. She's not taking it too well."

"Okay. I'll see if Indi has talked to her."

My mama and Uncle Storm called Vida, Syn's biological mother, Indi. Her middle name was Indigo and you had to be extremely close to her to call her Indi. Uncle Storm did what he wanted without invitation. However, since Maui spent a lot of time with her and her husband, they'd gotten close as well. "Okay, Ma. I'm about to ride a bit to clear my mind. I'll be at the diner in a lil while to help y'all transport food."

"Okay, baby. Thanks."

I ended the call and went back to Nesha's message. *I'm okay. I made peace with it a long time ago. You know that. You should too, Jakari. I'm worried about you.*

"Man, is we gon' ride today or what?" Uncle Jasper asked, causing me to chuckle.

"Yeah, man. That's Nesha. Now pass that shit. I only got one pull."

He passed it to me with a smirk on his lips. I took a pull and responded to Nesha. *I'm trying. For real.*

"Nigga, you gon' pass my shit back?"

"Hell naw. You didn't abide by the puff-puff-pass. The rest of this shit is mine. Na let's go."

I urged my horse forward with a gentle kick as Uncle Jasper said, "You muthafucka. You better be glad I'm the plug of Nome and got another one."

I laughed loudly. "I didn't doubt that, Unc."

As I sat toward the back of the crowd, I couldn't help but see when Yendi walked her fine ass in the barn. I'd been anticipating her arrival ever since Uncle Jasper had told me she was coming. She arrived a few minutes late, but she didn't know that the Hendersons were rarely on C.P. time. We were always ready to get the festivities rolling. If we said it started at three, people needed to get here by two fifty-five if they didn't want to miss anything.

I scanned her from her leopard print heels to her thick ass lips. That red lipstick she wore had my dick standing at attention. "Mm hmm. I bet yo' ass finna look alive around this bitch now."

I looked up and saw Uncle Storm standing over me. "You go worry about who Bali finna creep out of here with."

His head whipped around so fast that shit should have done a full three-sixty spin like the exorcist. I chuckled as I stood and walked toward Yendi. "That shit wasn't funny, nigga. Gon' have me in hurricane mode for nothing."

I chuckled again as I watched Yendi greet Nesha. When she saw me approaching, her eyes never left mine. Nesha was still yapping, and Yendi had zoned in on me. When Nesha realized what was happening, she rolled her eyes but smiled. Yendi looked to have stopped breathing. She seemed nervous, like she didn't know how I would react to her being here. I let a slight frown grace my face as I reached for her hand.

She slid it in mine, and I gently pulled her away from everybody. I turned to her when we got out of earshot of the nosy ass Hendersons. "What'chu doing here, Yendi?"

She cleared her throat, and her cheeks got red as hell. "Didn't you invite me?" she asked matter-of-factly.

"I did, but I said I would pick you up."

She slid her hand from mine and nodded repeatedly. I grabbed her hand again and said, "I'm glad you weren't waiting on me, otherwise, you wouldn't be here in this fire as jumpsuit, stuntin' on every woman here."

She smiled, but her eyes widened as I pulled her close to me and hugged her. As I held her, I asked, "Can we talk later?"

She pulled away from me, clearly surprised by my response to her being here, since her lips were still parted, and her eyebrows were somewhat lifted. A slow smile spread across her face, and that shit made my soul feel right. I lowered my head and kissed those pretty red lips. I couldn't resist them. As I pulled away, she grabbed my shirt and pulled me back to her. I bit my bottom lip, then gave her what she wanted... my lips again.

While her action was aggressive, her kiss was tender as fuck. When

I separated from her, I could see eyes on us, so I brought her over to my mama. "Mama, you remember Yendi, right?"

My mama smiled big. "I sure do. Hi, beautiful."

"Hello, umm..." Yendi glanced at me.

"I'm sorry, baby. Chrissy Douglas."

"Hello, Mrs. Douglas. It's great to see you again."

"Same."

My mama winked at me as I brought Yendi over to Uncle Storm, since he was waving us over. I took a deep breath as Yendi chuckled slightly. When we made it over to them, he said, "It's about time Jakari recognized greatness. I'm glad you're back."

"Thanks, Mayor Henderson."

That fool smiled and grabbed her hand, introducing her to everyone as my girlfriend. Jess walked over to me. "Nigga, she yo' girlfriend and you didn't tell me?"

"Jess, we haven't established what we have. You know how your loudmouth uncle is. She strokes his ego. At this point, she can do no wrong."

Jess laughed and said, "You better stay off Uncle Mayor. Let me go rescue poor Yendi."

She walked away, and Nesha approached me, wrapping her arms around me. "You look happy, cuz. I love that look on you. If Yendi does that for you, you definitely need to make it official."

Changing the subject, I said, "I thought you didn't want a shower? What happened to that?"

She rolled her eyes. "Evette, Sharon, and Olivia wouldn't hear of it, nor my sisters. They said the first of the next generation of Hendersons should be welcomed in style. Not to mention Lennox's mother was in on the shenanigans. I didn't stand a chance against all of them. They'll be doing Tyeis's shower in two weeks. I told them they could have done ours together. She might go into labor with those twins before then."

I chuckled. "Where are they?"

"On their way. Tyeis wasn't feeling too good today. I told them to just stay home, but she said Angel would have a heart attack if they didn't come."

I frowned slightly as Nesha continued. "She has a thing for your little brother."

"Aww shit. Rylan would hurt that poor girl. She wouldn't know what hit her. She way too innocent and too young."

"This I know," Nesha responded through her laughter.

Lennox approached and shook my hand then slid his arms around Nesha, caressing her belly. She was out there and could probably go at any moment. She was worried about Tyeis, but she had one foot in the hospital her damn self. Looking around the barn, I saw Uncle Storm and Yendi on the other side, talking to Malachi, Philly, Ryder, Legend, Zayson, and Red. Yendi had a big smile on her face, and I could see them asking her questions.

Legend, Red, and Zayson had might as well been my uncles too. They'd been around the family for nearly twenty years now. They were rodeo circuit legends, especially Legend. He'd groomed our cousin Malachi to be just as great of a bull rider as he was. Red was an amazing steer wrestler, besides being Legend's wingman. He broke record after record for the ten plus years he bulldogged. He and Zayson still team roped from time to time. I was pretty sure Yendi was being filled in on all that information.

I slowly shook my head and walked over there to go rescue her. Evidently Jessica's rescue efforts weren't successful while I was talking to Nesha. When I got close, I heard Uncle Storm say, "Here come his ass. 'Bout time. I was wondering how long you was gon' let me take her all over this barn."

I grabbed Yendi's hand as she said, "Nice meeting y'all. Good seeing you again, Philly and Ryder."

They all responded to her and before I could totally get her away from them, she said, "And Mayor, it's always good to see you."

"Take note, Jakari. Yendi, the pleasure is mine. You ever need a job or get tired of HJ, come see me."

I rolled my eyes, a common occurrence whenever I was around Uncle Storm. "Baby, Aunt Jen and my mama cooked the food. Nesha is stuck on spaghetti and fried chicken right now, so that's what they cooked."

"Sounds good to me."

I smiled at her as we went to the buffet style tables and fixed our plates. Spaghetti was the last thing I wanted to eat, but it would do its job and kill these hunger pains. I put a few pieces of chicken on my plate and only a little spaghetti. Everyone else had either already eaten or had already fixed their food so there was no need in being modest or considerate. Well, except for Decaurey and Tyeis. There was still more than enough left for them.

Once we sat, I slid my arm around Yendi's waist. "I'm sorry for pushing you away."

She put her finger over my lips. "We don't have to talk about that right now. Let's eat and enjoy the festivities. We can talk once everything is over."

I gave her a slight smile as Uncle WJ got everyone's attention. "We need some men up front, preferably ones closer to Lennox's age."

I slumped in my seat as Decaurey walked through the door with Tyeis and Angel. "Perfect, son. You right on time," Uncle WJ said.

Decaurey frowned as everyone else laughed. "Storm, Jasper, Mal, Jakari, and Christian, come on!"

Uncle Storm and Uncle Jasper frowned at the same time. "Nigga, I'm nearly fifteen years older than Nesha. Get Marcus to do it."

"Oh shit. Thanks, Jasper. Come on, Marcus," Uncle WJ said.

"Damn, Jasper. Just throw me under the fucking bus," Uncle Marcus said.

Meanwhile, Uncle Storm remained seated until Nesha said, "Please, Uncle Mayor?"

He stood but kept the frown on his face. *This nigga here.* I swore, he loved for people to kiss his ass. "What I told you about how to address me, CEO? Secondly, get Brixton's ass up here. You ain't get off, nigga."

Uncle WJ slowly shook his head as Brix stood while laughing. That laugh came to a cease when the door opened, and Nate walked through it with a huge ass gift. *Oh shit.* That nigga didn't tell me he would be here today. Although he and Lennox were friends, I didn't expect him to show up because of the situation with Jess. He went to where the gifts were and set the box on the floor then made his way to Nesha.

However, my eyes zoomed in on Jess. She was staring at the floor. When she lifted her head, her eyes went straight to Brix. Glancing over at him, I could see he was somewhat tight, but he seemed cool. Nate couldn't be trying to start shit. He said he wouldn't go to the private viewing simply to avoid Jess. So I couldn't understand why he would show up here.

He came our way and greeted Lennox and congratulated him. He then made his rounds greeting everyone. When he got to me, he shook my hand. "Nigga, what the fuck?" I asked.

"I know. I needed to see her, J. I was passing through, coming from New Orleans, and decided to drop off a gift."

I twisted my lips to the side. "You know she happy, right?"

"Yeah, but I'm not. Seeing her calms me, man. I feel like I'm about to lose it. What the fuck wrong with me?"

I walked off to the side, giving Yendi a wink, as she stared at Nate with wide eyes. Apparently, she knew who he was. When we got closer to the door, I glanced over at Jess to see her watching us. This wasn't good. Brix was too jealous and possessive for this shit. While Nate ignored Jess, but spoke to Brix, it didn't help matters. Brix's eyes stayed on him.

"You being here may calm you, but it sends Jess into a frenzy. First off, I believe she's still attracted to you, so she has to hide that shit in front of Brix. She loves him and doesn't want to do anything to offend him. You being here offends him."

"Lennox and I are friends. I won't ever approach, Jess. I just need to see her until my obsession wears off."

"That ain't an obsession, Nate. That's a fucking soul tie. You gon' have to get that out of your system."

He slid his hand down his face. "I know. Noah said the same thing. He said he went through something like this with that model, Sonya. J, how do I move on? I was smitten from the first time I saw her. I'll be okay for a while... like months, but then all of a sudden, she fills my brain and won't leave until I can either see her or talk to her." He paused and stared at the floor for a moment, then looked up and said, "She knew I was coming."

My eyebrows nearly hiked up off my fucking face. "Y'all talked?"

"No, not verbally. I sent her a message on IG saying that I would be swinging through to drop off a gift. She said okay and that Brix would have to understand that Lennox is my boy."

"Aww shit. I need to talk to her ass. I still don't think you should have come, but what can I say if she gave the okay?"

Nate shrugged his shoulders. He looked around me to steal a glance at her, then said, "Well, I gotta go. You still gon' make it next weekend?"

"Yeah, and I'll have a plus one."

I waved Yendi over because her eyes had never left us. I chuckled as she stood. She looked nervous as hell. Nate said, "Word? Who's the lucky woman?"

I nodded my head in her direction as she approached, and Nate turned to her. "Damn. She's beautiful, bruh."

"Mm hmm." Once Yendi got close, I grabbed her hand and said, "Nate, this is my lady, Yendi Odom. Baby, this is Nate Guillory."

She stared up at him and extended her hand. "Nice to meet you, Nate. My dad was a fan."

"Nice to meet you too. Is that right?"

"Yeah. You couldn't say shit about Nate around him," she said, then chuckled. "This is an honor. Do you mind taking a picture with me to send to my siblings?"

"I don't mind at all."

Yendi took her phone from her pocket, and I grabbed it from her and snapped the picture. I did my best to get all of Nate in the frame while standing so close to them. The nigga was six eight. I managed to accomplish the feat though. She took her phone from my extended hand and damn near inspected the picture. I slowly shook my head as Nate chuckled. He grabbed the phone from her and held it up to take another picture of the two of them.

When he gave it back to her, he glanced Jess's way once again. I looked over to where she was and saw that she was staring at us. *Fuck.* This wasn't good. "Can I speak to her? I mean, I spoke to her at the video shoot, and he was cool."

"That nigga was everything *but* cool. If you gon' keep staring at her, you might as well."

He nodded then made his way to Jess. I slid my arm around Yendi as I watched. "How do you know him?" she asked.

"He's Nesha's husband's friend. I met him at their wedding rehearsal. He has a thing for Jess, but she chose Brix over him. He can't seem to let her go though."

I watched Jess stand and give him a side hug then I brought my attention to Brix. He was watching, but he hadn't made a move in their direction. Jess was gonna fuck up if she wasn't careful. I turned my attention back to the beautiful woman next to me. "You wanna go to the game with me next weekend?"

Her brows lifted. "Sure. I would love to."

"Aww hell naw! Jakari, get yo' ass over here, cause I ain't doing this shit. I ain't being bare foot and pregnant for no damn body," Uncle Storm yelled.

When I turned to them and saw the fellas with balloons under their shirts to make them look pregnant and their shoes in front of them, I almost died in laughter. They should have known that fool would make a scene. He popped the balloon and went sat down. I slowly shook my head then noticed Nate heading back my way. "See y'all next weekend, bruh."

"A'ight, nigga."

He quickly made his way out. I gave Yendi's hand a squeeze then made my way to the fellas to get a balloon to put under my shirt. The deep frown on Brix's face didn't go unnoticed though. *What did I miss?*

CHAPTER 10
YENDI

"That man is way too dangerous," Jess said. "I made a mistake giving him the okay to come here."

I was sitting next to Jess as Nesha opened gifts. She just happened to be opening the huge box Nate had dropped off. I was surprised Jess was talking to me about that. We didn't know each other. I'd been sitting next to her since the game the men played, pretending to be pregnant. When Jakari walked over to them, I took a seat next to her.

I glanced over at her. "Why did you give him the okay then?"

She lowered her head for a moment, then said, "A few reasons. One, Lennox is his friend. He shouldn't have to miss out on events like this simply because me and Brix are here. That's not fair to him. Secondly, the only reason there's a problem anyway is because like a fool, I told Brix I slept with him. Thirdly, I miss Nate. He was an amazing friend that I could talk to about anything. I can talk to Brix about most things, but he tends to respond before he thinks when he's the subject of the conversation."

"So I suppose the question is how much do you value your relationship? If you wanted to hold on to Nate, you should have chosen him to be with. Jakari told me that it was your choice to make. He didn't give me details, but he said you chose Brix over Nate. There was a reason for that choice. Hold on to whatever that reason was. That's what's most important. It seems that Nate won't disrespect your wishes or Brix's unless you give him permission to."

I could clearly see her attraction to Nate when he was here. She'd stared into his eyes while he talked to her, and when he kissed her forehead, her eyes had closed for a moment, like she was filing the way his lips felt in her mental storage cabinet. She grabbed my hand and squeezed it then went back to watching Nesha open her gifts. She was still pulling shit out of the box Nate brought.

When she pulled out the Forces and Jordans, the awws could be heard all over the barn. Those little shoes were adorable, but when she held up the pair of cowboy boots, I placed my hand over my chest. I always wanted children, and seeing those little boots only had me imagining having Jakari's babies.

I knew we still needed to talk, but I could only hope that the talk was on the up and up. His response to me being here had shocked me. I expected some resistance, so when he frowned and asked why I was here, I was ready. When he pulled me in his arms and kissed me in front of everyone, I was totally caught off guard. The introduction to Nate as his lady had surprised me as well. I supposed Jasper's talk with him had gone over well.

He seemed to be the uncle Jakari confided in the most. Uncle Mayor Storm seemed to be the one always on bullshit. It was hilarious to me though. I quickly realized that flattery would get me everywhere with him. He was practically at the point where I believed he was trying to force Jakari to be with me by introducing me as Jakari's better half. I could only smile big because it was everything I was hoping to be. No one had dared correct him either, not even Jakari.

When Nesha opened the gift from me, her eyes widened and she said, "Mama, look!"

Three women looked her way, so I didn't know which one was her mother until the woman went and grabbed the crib toy from her. She held it to her chest and a tear slid down her cheek. She passed it to another lady, and she nearly did the same.

Nesha stared at my confused face and said, "I had one like this when I was a baby, and I held tightly to it until I was at least eleven or twelve. I ended up giving it to my baby sister when she was a baby. I loved this stuffed animal head, and I called this part his cape."

She giggled. "Thank you so much, Yendi. This means so much to me. Mama Sharon lost the other one during the flood. We both cried about it."

I brought my hands to my chest, feeling extra sensitive, like the gift meant a lot to me as well. I had an extremely empathetic spirit, and since meeting Nate, my sensitivity levels were at an all-time high. It was like I could sense my daddy's presence in that moment. Meeting him was like my dad saying he was always with me. Knowing that he was friends with Jakari made that moment sweeter. I would have a personal connection to one of my dad's favorite basketball players out of the 'young bucks'.

I chuckled at the thought of it. He said Nate played his role. He wasn't a superstar, but he ate whenever he got the ball. He took his role of a supporting cast member seriously. He said Nate was like the A.C. Green or James Worthy of the Lakers when Magic Johnson led the team to victory. They were key role players, and Nate embodied the position.

I was brought back to the present when Nesha said, "Oh shit."

Everybody froze as Lennox ran to her. "What's wrong, baby?"

"My water broke."

He quickly scooped her up and ran out of the barn as everyone applauded and screamed. Her mothers and dad all ran behind them as everyone else began gathering her gifts. Jakari's arms slid around my waist. "You cool with going to the hospital with me?"

"Absolutely. I'll go with you anywhere."

He slowly licked his lips, and I followed that tongue until it disappeared back into his mouth. Shit, I wanted to dive in after it. The things that long, thick shit did to my body had me about to cum from the sight of it. "If I didn't know any better, Yendi, I would swear that fat shit was juicing for me right now."

"Well, it's a shame you don't know any better."

He grabbed my hand and led me down a long hallway in silence. When I heard soft moans, I was somewhat confused. Then I heard, "Aww fuck! Give me that shit, Chas!"

Somebody was back here fucking? When the woman responded, "Take your shit, Jasper. Fucking take it!" I knew exactly who it was.

Jakari again licked his lips and opened the door to a private room. The minute he closed the door, he turned to me and pulled the straps of my jumpsuit off my shoulders and bent me over a table in the room. I glanced around and noticed that it seemed to be a conference room of some kind. "Oh shit. You ain't got on no drawz, girl."

I bit my bottom lip as I stared back at him. "If you weren't trying to see me, I had to be able to persuade you somehow. You gon' take advantage or not?"

Within seconds, he'd filled me to capacity, causing me to nearly scream out in ecstasy. "Oh fuck. Jakariiii."

"You ain't gotta be quiet around here. Fuck what anybody think. Let me know how this dick changed your life's trajectory. Fuck! This pussy got me by the fucking balls, Yendi."

His words took me out. I squirted every fucking where. "Oh my God! Look… what you… do to me, baby. Please… tell me… you're mine, Jakari. Shit!" I could barely get my words out, but I needed to know. I needed to hear him say he belonged to me. "Please… say it."

He leaned over and grabbed me by the neck, applying pressure that had me on the verge of cumming all over him again. "This your dick, Yendi, but so is my heart. You got me, girl. All of me. If you still want me, I'm yours."

My eyes rolled to the back of my head, and I came again. The pleasure of it was even more intense, but I didn't squirt. "Jakari, I will… always want… yooouuu. Shit! Oh my God, baby!"

He kissed my shoulder as he fucking twisted my insides out. This rough nigga was everything I wanted and had desired for the past few years. He was rough but tender at the same time. He was fucking the shit out of me, but making love to my heart and mind, gently caressing them with his words.

"Well, I'm yours, and you're mine. That shit gon' bring on a whole notha beast of a nigga. Don't fucking play with me, girl. This dick will tear you to pieces. You hear me, Yendi? I'm trusting you with my heart, baby."

"I won't... hurt you. Give me your heart, and I'll... take extremely good care of it."

He pulled out of me, so I turned around to see him admiring my body... every roll, stretch mark, discoloration, and the cellulite on my thighs... all of it. The parts of me that I'd grown to love seemed to be loved by him as well. He came closer and gripped my thighs, lifting me to the table behind me and dove back inside me.

His gaze into my eyes had my clit tingling, ready to express her love for him all over again. "Yendi, I can see the love you have for me in your eyes. What if I lead us to hell? You said you would go anywhere I went."

"I better prepare for the climate then. I will go to war with the devil for you. If I can see the value in you, then I need you to see it in you too."

I lifted my legs and wrapped them around his waist as he thrusted into me. He lowered his head to my nipple and sucked it as my pussy cried out in ecstasy. The sounds he had emanating from her filled the room and were just as loud as the sounds coming from my mouth. The man was sexually talented. I was more than sure he was talented in other ways as well.

He released my nipple and hooked my leg in the crook of his arm as he licked from my chest to my neck then my earlobe. "Damn. You taste so good. I could lick on this chocolate covered toffee all fucking day. You love me, Yendi?"

I nearly stopped breathing. I didn't know what made him ask me that. The words I spoke were saying it already, but I didn't want to admit that I'd fallen for a man I barely knew. What was that love based on? His looks? His dick? I didn't even know. It seemed spiritual, but again, I wouldn't be able to explain that shit to him or even myself. I remained quiet.

"You don't have to say it, baby. I feel it in my soul, I hear it through your words, and I see it in your eyes. I don't want to hurt you.

Be patient with me, Yendi, while I learn how you want to be loved." He lifted his head and stared into my eyes. "I wanna love you how you love me."

The tears fell down my cheeks as he long stroked me. He gently swiped them away with his thumb then leaned over me again, his mouth close to my ear. "I'm about to cum. I don't have on a rubber, baby."

I closed my eyes and allowed them to roll to the back of my head. It was no wonder this shit felt like it was on another level. He was fucking me raw. Maybe he'd gotten tested. He was trusting me fully. Before I could respond to what he said, he pulled out of me and allowed his ejaculate to hit the floor as he stroked it furiously.

His grunts were sexy as hell, but when he slowed down, long stroking his dick, and closed his eyes, the moan that left his mouth had my hand sliding down my stomach to stroke my pussy. That shit was sexy as fuck. It was like he started cumming all over again when he did that shit. I would have gotten pregnant for sure. He opened his eyes and his gaze lowered to my hand. He bit his bottom lip, widened his stance, and lowered his face to my pussy. "Let me fuck this beautiful shit up right quick."

He pushed my hand out of the way and sucked my clit up so good I screamed out my satisfaction. I came within seconds. He didn't let up until I started squirting. He pulled away, but he gently patted my clit, making me excrete even more. This man had control of my body in ways that I didn't. She submitted to his authority and was in awe of him every time I was in his presence. She gravitated to him in ways I didn't dare try to understand.

As I panted uncontrollably, he said, "Stay right here."

I nodded as he walked away. If every day with him would be like this, I'd be in heaven for sure.

HEALING FOR MY SOUL

WE HAD MADE IT TO CHINA ON OUR WAY TO BEAUMONT TO SEE Nesha. She was still in active labor, since the baby now wanted to be stubborn. I could tell Jakari was in his head about whatever he wanted to talk to me about. However, the way he kept glancing at me, I knew he was about to break the silence.

"About ten years ago, nearly two years after Avery got locked up, I met this chick in the club in Beaumont. It was twenty-one and up, so I knew I was good to fuck with whomever I wanted to. I was twenty-three and a ho. I'd fuck whoever. I wasn't looking for anything serious at the time. I was still young."

I slid my hand over his because I could feel his nervous energy. "You know I won't look at you any differently, no matter what."

"I get that feeling. This is just hard to talk about. My brother, Christian, and Uncle Jasper are the only ones that know exactly what happened that night. Christian saw most of it for himself. I just need you to know why I'm the way that I am. What sometimes influences the things I do. You already know about Avery, so I knew I had to tell you this too for you to fully get me."

He paused for a moment then squeezed my hand and continued. "This woman started dancing on me. I was feeling her. She was pretty and fine. In my mind, she would be my next conquest. My hands had graced every part of her. I was on the verge of fucking her right there in the club. Had Christian not gotten pissed and been ready to go, I probably would have. She'd ridden there with someone else and wasn't ready to go. I took her number and had planned to get at her the next weekend."

He pulled his hand away from mine and began tapping the steering wheel. Whatever he had to say was tearing him apart. "Jakari, pull over, baby."

He glanced at me, then turned into a convenience store in front of the Diamond D Ranch subdivision. I unbuckled my seatbelt and leaned over, cupping his cheek, gently sliding my fingers through his beard. "I got'chu, baby. Whatever you need from me. Maybe you getting this out will heal you in a way."

He nodded. "My youngest brother, Rylan, had a basketball game during the week before I was supposed to see her again. We were at HJ, trying to establish our presence in the sea of white folks that were there, and I saw her. She was a cheerleader for the other team."

My eyebrows lifted. He looked up at me, and said, "That was my exact reaction. She had to have a fucking fake ID to get in that club. She was sixteen years old, Yendi. I'd almost fucked a kid."

He dry-heaved. Knowing what his father was in prison for, I could understand why that shit affected him as much as it did and for this long. "I went through a period of thinking I was just a chip off the old block. Avery was the last person I wanted to be like after I found out he was a pedophile. My attraction to that little girl made me feel like I was just like him. Christian kept telling me that there was no way I could have known she was a minor. She shouldn't have even been in that club."

"God, baby. I know that had to be hard for you."

"It was. I talked to Uncle Jasper that night. He'd seen how she was looking at me and how I had looked at her. I was disgusted with myself. I literally had to go to the restroom and throw up. Thinking I could have slept with that lil girl made me so critical and extra careful around women. I swore off relationships, because women couldn't be trusted. The only women I trusted were the ones in my family."

I rubbed his hand between mine and asked, "Am I your first relationship since then?"

"Yeah. My only real relationship since my second year in college... since I was nineteen or twenty. I have some real issues to deal with because that shit bothers me. Plus, I found out earlier today that Avery got paroled. So he's out. I'm not sure where he is, but I'm hoping I don't ever have to see him."

"Have you thought about going to counseling?"

"I have. I was supposed to go to this lady named Serita Gardener, but I never made it to the appointment. She's who my mom and brothers went to, along with my Aunt Syn. Avery raped his adopted sister for years and Nesha as well. It's why I'm so protective of the two of them. Nesha seems to be okay with him. She's resolved her issues, but she works for the state and has a social work degree. She knew what she needed to do for herself."

He took a deep breath and shifted the SUV back to drive and drove away, getting back to Highway 90. "Aunt Syn isn't taking the news too well. He started messing with her when she was four years old. It didn't stop until she left for college. However, she became more sexual because of it, where Nesha was more withdrawn. I took it upon myself to be their protector. Aunt Syn knew I was watching her every move, but Nesha didn't. I felt like it was partially my fault for not noticing something was wrong, especially with Nesha. I was around her nearly every day, but I just thought it was girl problems."

He slowly shook his head. What his father did had fucked him up so bad. The situation with the young girl only amplified those issues. Glancing at me as we neared St. Elizabeth Hospital, he said, "Something about you is wanting me to say fuck all that. But my nature is to be protective of my heart. I've been that way for over twelve years now. Just that the mere sight of you makes me wanna do away with all that is worth exploring. I just hope I'm as ready as I think I am."

We'd gotten to the hospital, and he parked. Before getting out, I said, "If we are at this point, you're ready. You took me to your house to clean up a bit. You'd refused to do that before. You let me in, and I promise I will never make you feel regret. I have your back. Period. Like you, I don't know why I'm so drawn to you. I mean, you're handsome and all, but beyond the surface, I barely knew you. I feel like I know you well now though."

"What'chu mean I'm handsome and all? Girl, you know I'm a fucking Greek God in these streets. That body was saying I was on the verge of making the holy trinity a quartet earlier. Don't be minimizing my shit."

I burst into laughter as he smiled and got out of the vehicle. That was his way of deflecting. When he was done with a subject, that was what he did. I'd picked up on that a while ago. Just the fact that he was giving us a chance had me happy as hell. After opening my door, he helped me out of his SUV. He kept my hand in his as he closed the door then turned to me.

"I feel like you are the woman for me. The one that will help me through some shit. I'm just praying that my mind doesn't override my heart. I hope that I can keep my anger and hurt in check while I'm around you. I don't ever want to project that shit onto you. You don't deserve that shit."

"Stop worrying so much. I'm here, Jakari… through the good and the bad."

"What about the ugly?"

I smiled at him. "That shit too. You got me. I can feel your heart." I closed my eyes as I laid my hand on his chest. "That shit is pure. It doesn't know what it means to be in love or to love a woman beyond yourself. I'm glad to be the first that will get to experience that part of you. Now let's go check on Nesha."

CHAPTER 11
JAKARI

"He is going to be tall like his damn daddy," I said as Uncle Storm gave Lennox a cigar.

"And his uncle mayor."

I could have done without his shenanigans today. Yendi and I had been here for five hours when Nesha finally started pushing. The baby was nearly eight pounds and twenty-three inches long. I stared at him as I held him. This shit was dangerous, because I was standing here wishing I had shot the club up earlier. Yendi was perfect. While I knew she had issues to overcome with her family, she was still here for me and my fucked-up way of thinking.

As I handed Baylor back to Nesha, Decaurey and Tyeis walked in. They both wore frowns, and I knew some shit was about to pop off. Either they were arguing or something had happened that pissed both of them off. Tyeis's emotions had been everywhere, and Decaurey said they'd been arguing quite a bit lately. I slapped his hand and asked, "What's up?"

"That muthafucka is contesting paternity. She ain't been with that nigga in almost a year. He just tryna fuck with us."

"Tyrese?"

"Hell yeah. He called while we were on our way here."

"You know the ball is in your court, man. Whatever you wanna do about it, we got yo' back. If he was up to anything more, Ali would have called. Plus, Philly about to start working with them on the side."

"I'll let you know. It's like that nigga know Tyeis and I have been arguing lately. That shit had me questioning whether she was telling me the truth about when they last slept together. She said she hadn't been with him since she'd been with me."

"What do you feel?"

"Honestly, I feel like she's lying. I think she's scared to tell me the truth. If the babies aren't mine, this gon' be it for us. I'm not even exaggerating. It won't be because she was with him, because after the club incident, we weren't even a couple. It'll be because she didn't think I needed the truth. I don't want y'all to do nothing to that nigga yet, because of how I feel about what she's saying. If they are my babies, then I'll worry about that nigga then."

I glanced over at Tyeis to see her holding Baylor. She was smiling and cooing, but then a frown graced her face, and she nearly dropped Baylor onto Nesha's lap. Jess ran to her only to see the liquid puddle on the floor. Well, he wouldn't have to make special arrangements to do the DNA test. They could do it here, possibly.

Everyone crowded around Tyeis, and Aunt Olivia escorted her to the nurses' station. We were already on the third floor, so they didn't have far to go. I felt for D. This situation had to put a damper on the birth of the babies. I could imagine he wouldn't want to bond with them as much until he found out the truth. That was probably one of the reasons they'd been arguing a lot too. I glanced over at Yendi to see she'd sat in a corner and had fallen asleep.

I made my way to her and kissed her lips. Her eyes fluttered open, and she smiled at me. "Sorry."

"You ain't gotta apologize, baby. It's almost one in the morning. You want me to take you back to your car so you can go home?"

"No. I'm good here with you," she said then rested her hand on my cheek.

"Good, because I want you here with me. Get you a nap in. I'm

HEALING FOR MY SOUL

gonna go check on Tyeis and see how far along she is in her labor. She's early by a month though. So hopefully the babies will be okay."

"I'm sure they will. Go ahead, baby. I'll be right here if you need me."

I smiled at her beautiful face and kissed her luscious lips. *Damn, her lips soft.* Her lips were one of my favorite parts of her body. That pussy claimed the number one spot, but those lips were definitely a close second. Feeling them on mine and on my dick was like having a cold glass of water on a hot day after working cattle. *Shit.*

I kissed her again, and Nesha said, "Keep it up and y'all gon' be taking a trip this way sooner than you anticipate."

I chuckled. "I won't shoot you the finger since you just pushed out a baby giant."

I turned back to Yendi. "I'll be back, baby."

I kissed her again just for Nesha's viewing pleasure then headed to find where they took Tyeis. Once I was outside of the door, my phone rang. Pulling it from my pocket to silence it, I saw it was Ali. *Shit.* "What's up, dude? What'chu got?"

"What's up? I called Philly, but he didn't answer. I know it's late, but I found out some shit. Tyrese is kin to Tyeis's baby daddy, Kelvin. That's his cousin. He's kin to the cop on his mother's side and kin to this fool on his father's side. Anyway, they are working together to try to bring down the Hendersons."

What the fuck!

"He messed around and made a move to set up some minor shit at a grocery store, destroying product with an employee. He's planning to make his rounds at all the local grocery stores and has the rice farms on his hitlist. I'm gonna move this shit to the top of our list of priorities. I'm also gonna have someone at each store near inventory, and I'm coming to Nome to the rice farm in a few hours."

"That muthafucka. So this issue with paternity of Tyeis's babies?"

"That's just to distract y'all from what he's really after. I saw them going to the hospital. She in labor?"

"My cousin Nesha went into labor. Tyeis was coming to visit her and ended up going into labor while she was here. Decaurey is going to submit DNA for a test to shut this nigga up."

Hopefully. With the way that nigga was talking, for Ty's sake, I prayed those babies were his. If they weren't, this shit wasn't going to be good. However, Grandma's word had to mean something. She was the one that had said Ty was pregnant. Surely, she wouldn't spill the beans on that if she thought she was pregnant by someone else, would she? Maybe she didn't get a reading on that. I chuckled to myself as I thought of my grandmother as a damn psychic or something.

"A'ight."

"I'm going to call a meeting in the morning so you can meet everyone. They are all here at the hospital, so let me get with my uncles."

"Okay. See you later."

"Bet."

I ended the call and wanted to throw my fucking phone. This nigga was just as shady as I thought he was. I made my way back inside Nesha's room and called Uncle WJ out of there. He'd stayed with her, and Aunt Olivia had gone with Decaurey and Tyeis. Yendi was sound asleep, her head resting against the wall. When he walked out of the room, he immediately asked, "What's going on?"

"That guy, Tyrese, is trying to hit grocery stores and destroy inventory. He has inside people working at each fucking store. Ali has guys that will be at every store in the area to stop shit from happening, and he's coming to Nome in a few hours to meet with us and man the rice farms. Most likely around nine or ten."

"Fuck," he mumbled. "All this shit got to with Reggie?"

"Yes, sir."

"Yeah. His ass needs to disappear like his uncle. Let's go tell Storm, Marcus, Jasper, and Kenny."

I followed him to the waiting area to see my uncles all seated and talking amongst themselves. "I need to talk to y'all," Uncle WJ said when we approached. "Y'all too, Jen and Tiff."

My mama had stayed behind with my other aunts and uncles to get the barn cleaned up and food put away. She was probably sleeping now so she would hear this shit later, along with Philly and Nesha.

Everyone stood and followed Uncle WJ to a far corner of the room. They all wore frowns, showing their confusion. That was when I realized just how much they all looked alike, especially Aunt Jen, Aunt Tiff, and Uncle Storm.

"Spit that shit out, WJ. I can see the disgust all over your face," Uncle Storm said.

"That nigga that used to talk to Tyeis and that attacked Decaurey is making moves. Ali from Watchful Eyes is coming around nine tomorrow morning to talk to us about what we want and expect to be done."

"What's he doing?" Uncle Jasper asked.

"He's trying to attack our inventory shipments and the rice farms in general. We gon' have to keep our eyes open at all times. That means he has help if he's planning to do all that shit. Ali will fill us in on the details in the morning. I just wanted to give y'all a heads up."

"My eyes always open, and my ear is always to the streets. 'Bout time y'all get on my level," Uncle Storm said and walked off.

Everyone rolled their eyes at nearly the same time, but Ty's screams claimed all our attention. My aunts ran toward the room she was in, and I ran behind them. When we got to the room, they were wheeling her out. "What's going on?" Aunt Tiff asked.

"C-section. Both babies are breeched," Decaurey said as he hurriedly followed them.

It seemed in this moment all bullshit was at the back of his mind and the well-being of the babies and Ty were at the forefront. *Thank God.* As I made my way back to Nesha's room to get Yendi, Uncle Kenny said, "I'm gonna get with Price to be on the look out when he and his drivers are making deliveries."

"Okay. I appreciate that, Unc."

We slapped hands, and I continued to Nesha's room. Uncle Kenny, although quiet, was the smartest of all of us, especially when it came to criminal shit. That nigga also had a spirit of discernment that couldn't be fucked with now. I supposed his past with Reggie had afforded him that gift. When I stepped into Nesha's room, the baby was lying on Lennox's chest, Nesha was sound asleep against

Lennox, since he was in bed with her, and Yendi was staring right at me.

She gave me a soft smile and asked in a low voice, "How's Ty?"

"They are about to perform a C-section. The babies are breeched."

"Oh wow."

I gave her a soft smile then went to Lennox to see my little cousin again. He had a head full of hair like Nesha. "Can you put him in his incubator thing? I'm gonna try to get some rest, but I don't want to wake Nesha up."

"Yeah, sure."

I slowly scooped Baylor up and listened to his little whimper. His lips were purple looking and pursed. I slid my finger over his head, suddenly filled with love. One day, I would have my own, and I couldn't wait. When Yendi appeared next to me, I realized I'd just been standing here with him for a while, staring at his angelic face that I was sure would soon be a little terror, fucking Nome up.

"A baby looks good on you. Do you want one someday?"

"Yeah. I didn't know until now though. What about you?"

She nodded as a smile spread across her thick lips. I brought Baylor to his bed and finally laid him in there then turned my attention back to Yendi. "Let's get out of here, baby. I'm tired, and I'm sure you are too. I just wanna lay next to you and hold you in my arms."

Her eyebrows lifted slightly as I looked away. I was becoming way too soft and expressive. I surely had to get away from this baby. He was only making things worse. She lifted her hand to my cheek and gently stroked it. "Are you saying you want me to stay with you tonight?"

"Yeah. You good with that?"

"Mm hmm. Better than good."

I grabbed her hand and led her out of the room. I supposed turning myself inside out for her earlier only increased my sensitivity. As we walked down the hallway to the elevator, I brought our joined hands to my lips and kissed hers. Letting go with her felt better than I thought it would. It was actually taking way more effort to resist her. She smiled at me, and I pulled her in my embrace. "How do you feel so strongly for me? How are you so strong? Seems like that should be my position as a man."

"I'm not always strong. Honestly, I'm fragile. That's why this shit between us has to be God. I'm not the type of woman that can handle tough battles with grace. I would crumble. I literally ran and moved over a thousand miles away. To me, someone calling me a strong black woman is like giving someone permission to fuck with me to test that theory. I don't like that. The problem with me running away is that I now feel hyper-independent, because I don't have any family here. I don't like that either."

I learned something new about her in this moment. I supposed my issues and situations had clouded my vision concerning her. I couldn't see how weak she was feeling because I thought I was feeling weaker. "There's no need for you to be hyper-independent with me around. You are so important to me. Never be afraid to depend on me. I'm here for whatever you need. I promise."

She leaned against me and wrapped her arms around my waist, hugging me tightly. I already knew that before we went to sleep, I would be loving her gently. It seemed this moment called for it.

THE RINGING PHONE WOKE ME UP. I LOOKED AT THE CLOCK TO SEE IT was seven. We'd only gone asleep about three hours ago. We got to my house about three, and I made love to Yendi for nearly an hour before we crashed. I'd planned to wake up by eight, so I was extremely irritable now. As I wiped my eyes, I realized it was Yendi's phone ringing. She sat up with a frown on her face. "Ugh! Who the fuck calling me so early?"

My eyebrows lifted slightly. It wasn't often that I heard her curse like that outside of sex, so it caught me off guard. She went to her phone and by the time she got to it, it had stopped. She looked at it and rolled her eyes. Giving her attention to me, she said, "I'm sorry. I thought I'd silenced my phone while we were at the hospital. Some people have no consideration for other people."

She came back to the bed and snuggled against me. I kissed her forehead. "It's okay." When I wrapped my arms around her, she trembled. "Yendi, you good?"

"Yeah. Thanks."

"No, you aren't. That's that hyper-independence you talked about earlier. What's up?"

"That was my mother. She called from my father's phone."

She broke down in my arms, and I hugged her even tighter as I closed my eyes. Why would her mother call her from her father's phone? That was fucked up. I could imagine how her heart probably hopped in her throat when she saw his name appear on her phone screen.

"What can I do, baby?" I asked her as I rubbed her back.

"Just what you're doing now. Thank you, Jakari."

"You don't have to thank me. I'm your man now. This shit is my job. I got'chu."

She stared up at me. "I got'chu too, baby. I don't know why this is so strong between us, but I'm willing to go with it and see where it leads."

I leaned over and kissed her lips. However, I didn't know why I did that, because I could never just kiss her and move on. I had to explore more. It didn't help that we'd slept naked. I slid my hand over her ass and closed my eyes, fully concentrating on what I was feeling, hearing, and smelling. The scent of her sex filled the air, and I was like a fucking hound dog after that... a gentle one.

I kissed her neck and slid my body atop hers. I opened my eyes and for the first time in my life, I spoke the abundances of my heart to this woman God blessed me with. "Yendi, I need you. I feel so free with you. Free to be me without the hard shell."

I looked away, my mind trying to force me to evaluate what I was about to say. My heart won when I said, "I love you... every part of you. I feel soft as fuck for revealing that to you, but there is no one out there I'd rather seem like a weak ass nigga in front of. I feel that you love me too. You can let go with me, baby. We can get over our hurts together, propping one another up where we're weak, being the best therapy either of us has ever gotten. I need you more than I've ever needed anybody. You make me better. My family sees it, so I know you see it when you compare how I am now to how I was when we first met."

"Yeah. You told me you wanted to give me the best orgasms of my life. You backed that shit up too." She paused and closed her eyes, taking a deep breath and slowly exhaling. "I love you too, Jakari." Her eyes opened and she said, "Please don't hurt me. Be gentle with me, baby. I don't want to have to deal with heartbreak on top of everything else."

I slowly slid my dick into her and bit my bottom lip trying to handle the intensity of that shit. "I will never intentionally hurt you. If by chance I do, I'm gonna try to move the earth, moon, and stars to make that shit right. You mean so much to me, and I know with time, that feeling will only grow stronger. You said you would go to hell with me. That's some strong shit, baby. Just so you know, I'd go for you too, but I'd fuck the devil up in your defense while I was there. Anybody can catch a fade. And this pussy? This shit would make hell hotter. Fuck!"

My stroke became stronger as Yendi moaned loudly. Her walls clenched me and had its way with me as I dunked my shit repeatedly in her baptismal. I swore I was having an outer body experience, my spirit man hovering over us watching the action. There was no way this angel could take me to hell. I entered heaven's gates every time I pushed inside of her.

I gripped her thigh and pushed it toward her as she curled the other around my waist. "Jakari, shit, I love you. Ooooh fuck! I'm cumming!"

I increased my pace a little, torturing myself as she squeezed the fucking life out of me. I wanted to fire off in her depths so badly. Just the fact that I'd been having unprotected sex with her had spoken volumes to me. I was always careful, but with her, I didn't give a shit about any of that. I knew I was clean, and I trusted that she was as well.

Her nails dug into me. I released her leg and lowered my head to her lips as her hands slid around me to my ass. She pulled me into her, and I stilled my movements. I was balls deep in her pussy, and I could tell that I nearly took her breath away. "Jakari?"

"Yeah, baby? You good?"

"Good as fuck. Please fuck me. I don't want to be able to walk out of here for hours. Give me that 'you ain't going no fucking where' shit."

I frowned at her. "So you want that disconnected shit?"

"No. I want that let me teach you a lesson shit. You think you can handle that?"

"Have you met me? I can handle whatever I choose to handle. I don't fuck with shit I can't handle. I'm finna handle yo' ass all over this fucking house."

I pulled out of her and pulled her to the edge of the bed then turned her over. My dick took over, and I nearly zoned out on her ass. Making sure I didn't cum too quickly, I switched positions. I lay in bed and said, "You want me to fuck *you*, but what if I want you to fuck *me*?"

"Then I'm gonna get up here and do my best work."

Man, she straddled me and slid that hot pussy on me, making me shiver. "Damn, girl."

Her eyes rolled to the back of her head and her hips rolled too. I lifted my hips slightly, gut checking her cervix while she stroked me just right. Feeling her juices leak to my balls had me about to detonate. It was getting to the point where I couldn't contain it. Seeing her big ass titties slightly bounce and sway with every roll her hips took was mesmerizing as hell. I lifted my hands to them and teased her nipples.

My hands journeyed to her ass and smacked her hard, showing her just how aggressive she was making me. "Fuck, Jakari!"

Apparently, she liked a little pain with her pleasure because she detonated all over my crotch area. "Oh fuck, Yendi. I'm about to nut, baby."

I expected her to stand, but instead, she stretched her legs out and completely sat on my dick as I fired off within her depths. My eyes widened slightly. I could only hope that she knew what she was doing, because I sure in the fuck didn't. We were both sensitive to this morning's events, but shit. Thoughts of doing this shit had crossed my mind, but I didn't think I would be taking a leap tonight.

She lowered her head for a moment. "I'm... I'm sorry. Fuck! I don't know what I was thinking. We just became a fucking couple! Oh my God. Shit!"

She was panicking. She slid off me and was about to get out of the bed until I pulled her back. I was in shock somewhat, but whatever happened, just happened. "Yendi, calm down, baby. It's okay. Last night and this morning had us both sensitive. It's okay. You may not even get pregnant. I mean... I do have Henderson running through me and our shit potent as fuck. You saw all the kids running around at the baby shower. So my suggestion is for you to get your mind right. I'm gon' help you with that shit too."

She took some deep breaths as my phone rang. It was eight o'clock so I knew it was probably Ali. Yendi stood from the bed and got it from my pants pocket on the floor. I didn't even charge that shit last night. I had a one-tracked mind... making love to Yendi. When she handed it to me, I said, "Thanks, baby."

"Hello?"

"What's up, man? I'm about to head that way. The entire crew is going to roll with me."

"Okay. How many of y'all should we expect?"

"Including me, nine."

"A'ight. Let get myself together."

"A'ight."

I ended the call and got out of bed as Yendi snuggled back under the covers. I quickly texted Uncle WJ, letting him know that they should be here by eight thirty, but we would take them around to the rice, hay, and grass fields first. By the time we got to the boardroom at the barn, it would be nine. Once the thirteen of us joined them, the barn would automatically go into party mode, thinking an event was happening. That was the only time more than twenty people was there at once.

After quickly showering and getting dressed, I made my way to

Yendi. "I'll be back in a couple of hours, baby. You gon' be good alone? I can call Jess to come hang with you until I get back."

"I'm okay. I'm gonna go back to sleep. Hopefully you will be back before I get lonely."

"Okay. We can go get lunch or something."

"Okay," she said and puckered her lips for a kiss.

I obliged her a few times then made my way out the door before I ended up naked all over again.

"THIS IS SHYRÓN BEROTTE, PART OWNER OF WATCHFUL EYES, AND he's also an attorney. That's how we skate around shit. This is Jericho Marcellus, Chad Berotte, Seneca Roberts, Rondo Simpson, Dinalee Simpson, Jungle Patterson, and Vegas Knight. Jungle and Vegas live in Houston so they primarily handle that area along with Seneca," Ali said.

I nodded and everyone shook hands as I introduced my family. "WJ Henderson is our CEO, and our board members are Jenahra Wothyla, Chrissy Douglas, Kenny Henderson, Jasper Henderson, Chasity Henderson, Tiffany Semien, Storm Henderson..."

"*Mayor* Storm Henderson," Uncle Storm interrupted.

There were heavy sighs from the family and a slight smirk from Ali. I slowly shook my head then continued. "Philly Semien, Marcus Henderson, and that's Nesha Guilman on Facetime. Decaurey Franklin is also on Facetime over there. I'm Jakari Bolton, the CFO. So, the siblings started running the business some years back, but they had some issues with a jealous muthafucka named Reggie. I'll let Uncle Kenny fill y'all in."

I took a seat at the table and put hot sauce on the breakfast burritos Aunt Jen and my mama had prepared for everyone. Thankfully, I probably wouldn't have to say another word. I planned to listen and eat my belly full. Uncle Kenny, Aunt Jen, Aunt Tiff, Uncle Storm, Uncle WJ, and Uncle Marcus all gave the rundown on Reggie's punk ass. The only ones he hadn't personally fucked with was my mama and Uncle Jasper. That didn't matter though. You fuck with one, you done fucked with us all.

"Sound like that muthafucka fucking wit' y'all from the grave," Shyrón said.

"Hell yeah. Honestly, I just want y'all to take Tyrese out, but I know we have to find out who all is involved first," Uncle Jasper said.

Ali nodded. "Dinalee and Rondo are going to stay out here in Nome. Rondo is familiar with rural areas and since Dinalee is his wife, she gets to stay too. I'm gonna float around. Y'all have a lot of property, and I wanna make sure everything is covered. I have a tracking device on Tyrese, a nigga named Kelvin, and another one named Creed."

"Creed?" Decaurey asked from Aunt Tiffany's phone.

"Yeah," Ali confirmed.

"Fuck. That's my bonus daughter's brother. He can't know Angel is connected to this."

This shit was getting way to deep. "I'm letting y'all know now that if a muthafucka cross me, I'm shooting first and asking questions later," Philly said. "If they're innocent, they were too fucking close to action they had no business in. Period."

"Nigga, you still the same, huh?" Jungle asked and chuckled.

"Hell yeah. Minus the drugs and shit," he said, glancing at Aunt Tiff, his sister-in-law.

He knew Aunt Tiff would report back to her husband Ryder, and he didn't want no shit with his older brother, even at their grown ass ages. There were laughs and surprisingly, Uncle Storm didn't have anything smart to say. Ali seemed to have a good plan in place to catch these fools. He said he had a few guys that worked off contract, so he would be pulling them in as well. We would need all the help we could get to diffuse of this situation quickly.

CHAPTER 12
YENDI

I lay in Jakari's bed staring at the ceiling. That call from my mama had really pissed me off. I didn't reveal just how pissed I was in front of Jakari, because I didn't want him second guessing his decision to be with me. It was bad enough I broke down in tears in front of him. I wanted to answer the phone and go the fuck off. Why the fuck would she call me from my dad's phone? When I saw 'Daddy' go across my phone screen, my heart nearly burst out of my chest. Although I knew he was no longer here, for that split second, it felt like he was here again.

I grabbed my phone and decided to call my sister, Janay. I hadn't talked to her this past week, but that was normal. We didn't talk verbally every day, but we texted each other at least every other day just to check in. I'd already had a whole crying session after Jakari left, but now the anger had come back to the forefront.

"Hello?"

"Hey, Janay."

"Hey, Yendi! How've you been?"

"I've been good. You sound so upbeat, and I'm calling to drag you down with drama."

"Girl, I don't care. I'm just glad to hear from you. Apparently, you and that country man have gotten even closer since you gave him the goods. You ain't got time for me and poor JaCory." She giggled. "What happened?"

"Well, that country man is now my man. I'm laying in his bed as we speak. He had to go to a meeting. His name is Jakari, by the way."

"Oh shit! Congratulations! I'm happy for you! With news like that, whatever has you down has to involve your mother."

"Your mother, not mine. She called me from Daddy's phone."

"She did what?" Janay yelled.

"You heard me. She called from Daddy's phone. For a split second, I got excited, only to be dropped right on my big ass head."

"Oh, man. I'm sorry, Yendi. That would have pissed me off. I'm sure it hurt too."

"Yeah… both. I keep going from one extreme to the other. One minute, I'm angry and the next, I'm crying because I miss daddy so much."

"Yeah, me too. My weekends feel so empty, so I can imagine how you feel."

"It's like every day, I'm missing something. Either he was calling me, or I was calling him. So for that split second, things were back to normal. Anyway. How is JaCory?"

"He's okay. He's with his daddy. He'll be back this evening."

"Oh okay. So what did you do this weekend?"

"Nothing. Got some much-needed rest. Maybe one weekend, I can fly out there to see you."

"That would be so great. We keep talking about it but haven't made any moves yet. I would pay for half your ticket."

"Yeah, let's arrange that soon. I can leave here on a Friday afternoon and be back before Terrence brings JaCory home Sunday evening."

"Sounds good to me. Let me check some things and see what weekend would be good."

"Yes. I have to see what Friday I would be able to take off work. Are you gonna call her back?"

"Hell no. Have you talked to Marie?"

"Yeah, a couple of days ago. I haven't talked to Pete though. Have you?"

"No. You're the only one I talk to regularly, unfortunately."

"I hate that, especially with you being way out there away from everybody all by yourself."

"Yeah, it is what it is. I have a couple of acquaintances that could possibly turn into friends. Jakari has an extremely large extended family. I met a lot of them at his cousin's baby shower yesterday. Don't worry about me, Janay. I'm okay."

"Then you don't worry about me either. JaCory and I are okay. I haven't seen Mama since you saw her. Thankfully, she hasn't reached out, although Terrence is talking about inviting her to JaCory's birthday party. He can kiss my whole ass if he thinks I would be cool with that."

Her ex-husband and our mother had suddenly gotten so close since Daddy died. That shit pissed me off to no end, because he rarely came around when daddy was alive. I felt like there was more going on that we didn't know about, but whatever. She could ride off on a white horse with his ass into the sunset for all I was concerned. Janay surprisingly felt the same way. "That jackass."

"Right."

"Well, I won't hold you any longer. Let me know what Friday you can come, and I'll check my schedule. Oh! Wait! You won't believe who I met yesterday."

"Who?"

"Nate Guillory."

"You're lying!"

"No. He and Jakari are friends. We're going to a basketball game next weekend. I'm gonna send you the pictures we took."

Not long after I sent them, she started screaming. I laughed until she quieted down. "You okay?" I asked.

She burst into tears. Hearing her crying audibly was hard. She always kept it together in front of me. I supposed she was hyper-independent too. She rarely showed negative emotions that would make one assume she needed help. "Janay, please don't cry," I said as I wiped my tears.

"I'm trying not to, but Daddy would have been in heaven standing next to Nate."

"I know."

"I'm sorry for breaking down on you. It's just hard."

"Believe me, I know. You don't have to apologize. It doesn't seem like it's been nearly six months already."

"Right. Okay. I'm gonna get on that schedule check. Thanks for these pictures, Yendi."

"Anytime. I love you, sis."

"I love you too."

I ended the call, feeling more emotional than I was when I called. This had to get better. Out of everyone in my family, I talked to my dad the most. I got out of bed and went to the bathroom to clean up a bit. I was sure Jakari would be getting home soon. Since we didn't go to my place before coming here, I had to "brush" my teeth with my finger. Thankfully, I really didn't sleep long enough to have morning breath. So I would be okay if he wanted to kiss me before we went to my place.

After straightening his comforter and tidying up his room a bit, I wrapped myself in his flat sheet and went to the kitchen to grab a bottle of water from his fridge. To say he lived alone, he had quite a bit of food in the refrigerator. Immediately after the thought graced my mind, I remembered his mom was a cook. *Duh, Yendi.* Of course he would have plenty of food. He never had to cook with a mom like her. I could tell that she spoiled him too. He wasn't rotten, but there were things she still did for him… like cook.

If he didn't get home soon, I would dip into what was there, because my stomach was talking mad loud. I hadn't eaten since the baby shower yesterday, and it was coming up on a whole twenty-four hours since then. When I heard the door open, I smiled. Despite all the turmoil my soul was in, it was still happy about where Jakari and I were in this relationship.

I couldn't dare tell Janay that I was already in love with him. I still couldn't believe he said it first. My mind wanted me to believe that he was bullshitting me, but then I talked myself out of that reasoning. What reason would he have to lie about that? He'd already gotten the pussy and my fucking devotion without even a promise of us continuing to see each other. I didn't know what had come over me regarding this man.

Everything I said I would never do... I was doing. Jakari had my heart before I could count to ten. I was willing to do shit for him that I had refused to do for anyone else. *Me wait for who?* There was no way in God's green earth I would have told a man that I would wait for him to get his shit together. No way in hell. My behavior was shocking to me, but I wouldn't change it for the world.

Jakari's love was passionate and gentle. I loved that. However, that shit could get aggressive as well. I'd sensed that he loved me, because I could tell he didn't even understand why he was explaining so much to me, like that night he came to my house to tell me we couldn't see each other anymore. He should have known better. We were both miserable for days after that.

I heard the back door open and close again, then he rounded the corner. He smiled when he laid eyes on me, wrapped in his sheet. "Damn. You look sexy as fuck."

"You're only saying that because you know I'm naked under here."

"I *do* know that, but it's not the reason you look sexy."

He walked to me slowly and leaned over to kiss my lips, just as I figured he would. At least he had mouthwash I could gargle with. His fingers slipped in between my breasts and pulled the sheet from my body. "Mm. You can walk around just like this, baby."

"I bet I can. My pussy would never recover from such a thing."

He laughed. "Let me find out though. I'll be sure she recovers so I could do it all over again."

I joined him with my laughter as he swatted my ass. I bit my bottom lip while he slowly shook his head. "What?" I asked.

"You got them dimples winking at me. That's gon' make me eat *you* for lunch. I love those dimples."

"Do you now?"

"Mm hmm. I told you I love everything about you, woman. Go put some clothes on though before I take advantage and we not go anywhere."

I smirked at him and walked away as he admired me like I was a runway model. I supposed I was… *his* runway model.

When Jakari stopped and picked up the girls, I was in awe of him. I thought lunch would be just the two of us, but he surprised me and picked up Ashanni and Maui. We talked the entire time about reading and school. Then, of course, they had to mention how happy they were about Jakari and I being a couple and how their plan worked. We'd laughed at what they thought they were hiding and explained how we both knew what they were up to.

Jakari was in his own world, tuning us out for most of the conversation. I noticed he was on his phone a lot, but I didn't pay it any mind. They'd had a meeting today, so I was sure he was still handling business. Maybe he brought them along to keep me company. However, if he had business to tend to, I wouldn't have been upset if he had to cancel our outing. Although it was Sunday, I knew business didn't stop for the type of business they ran.

We were on our way up to the hospital to see the babies. Tyeis's babies were in the NICU, but Nesha and her son would be going home tomorrow. Ty and Decaurey's babies were only around three pounds and seven ounces each, so I knew they would be staying in the hospital for a while. We didn't get to see them before we left so I was anxious to see them now.

Once Jakari parked, he said, "Sorry I risked y'all's safety by texting and driving, but the mayor is on my last nerve. He's wearing our group thread out about what we need to be doing tomorrow. He's up there with Decaurey, so Maui be sure to lay the charm on so that nigga can calm down."

"What's he saying?" Maui asked.

"How if we listened to him like Marcus does, we wouldn't have half the problems we're having. Just stupid shit, as usual."

The girls chuckled. Maui said, "Hey na, Jakari. That's still my daddy. He may be bold and aggressive, but he *is* smart."

"I didn't say he wasn't. They are all smart, but his ass is annoying, and you know it."

She laughed more. "Again, watch yo' mouf though. I'm still his daughter. Don't push that storm out of me."

Jakari stared at her for a second and said, "Aww hell naw."

He got out of the SUV and opened our doors. After he helped me out, he pressed his body against mine and kissed my cheek. "Don't get carried away with those babies today unless you are truly prepared. Remember what happened earlier. If you want me to be your baby daddy, just say that shit."

I giggled as I wrapped my arms around his waist and stared up at him. "You would be cool with that, cowboy?"

He smirked, I assumed at me calling him cowboy. He was wearing jeans, boots, a belt with a rodeo buckle, and a hat. On top of that though, he wore a T-shirt, diamond studs, and a diamond piece and chain. I didn't know whether to say 'howdy' or 'what's up, nigga?'. I liked it though. This style was new to me since I wasn't southern or country. It was sexy as hell.

"Cowboy, huh? Keep it up, and I'm gon' take you back home for a bedroom rodeo."

"Are y'all coming or nah? We can go up there by ourselves," Ashanni said, interrupting us.

"Y'all better be glad I like y'all and that I owe y'all for introducing me to this fine ass woman."

They laughed as my cheeks heated up. He grabbed my ass right in front of them and kissed my lips then pulled away. "If I didn't know any better, I'd think you were trying to incite a rodeo in this parking lot," I said before releasing him from my grasps.

"Girl… You better quit playing before you be bowed up against this Suburban in the broad daylight."

I laughed, but he was serious as hell. "Okay. Let's go."

He bit his bottom lip and nodded repeatedly as he grabbed my hand. "Good, 'cause I don't want nobody seeing what belongs to me now. I'm a selfish muthafucka when it comes to my cake, Yendi. I hope you can deal with that."

"Mm. I can more than deal with that. I'm one in the same. All of you belongs to me too. So you only diving in one lake."

"Shiiiid, I'm deep-sea diving in an ocean. Don't undermine that gripper. That's a fucking maneater between your legs, girl," he said in a low voice near my ear.

Maui turned to look at us with her face scrunched up like something stank. "Are y'all being nasty?"

"We're being grown. Stay in a child's place, lil girl," Jakari said.

She rolled her eyes and stopped to push him. "If this is your way of paying us what you owe us, I'm not feeling it one bit."

I giggled as she continued. "Oh! My dad has an iPhone for us to give away."

He'd already donated a phone to fulfill the plans this past Friday before the pep rally. "Another one?" I asked wide-eyed.

"Yeah. You get whatever you want when he likes you," she said, then winked.

Jakari slowly shook his head. "I guess I should've told *you* to kiss up to his ass so he can calm down. He better be careful though. I'm possessive too."

It was my turn to shake my head. I felt good. Even after the bullshit from earlier, today was shaping up to be a good one. I felt like I had a family again, and I would do whatever I had to do to make sure that didn't change. I couldn't lose that twice.

CHAPTER 13

JAKARI

When we got to Houston and had gotten inside the arena, I had a surge of nervousness overcome me. I didn't know why, but I was on guard for bullshit. Yendi was beyond excited. It was her first time going to a professional basketball game. Knowing that we were personally invited by her dad's favorite player was the icing on the cake. Her excitement was contagious, and she had me lowkey excited.

Nate had gotten us box seats, and after a minute or two, I saw why. Noah and his wife, TAZ, had joined us. I'd gotten a chance to meet him for the video shoot months ago. After seeing how excited Yendi was to meet him, he probably knew she would be beyond excited to meet Noah and TAZ. Her back was to them so she didn't see them walk in.

I approached him and his guard halted me. When Noah saw me, he smiled, and invited me into his presence. We shook hands. "Nate told me you would be here with a lady friend. How are you?"

"I'm good. What about you?" I asked as I noticed Yendi staring wide eyed.

I chuckled and said, "That's her over there, looking like a deer in headlights."

He laughed. "Well, this is my wife Taryn, aka TAZ."

She extended her hand and smiled big. "Hi, Jakari. It's nice meeting you. I've already heard your name a few times tonight."

"I chuckled. The pleasure is mine."

I glanced back at Yendi and invited her to join us. We were sitting right next to them anyway. Once she got next to me, I kissed her lips. "Noah... TAZ, this is my lady, Yendi. Yendi, this is Noah and—"

"Umm... I know who they are, Jakari. Thank you so much."

I chuckled as she extended her hand to shake Noah's. He chuckled then pulled her in for a hug as I took pictures. TAZ hugged her as well, and I took pictures of the three of them. Noah's bodyguard then offered to take pictures of the four of us. When Yendi realized we would be sitting next to them she nudged me. "Jakari! Why didn't you tell me?"

"Because I didn't know either. I knew he would be here tomorrow for the private viewing of the video Jess did with him, but I didn't know he would be at the game. I surely didn't know TAZ would be here."

She rolled her eyes. I'd invited her to the viewing but told her that Noah wouldn't be there. I chuckled as she took her seat next to TAZ. I could see how nervous she was with how stiff her shoulders were. Noah and I walked to the glass, and he said, "My brother gon' self-destruct if he ain't careful. I nearly did a few years ago. I was at rock bottom, and I knew part of the reason why was because I couldn't let go of Sonya. The other part was that Jah couldn't let go of Kermit."

He side-eyed me as I chuckled. That man's name was Kahmad, but he insisted on calling him Kermit. "He so in love with Jess his ass can't function. I don't even know how he's playing as well as he is. That woman is pregnant and engaged. She has moved on with her life," he added.

"She ain't innocent though. That's my cousin, and I love her, but I have to talk to her. Although she isn't the one reaching out, she's allowing him to be in her space, knowing how Brix feels about it. She looks at Nate as a friend, but if she's that attached to him, she should have chosen him. Real shit."

When I heard TAZ hit her signature harmony, I turned to look at her and Yendi. Yendi's eyes were closed and when I turned back to Noah, his eyes were closed too. "That was amazing. Thank you so much," Yendi said with tears streaming down her face.

I took a quick picture of her then looked out at the court as the players warmed up. "God said that a soul tie is hard to break. Nate and Jess entered into one another's soul when they had sex. Their interaction was so full of passion and lust, it has a hold on them. Only prayer can change it. I have a feeling this is going to go from bad to worse before it gets better."

I didn't respond to what he said, but I could only hope that he was wrong about that. As if sensing my doubt, he said, "Most times when she hits that polyharmony thing she does, I can hear God's voice. It's clear, as if you were talking to me. The first time I heard it I was blown away. That was how I knew she was the one. God told me through her voice. She helped bring me from the depths of depression... just like that woman is doing for you. Satan gon' come for that. Don't let him win."

I didn't realize just how spiritual Noah was, but I couldn't help but nod in agreement and shake his hand. When the buzzer sounded, he said, "Let's watch this nigga run this score up."

I chuckled. "Hell yeah."

I sat next to Yendi and kissed her cheek, replaying what Noah had said. What did God tell him was coming to test my love for her? I glanced over at him, seeing he was totally wrapped up in his wife. "Thank you for bringing me along with you, baby. This is amazing."

"Girl, you ain't gotta thank me. You my baby. You are always invited to be where I am."

I kissed her lips and did my best to relax and forget about his warning. Seemed like Jess and I were both in trouble.

IT WAS HALFTIME, AND DALLAS WAS UP BY TEN POINTS. NATE HAD fifteen points and six assists. He was on his way to a double-double.

HEALING FOR MY SOUL

Yendi wanted to step out and buy a couple of souvenirs. We left out and headed to a store that sold jerseys, key chains, and whatnot.

Once she'd picked out the things she wanted, we headed to the register and paid for everything. She lifted her camera and took a selfie of us then one of herself. Her smile was big, and I couldn't wait to wipe that shit right off her beautiful face. Her titties were on display every time her duster sweater thingy fell open.

"See, I'm gon' have to punish you tonight for wearing this shit, showing off my goods. That's my pleasure bags, Yendi."

She giggled and tilted her head back, puckering her lips. She knew I couldn't resist those soup coolers. I leaned over and kissed her then pulled away with a smile on my face. It didn't take long for that shit to fade though. I was hoping I didn't see who I thought I'd seen. Grabbing Yendi's hand, I pulled her harder than I'd intended. "Whoa, Jakari. What's up?" she asked.

"I'm sorry. I'm tripping."

I slid my hand over my face then brought her hand to my lips and kissed it. She gave me a soft smile, and we made our way out of the store to head back to the box. Before we could get there, I nearly walked right into him. I stopped in my tracks and stared right at him. Yendi looked from me to him and him back to me then brought her hand to her mouth.

He swallowed hard, and said, "Hey, son."

My jaws flexed as I gritted my teeth, doing my best to control myself. I always wondered what I would do if I came face to face with him. When my mama told us about him and what he'd done, the only time I saw him after that was in court. The only reason I'd even gone to the hearing was to support Nesha, Chenetra, Shakayla, and Aunt Syn.

I'd imagined that I would punch him in his shit or curse him out. Right now, I couldn't seem to move or speak. This was the last place I expected to see him. Yendi wrapped her arm around mine, clearly nervous about how I would respond. She knew who he was because me standing face to face with him was like looking in the mirror. We were the same height, same complexion, had the same hair and smile. My fingers even looked like his. Everything about my looks was a carbon copy of Avery Bolton.

"Avery, are you ready to go be seated?"

I turned my attention to the woman that was speaking and jerked away from Yendi. "You have got to be fucking kidding me."

Avery looked confused, but the woman knew what the fuck was going on. It had been ten years, but Shakari looked almost the same as she did back then. The only thing different about her was her hair. I didn't understand why the fuck he was with a twenty-six-year-old woman. She was younger than his youngest son.

"Umm... hey, Jakari."

"Man... don't fucking speak to me. Why are you here, enjoying yourself, while you being free has nearly destroyed the woman you raped for fourteen years. Didn't you have to register as a sex offender? You a fucking pedophile. Ain't no reason you should be allowed at a basketball game around little girls. Your parole officer know you here?"

All I saw was red. We had an audience, but I didn't care. "Jakari, son... Can we talk?"

"Talk about what? Talk about how you're a sick ass muthafucka that like lil girls? You gotta be a good thirty years older than the woman you with. You ain't changed! You lied to them people at the prison. You need to still have your ass locked up. I can't believe this shit," I said as I paced,

"Jakari."

I turned to Yendi as she silently pled with me through her gaze. Just as I was about to walk away and just go with her, he grabbed my arm, trying to pull me into an embrace. I shoved him to the floor. I didn't know who the fuck he took me for. "Don't you ever in your fucking life put your hands on me. Period!"

I walked away, practically running as security guards and cops came our direction. One caught up with me. "Sir, what's the problem?"

"A misunderstanding with the man over there. I'm leaving because this arena ain't even big enough for the both of us."

"Okay. Let me escort you to the door."

I nodded and headed that direction as I heard Yendi yelling my name. I couldn't turn around to even acknowledge her. If I had to look at him again, I knew I wouldn't be able to control my actions. The surge that I felt when he touched me had me dangerously close to going to jail tonight. I made my way out of the doors and called one of the people that always had my back. "I saw y'all in the box, nigga!"

"I need you to come get Yendi. Now. I gotta go."

I ended the call and went to find my SUV. The voices in my mind were speaking loudly. If I went back in that arena, I would definitely kill Avery. Uncle Jasper was calling me back, but I couldn't answer. I sent him Yendi's contact information and hopped in the Suburban. I rested my head on the steering wheel for a minute then lifted my head and punched it.

I felt like I could barely breathe, but somehow, I was able to burn the fuck off. My phone was ringing again, but I didn't bother looking at it because I knew I wouldn't answer it. The voices in my head were telling me that Yendi didn't deserve this, and I knew she didn't. I thought I had this shit under control. Allowing her access to all of me was a mistake. She deserved better than this.

They were also telling me to track Avery down and do what the system should have done. I hoped he got raped in prison. Thoughts of him being somebody's bitch gave me a little relief, but not enough to stop the pounding in my head. My phone was ringing again, and I could imagine it would be doing that for the rest of the night.

I grabbed it and powered it down, but not before seeing Yendi's beautiful face. Noah's words had found me quick as hell. I failed the test. I wasn't ready for a relationship. I was no better than Avery at this moment. I literally just left Yendi stranded in Houston. I couldn't see past my anger. Leaving was what was best. She needed to move on with her life and find someone that was better for her.

You should have punched that muthafucka in his slick ass mouth. That was the same mouth that coaxed little girls out of her panties.

I quickly pulled over and threw up. My mind created visuals for everything and at this moment, that was a curse. Seeing what he did to a young Nesha and a young, impressionable Aunt Syn was too much.

Knowing he'd gone all the way with them and had the audacity to come home and sleep in the same bed with my mother after that, only made me regurgitate more.

I grabbed the bottle of water from the cup holder and rinsed my mouth out. When I closed the door, I rested my sweaty forehead on the steering wheel once again and cried. My hatred for him had taken over my life. That was something I'd allowed. When my hatred for him overpowered my love for Yendi, I realized I wasn't doing as well as I thought I was. I'd brought her into my world of hurt, anger, and dysfunction and left her alone to fend for herself through the mess I put her in.

I drove to the Hilton I saw in the distance and sat in the parking lot, trying to make sense of what happened and how I handled it. *Fuck!*

CHAPTER 14
YENDI

I stood there in disbelief as I stared at Jakari's father and the woman. I wasn't sure what she had to do with anything until his dad asked, "How do you know my son?"

"I tried to trick him into being with me when I was sixteen. We were at a club for twenty-one and up, so he never asked my age. We agreed to hook up at a later date but before that day came, he saw me cheering at a basketball game."

Jakari's dad looked at me with sorrow in his eyes. He looked like he wanted to say something, but I didn't have a desire to listen. I walked away, not able to stop the tears. Jakari had left me stranded in Houston. How was I supposed to get back home? I knew that if push came to shove, I could get a ride home, but I wanted to get back home the same way I got here. Before I could walk to where the box seats were, I had to sit for a moment.

I was getting stares from people all over the place who'd witnessed what had gone down. I wasn't angry for how Jakari responded to his dad. He was caught completely off guard. That would have been like seeing my mother here. I couldn't say that I wouldn't have gone off just as he did. The problem was that he forgot about me. He let his anger push me away from him instead of letting his love pull me *to* him.

After going to the bathroom to clean my face, I made my way back to my seat while repeatedly calling Jakari, only for it to ring until it went to voicemail. When I walked in alone, Noah frowned. TAZ looked at me and frowned as well. Noah stood and approached me. "What happened?"

"He left me. He left."

"Why?"

"He was confronted by his past, and he couldn't handle it. He's living in the past right now. The problem with that is I don't exist there. I don't want to go into detail, because it's more than that, but it's not my business to tell."

"I understand. Come here."

I fell in his arms and cried my eyes out. When I realized I was wetting *thee* Noah's clothing, I pulled away. "I'm sorry."

I wiped his shirt as he frowned. "We can make sure you have somewhere to sleep until morning. I'm sure the hotel we're staying at has availability."

I sat in my seat next to TAZ as the second half started. I couldn't focus on anything but how Jakari was feeling. When my phone rang, I quickly pulled it from my crossbody. I didn't recognize the number, but I answered anyway, expecting the worst. "Hello?"

"Yendi?"

"Yes."

"This is Jasper. Jakari called for me to come pick you up. He didn't stay on the phone long enough to explain what happened. I know y'all are at the game, so I'm on my way there. I should be arriving in about forty-five minutes to an hour."

"Okay," I said, hearing my voice quiver.

"It's gon' be okay, baby girl. We gon' figure this out. Okay?"

"Okay. Mr. Henderson?"

"Call me Jasper. What's up?"

"Thank you. I'm worried about him though."

"Don't worry. Jakari gon' be alright. Start getting to where I can get to you easily."

"Okay."

I ended the call and closed my eyes. He cared enough to get me a ride home. He hadn't completely forgotten about me. I tried to call him again, and his phone went straight to voicemail. My heart was so hurt. Even in this moment, I wasn't angry. I loved Jakari so much. All I wanted to know was if he was okay. He was so angry when he left. I was scared he would get in a wreck. I could only imagine the way he probably burned out of here.

I turned to TAZ and Noah as they quietly watched the game. That was totally different from the first half. Noah was up, yelling out his excitement earlier. "Thank y'all for being so kind to me. Jakari's uncle is on his way to get me. He said he would be here in less than an hour so I'm gonna go find out where I need to go for him to pick me up."

TAZ reached over and hugged me. "Kindness is in our nature. You don't have to thank us for that. I wish y'all the best."

Noah stood when I did and hugged me as well. "Enjoy the viewing tomorrow," I said.

His eyebrows lifted and scrunched together in a sympathetic type of way. I could imagine that I wasn't invited anymore. I didn't want to be there without Jakari anyway. I made my way out of the room, and when I saw an employee for the arena, I asked for directions. As I walked in the way I was directed to go, my phone chimed. I looked at it to see a message from Janay.

Your mama pulled that shit with me, and I answered and cursed her ass out. How dare she play with our emotions? Just because she wasn't as hurt about Daddy's death doesn't mean we aren't. Although I hated to do it, I blocked Daddy's number.

The tears slid down my face. I couldn't handle dealing with that right now. The only person I wanted to think about was Jakari. He was the man I loved, and I knew that he wasn't in a good place mentally. His well-being was the only thing I was concerned with right now. I told him I would be with him through this, and I truly planned to if he let me.

Jasper opened the door of his Escalade for me, and I slid into the plush seating. It had cooled off outside, and I was freezing since my legs were exposed. I'd worn a somewhat long-sleeved all-in-one with heels, since I knew we'd be in the box. I said somewhat because the sleeves had slits in them to where my arms could be seen. The legs of it were made the same way. I had my hair pulled up and had added a ponytail to it. So I didn't even have a wig on to keep my head warm.

When he got into the truck, he reached over and grabbed my hand, giving it a squeeze then took off. As he drove, I stared at my phone, looking at the text message I sent Jakari.

Baby, I'm not angry. Please call or text me and let me know you're okay. Please... I love you, and I'm worried about you. I didn't hang around to even talk to your dad and that woman. If you have an issue with them, then so do I. I'm here for you. Please don't shut me out, baby.

As I read it repeatedly, the tears slid down my face. Thankfully I had great skin because I'd long ago cried my makeup off my face. What the tears didn't eliminate, I'd wiped off when I cleaned my face in the restroom. It was like I could feel how hurt and angry he was. The two people he had the most issues with were together, overwhelming his mind and sending his heart into an emotional cardiac arrest.

I was standing there with the paddles though, ready to shock him back to life with my love, only to be ignored. When I yelled his name, I just knew he would snap out of it and realize what was more important, but he didn't. That shit hurt so bad. Breaking the silence, Jasper said, "So you got to meet Noah, huh? I saw y'all on TV during the first half."

"Yeah. Him and his wife. I love both their music. She even sang for me. God, it felt like I'd stepped through the gates of heaven and was listening to a chorus of angels. Nearly brought me to tears."

"I know what you mean. Listening to her recorded vocals does that to me, especially when I'm high. So I can only imagine what it sounds like in person."

I bit my lip, trying to contain my smile. "You listen to her while you're high?"

"Maaaaann, I swore I was sitting at the feet of Jesus. I had to put my blunt out and apologize to the Lord for giving him a contact high."

I could no longer suppress my laughter. I hollered. Jasper was funny as hell. This was where Jakari got his sense of humor. The mayor was funny too, just in a cynical sort of way. Jasper was a fun, laidback funny. "You are a mess! I can't wit'chu!"

"Girl, you better start dropping by on Fridays and get in the Lord's presence with me. You'll never be the same."

I laughed more, and he chuckled with me. "Jakari has a great support system. I just wish he would use it."

"Yeah. Our last talk went well. So I thought he was good. I suppose he *was* good at the time. What happened?"

I lowered my head, trying to figure out if I wanted to say since Jakari hadn't told him. "He uhh… he saw his dad at the game."

"Ooooh shit. Yeah. Had I been there, we would have gone to jail tonight. I wouldn't have been any help at all. We would have fucked his ass up. How was he at a game?"

"That was the same thing Jakari asked him. It gets worse Jasper. The girl from ten years ago was with his dad."

"The fuck? Oh, my boy did good by not fucking that nigga up. Not saying it was good he left you, but shit. Had he taken you with him, I would have given his ass an A plus. That girl gotta be younger than his youngest son. Rylan is twenty-seven I think."

"He said his dad had to be nearly thirty years older than her and that he hadn't changed and should still be locked up."

"Damn. I hate he turned his phone off. It's going straight to voicemail. I said a special prayer for him while I was at the feet of Jesus before I left."

My eyebrows lifted. "You're high right now?"

He chuckled. "I was flying like sheets in the wind on a clothesline on my way here, but I'm coming down now. Girl, you in more danger when I'm sober. I'm relaxed right now and don't give a fuck what the rest of these people doing on the road. You gotta be high to drive in Houston anyway so you don't have a fucking aneurism yelling at these no-driving fuckers."

I swore I could get used to Jasper's ass. Just thinking about how Jakari was pushing me away and about to take the only family I had now away from me, produced tears all over again. "Whoa, did I say something wrong?"

I shook my head rapidly. "You just feel like family. If Jakari pushes me away, I'm gonna lose the only sense of family I have. My dad died months ago, and my mother is a fucking mess, so I had to block her. I moved here to get away from her. So it feels like both my parents died. Y'all have filled a void in my life and knowing I may lose that already is heartbreaking."

"Listen to me, Yendi. It don't matter what happens between you and J. We gon' still be cool. But... I believe y'all gon' work it out. You seem to be so understanding of his turmoil and from what you just told me, I can see why. He's going to talk to me in his time. Knowing him like I do, he's probably overthinking shit. Thinking you deserve better than him and what he can give and all that bullshit. He's been like that since he was a kid... always so hard on himself."

"Jasper, I'm trying to be optimistic, but I don't feel good about this. After he'd given me all of him, I know he's embarrassed about this. He said he would never intentionally hurt me. He glanced at me and walked out on me anyway. He said he loved me. Why would he do this? I told him I was here for the long haul and to help him through all that shit. Did he think I was just saying that because it sounded good to say?"

"J has been the man of his family for a long time. When that shit happened with his daddy, he didn't show weakness. He was always trying to be strong for everyone else. It nearly killed his mama. She started smoking and drinking a lot after that. She wasn't a smoker, but she was at my house more often than not, getting fucked up with me. So he felt he needed to be there for her, his brothers, Nesha, and his aunt. He never got to address how what his dad did affected him. He doesn't feel comfortable being vulnerable. Don't stop coming around. Show him that you meant what you said."

I nodded once again and dried my face. "You're right. You give amazing advice. Does that only happen when you're high?"

He smirked. "Naw. I'm an intelligent nigga. The advice does get better when I'm high though because my mind is clear."

I chuckled, trying to force myself into a good mental state. "So should I show up at the viewing tomorrow?"

"Hell yeah. Everybody gon' be there, ready to turn up. It's gon' be at the family barn, where all the big shit goes down."

"Okay. If I didn't work at the school, I'd ask for a sample of your product."

He pulled a blunt from his console. "Girl, fuck them people. You associated with the Hendersons now. The mayor got you covered."

He chuckled as he passed it to me. "Jasper, I don't even know how to smoke. I was just kidding."

"Oh shit. Give me that back. You can't be wasting my shit. I'll show you though if you wanna learn. When we get to Liberty County, I got'chu."

"Why Liberty County?"

"'Cause I got the judge on speed dial. I can get out of shit out there. Them people out here will throw me in jail without question. They don't give a fuck who you are out here."

I slowly shook my head as a smile played on my lips. I could chill with Jasper anytime. I would have never guessed Ashanni's dad was this cool. Looking down at my phone, I picked it up from my lap and tried calling Jakari. It went straight to voicemail again. I sighed then set it back on my lap. "So how many kids do you have?"

"Two boys after Ashanni. So three total. Royal and Crew. Royal was hell on wheels, but he's calmed down now. He's thirteen and Crew is nine. He's the typical, active boy. You want kids?"

"I do. I love kids."

"You obviously ain't spent much time around Storm's other kids. Maui will make you think they are all like her. She's the only one that turned out like her mother. Those twins and her two younger brothers will make you snatch your ovaries and fallopian tubes out yo' damn self."

I hollered with laughter as he continued. "You think I'm lying? I'm not even halfway playing. Bad ass kids."

By the time I caught my breath from laughing so much, Jasper had pulled out his lighter and sparked up. He took a huge inhale then blew it out slowly and passed it to me. I stared at it for a second, then took a slow pull from it. Although I didn't smoke, I could follow directions. Jasper's silent instructions were great. A smile formed on my lips as I exhaled. I could see his eyebrows lift in my peripheral.

"I thought you'd never smoked before."

"I haven't. I just watched you. I'll try to truly inhale and blow it out my nose next time."

"A'ight. Don't be getting choked. You gon' be at Jesus feet for real."

CHAPTER 15
JAKARI

I'd fucked up... just what I was afraid I would do. I didn't know why I thought I could handle a meaningful relationship with anybody. Yendi, although she had issues as well, she was perfect. She knew how to separate that situation from what we had. If she was angry at her mother, she didn't take that out on me. While I could see she had a problem, she didn't distance herself from me. I didn't know how to do that yet.

I'd already called Serita this morning and rescheduled my appointment instead of doing it on the website. It was past time. When I told her who I was and what my issue was, she seemed to be stunned into silence. I knew she remembered counseling my mom, brothers, and Aunt Syn. Sometimes she still counseled Aunt Syn. After I gave a rough explanation of why I needed to see her, she said, *I waited to hear from you for a while. When I didn't, I assumed you had a handle on things.*

Yeah, I thought I was handling it too. I wasn't handling it in a healthy way though. After twelve years, I still felt guilt, anger, hatred, and hurt. I hated Avery Bolton and everything the image of him now represented. Seeing him with Shakari was the straw that broke the camel's back. Everything came crashing down on me. I lost my heart. I truly believed that what I'd done to her last night was bothering me more than it bothered her.

I knew she was hurting, although she probably wouldn't verbalize that to me. She said before that she needed to be handled with care... gently. What I did was everything but. It was like I couldn't control my actions at that moment. I'd always been able to control myself until I met Yendi. Love found me, and I couldn't stop the inevitable. The problem with that was I didn't know how to handle her love for me or my love for her. Again... I thought I did until last night.

It had only been a week of us being together, and I'd already fucked things up. The odds of me hurting her again were great... overwhelmingly great. I promised her that I would never intentionally hurt her. While I made a conscious decision to leave her at the arena, I couldn't force myself not to. I supposed I was a creature of habit. When I was hurt or offended, I needed to be alone. I didn't like anyone seeing me in the state I was in last night, not even the people closest to me. On top of that, I was now embarrassed about what happened and my behavior afterward.

As I sat outside of the room Jess would be in, I lowered my face to my hands. I'd just gotten back to Nome an hour ago. I went home and showered then came here. Focusing on Jess's issues would possibly keep the attention off my own. *Typical Jakari. Deflect, ignore, and suppress.* Noah probably thought I was a fucking fool. I was more than sure Yendi had gone back to her seat without me. Seeing Noah today would bring all that shit crashing down. Plus, we were supposed to go turn up with Nate after the game, whether they won or not.

I didn't know how the game turned out, because I never got a hotel room. I sat in that Suburban all night and drove around, burning all my fucking gas, trying to rid myself of the reoccurring thoughts of failure, anger, and hostility. I wanted to fuck Avery up. To say I couldn't control myself, I somehow kept myself from choking the fuck out of him. Maybe because it was something that just wasn't in my nature to do. I rarely resorted to violence.

I pulled my phone from my pocket and stared at it. This morning, when I powered it on, I had so many messages. Most of them were from Yendi. There were also messages from Uncle Jasper and Nate. Apparently, no one else knew of my disappearing act, which meant they kept it to themselves. I couldn't be more grateful for that. I didn't need everyone blowing me up and trying to give me advice. Uncle Jasper knew that much about me, and either Yendi understood me more than I thought she did, or Uncle Jasper had told her to keep it to herself.

"Jakari what are you doing here already?"

I looked up to see Jess and Brix approaching. I stood from the chair I had pulled to the hallway and shook Brix's hand. "I wanted to holla at'chu about something."

She frowned slightly as she hugged me. "Okay. You okay? You look bothered."

Great. I supposed I could make it seem like I wanted to talk about me so Brix would leave. "Naw. I ain't okay."

Brix kissed her head and said, "I'll let y'all talk. The mayor is outside, so I'm sure he'll keep me entertained."

Jess giggled then lifted her head and kissed his lips. "Okay, baby."

Brix gave me a head nod then walked away as Jess opened the door to her room for the day. I walked in behind her and saw that it was fully stocked like she was a fucking star. I supposed she was. The family had really done this shit up to make her feel special, and I loved it. There was a vanity area with lights around the mirror and everything.

"This is beautiful!" Jess said as she sniffed the roses on her vanity.

"It really is. They did an amazing job in here."

She turned to me with a slight frown on her face and extended a hand toward the couch. I went to it as she followed me, and we sat at the same time. "What's going on, J?"

"I have plenty going on, but this ain't about me. I said that so Brix would give us some alone time. Why are you giving Nate clearance to be where you are when you know how Brix feels about it?"

She lowered her head. "Because Brix is being insecure. He knows I love him. I chose him over Nate. That should stand for something."

"Nate is trying to be respectful. You know that man loves you, Jess, and I feel like you have something for him too for you to keep allowing this. You tryna fuck up everything with Brix? He has a right to feel the way he does about Nate. Thanks to you, he knows y'all fucked... and that it was after y'all reconnected. If you wanted to remain friends with Nate, that was some shit that you should have kept to yourself."

"That wouldn't have changed anything. Nate can't control his facial expressions. When he looks at me, I can see and feel the love he has for me. It wasn't an easy decision. Nate is a great guy. I had to factor in situations though. I didn't want to be with someone who was famous, although that's the arena I'm trying to be in. Brix was way more familiar than Nate as well. I didn't give Nate enough time to show me exactly who he was and what I would be dealing with if I were his."

"So you made a decision without knowing what Nate would bring to the table. Are you regretting that?"

"No. I love Brixton. My soul just wants to hang on to Nate. You may feel like this is TMI, but the time I slept with Nate was so fucking passionate. I was vulnerable because Brix had hurt me, but being with Nate was something I'd wanted to experience before I gave in to Brix. It was selfish, and it was something I shouldn't have done. Nate is a great person from what I know about him, but every time I see him or he messages me, my sensitivity comes out because I know I hurt him that night."

"Jess, he knows your position. You can't keep doing this dance. You can't hurt him any more than you already have. This shit is getting dangerous. He won't move on if you keep letting him in, baby. I know the shit will hurt, but you can't keep hanging on to him. Brix will notice and that will cause problems for you."

"I know. You're right. He's coming today though. It will be the last time I give him permission to be where I am." She closed her eyes and took a couple of deep breaths. "He took care of my soul when I needed it most. It's hard to let him go, but I know I have to. I'll never forget how he made me feel though. Hopefully, my memories with Brix will start to overpower that one. It makes it hard that at the time, Brix was the one who had hurt me. I was tired of being hurt by men I loved. The shit with Decklan was still somewhat fresh too."

"I get it. But you'll get through it, because you are Jessica muthafucking Monroe."

She giggled. "You got damn right. Now what's up with you?"

"I saw Avery last night. When I saw him, I lost it and left Yendi at the Toyota Center."

Her eyebrows lifted as I continued. "I called Uncle Jasper to go get her. She's been calling and she left a lot of messages, but this text message hurts. I don't want her settling for a broken man. A man that can't give her what she needs. I don't want to keep hurting her. We've only been together a week."

"Let me see the text."

I took a deep breath and pulled my phone from my pocket and opened it up. I read it all over again as I felt the lump form in my throat.

Baby, I'm not angry. Please call or text me and let me know you're okay. Please... I love you, and I'm worried about you. I didn't hang around to even talk to your dad and that woman. If you have an issue with them, then so do I. I'm here for you. Please don't shut me out, baby.

I handed the phone to Jess and as she read it, the tears fell from her eyes. "Wow, J. She loves you."

"Yeah. I love her too."

"Then get help and be with her. It seems like you need her. She clearly needs you. Stop denying yourself happiness."

"I talk to Serita Monday. I'm trying to get on track. What bothered me the most is that I chose to focus on my hatred for him than my love for her. I'm no good for her right now, but she won't let go. I need her to let me go."

"No, you don't. You need to be vulnerable with her. Let her be there for you if she wants to be. If she still wants you through everything that has happened, who are you to tell her she shouldn't? I'm glad you're going to talk to Serita. I really pray she can help you get your mental to match your heart. You have a beautiful heart, J. It deserves to receive the love Yendi is offering."

I nodded then stood from the couch. I couldn't have this conversation with her. Talking about it always put me in shut down mode. "Well, I can't wait to see the video tonight. Think about what I said."

"Yeah, me either. I will, but you think about what I said too. I love you, J."

"I love you too, baby."

I hugged her, and she kissed my cheek. I gave her a slight smile. "I'm proud of you, superstar."

After winking at her as she blushed, I left the room, letting the smile fall from my face. I had to get to Uncle Jasper's to smoke before the private viewing. I needed to mellow out ASAP.

I WAS SO RELAXED BY THE TIME I GOT BACK TO THE VIEWING. UNCLE Jasper and I got lit as fuck. I had to have smoked three blunts. When I got home, I could barely function enough to shower and get dressed. I ended up taking an hour nap then handled my business so I could get back to the barn on time.

Instead of dressing up, Noah and Jess suggested country attire for the evening. I was just fine with that shit. After the viewing, J. Paul was gon' kick the party up a notch, and we were gon' show Noah how we did it in Big City Nome, Texas. Watchful Eyes would be on the premises as well, securing the event.

No one had made any moves as far as our inventory went, nor had anyone shown up in Nome to fuck with anything. Maybe Tyrese decided not to go through with it. I didn't know, but I wouldn't let my guard down so soon. As I walked around, making sure everything was straight, I saw Decaurey walk in.

"What's up, nigga? What'chu doing here?"

"I had to show my face for a little while. I'm not staying long. My babies need me."

I stared at him and realized what he was saying. I smiled and slapped his hand. "Congratulations, big dawg."

"Yep. So I guess I'll never know if she's telling the truth or not."

"Did you tell her you were doubting it?"

"Naw. I told her if I did a DNA test, we wouldn't have to fool with Tyrese. That was proof enough."

"Good."

"Yeah. Well, let me mingle a lil bit before the video comes on, because I'm leaving right afterward."

"A'ight, man."

Nate had already arrived, and he was seated toward the back... with a woman. That was shocking as hell. I hadn't had a chance to talk to him so I made my way over to him. He stood from his seat, and I saw he had on Cinch jeans, a huge ass blinged-out belt buckle, and boots. I nodded repeatedly as he smiled. When I got closer, I slapped his hand.

"What happened to you last night, man? Noah said some shit popped off, but he didn't know details because Yendi wouldn't say exactly."

"What *did* she say?"

"That something from your past basically had you fucked up. I don't know her exact wording, because you know Noah uses a lot of words and shit sometimes. So I forgot exactly how he said it."

I nodded repeatedly. She was protecting me even in that moment. That woman was so damn perfect. "She was right. My dad and I have a rift because of something he did in the past. He was locked up for twelve years. I saw him at the game. You know I trust you if I'm telling you that much."

"Absolutely. I know you're pretty private, so I'm shocked you said that much. I hate that happened. I was looking forward to turning up with y'all. We beat them by fifteen so the turnup would have been even better. I cut up for y'all though."

I chuckled. "Congratulations. How many points you ended up with?"

"Twenty-five points, eleven assists, and three blocks, my nigga."

"That's what's up! Congrats again. So, umm... who's the woman?"

"A decoy to make Brix comfortable and to help Jess move on. If she thinks I'm done, then she'll be done." He slid his hand over his face. "She's my cousin's homegirl. We practically grew up together. She knows the deal though. So if I kiss her or be affectionate, she knows it's an act."

"Wow. That's big of you. I hope it's an act for her too."

"It is. She has a man. This shit was hard, but I listened to what you said, and I'm trying to do something about it. I want Jess to be happy. Real shit. Even if she's happy with someone else. I love that woman, for real."

I patted his back as some lady went to the mic to announce the entrance of Noah and Jess. Finding my seat, I watched my cousin strut out in some too small cut-off shorts, knee-length boots, a plaid halter top, and a Stetson. My frown was way too deep. Jess sure knew how to push the limits, walking in here looking like a fucking buckle bunny. I glanced around the room to see frowns on all my uncles' faces, especially Uncle Storm's. However, Nate was stuck... eyes fucking glued to her.

Once they got to their seats, Jess hopped back up and went to the mic. "I just had to come up here, big belly and all, and say calm down Uncle Mayor, Uncle Jasper, Uncle Kenny, Uncle WJ, Uncle Ryder, Uncle Philly, Uncle LaKeith, and Uncle Marcus. Lawd have mercy! This is business. Get those frowns off your faces. Y'all too, Jakari and Decaurey!"

The crowd laughed as cameras flashed. There was so much fucking paparazzi in this bitch it was ridiculous. She went back to her seat on the hay bales next to Brix, Noah, and TAZ. The lady that introduced them went back to the mic, explaining just how perfect the video was and how it was going to blow up in the industry.

"Jessica told me to label this genre of music country hood. We're getting it trademarked as we speak. Noah plans to do a few more songs and videos like this and plans to give women from this area a chance to be featured, and a couple more artists on his label are looking into tapping into it as well."

The crowd applauded loudly as Jess blushed. Nate was just staring at her. He wasn't clapping, but I could see the longing in his eyes. Thankfully, where Jess was seated, she couldn't see him. What caused me to pause was the woman I saw being seated near Nate. It was Yendi. *Fuck!* She said something to Nate, and he hugged her with one arm then nodded his head in my direction. She looked right at me.

She brought her hands to her chest, I assumed indicating her relief that I was okay. She didn't know it was a country theme since I didn't tell her. She wore a long black dress with a split on one side nearly to her waist. I noticed her shoulders were out when she slid her shawl off. I turned toward the screen when the lights dimmed, doing my best to ignore her.

She didn't know what was good for her. I wasn't it right now. Once I got myself together, if she was still single, I would shoot my shot then. When a picture of my grandmother came across the screen, you could hear the gasps throughout the room. Then there was a video. I was stunned and Jess seemed to be also, like she didn't know.

"This is how we do things in Big City Nome, Texas," my grandmother said and chuckled. "I don't know why them chirren say that shit. Baby, yo' bathtub probably bigger than Nome."

The crowd laughed loudly. "One thing about Nome is that we all we got. We family. We fuss, we fight, we do stupid shit, but we love each other. We fix things. We heal from things. That's what the Hendersons do."

As Noah recorded, he asked, "So how do you feel about Jess being in this video with me?"

"Listen, I'm proud of my baby. That girl been fierce since she was little. I'm glad Shylou and Carter helped her to follow her dreams. She deserves this. Just don't be grabbing on all that ass she got, Noah. Her fiancé gon' fuck you up. That boy don't play about Jessica Monroe, baby."

Everybody laughed again, and the video cut to her saying, "I'm so proud of you, Jess. This is only the beginning. You gon' have all these city slickers tryna be country. This shit is born into you." She said in a lower voice, "Don't insult the people, Joan."

Noah cracked up like it was his first time seeing it as well. The video cut again, and she said, "Jess, the Hendersons have always been known for farming, ranching, and rodeos, but you taking the name to an entirely different arena and letting people know what it stands for. I can't wait to see the finished product. Girl, you gon' fuck these people's minds up, because you a product of Jenahra Henderson Wothyla and her fine ass mama, Joan Henderson!"

She struck a pose and tilted her Stetson, causing the room to laugh again. "Congratulations, Grandma's baby!"

I swiped the couple of tears that fell. Seeing my grandmother again that way was a blessing. That woman was something else. My grandfather was seated up front with Uncle WJ, and I could see his shoulders quaking. He hadn't been doing all that well since she passed. He wanted nothing to do with nothing. Aunt Tiffany, Aunt Jen, and my mama spent the most time with him, making sure his needs were taken care of. He rarely left the house.

Another picture of my grandmother came on the screen as she was rooting Malachi on. The bull was in the air and Mal was holding on for dear life. Then the words 'Rest in Heaven Grandma Henderson' and her birth and death dates appeared on the screen. There was thunderous applause as Jess leaned into Brix.

I hated Nesha had to miss this. She and the baby were home, but she felt it was too soon to have him out and about, around all these people. I could agree with her on that. Once the video started, I smiled. I remembered seeing everything that unfolded. Seeing Aunt Tiff and the girls do their thing was fun to watch. The rodeo relay, and Legend, Red, and Zay cutting up was cool to see on the screen as well. When I caught a glimpse of myself, I smiled. I was walking to my seat, rubbing my hands together like I was ready for action.

It cut to them horse riding and laughing at Noah. He looked so uncomfortable on that horse. Jess looked so beautiful. She was smiling big for most of that scene, and I felt like that scene was her in her element. It was like they told her to just be herself. She kissed Noah in the scene, grabbing his locs to pull him to her. It was just a peck on the lips though. However, with the way he looked at her, I knew more was coming later in the video.

The part we were all waiting to see though was the part they filmed here in the barn that no one was able to see. Jess had on a red dress that showed a lot of her womanly parts. My face scrunched up as Noah's eyes graced every inch of her. It cut to them slow dancing and him gripping her ass, then the kiss. That shit was nasty. Jess gave that man her whole tongue.

I rolled my eyes as the women in the crowd screamed. However, when her shoulder straps came down, my eyes bugged out. Then there was a flash of her in her bra and panties and Noah shirtless upstairs in the hay. My eyes went over to Brix, and he looked tight as fuck. Jess grabbed him by the chin and kissed his lips, forcing him to cool out. Thankfully, the video didn't go through every moment of what they were insinuating happened.

When it was over, I could see Yendi staring at me. I quickly made my way closer to the front as Jess and Noah went to the mic to talk. I slipped right out the door and to my truck parked in the back. Before I could pull away, she'd made it to me. *Fuck!*

"Jakari, what are you doing? Did you listen to any of my messages? Did you read my text? Why are you running from me?"

I swallowed hard and got out of the truck. Grabbing her hands, I brought them to my lips one at a time, kissing them. "Baby, you're perfect in every way. But you having to suffer through my bullshit ain't where it's at. You better than this shit. I'm fucked up. I told you that a while ago. You wanna keep getting hurt? Huh? My soul is dark, Yendi. Quit fucking chasing after a man that's beneath you!"

She wrapped her arms around my waist. "I can't let go, Jakari. I love you! How am I supposed to turn that shit off? You got me to admit that shit to you so soon. You said you loved me! Don't do this. Don't let hate win. I want to help you through this. If I didn't want to be with you through this, I wouldn't be here. Please, baby."

She laid her head on my chest as my arms rested at my sides. She was making this shit so difficult. I didn't want to let her go, but I couldn't understand why she wanted to sign up for the shit show going on in my life. That was more than love. Fuck love. Who volunteered to be miserable in the name of love? Fuck that.

I put my hands to her head and tilted it back and kissed her soft, thick ass lips for the last time then pushed away from her and got in my truck, burning off. This was what was best and one day, she would thank me for helping her dodge this bullet.

CHAPTER 16
YENDI

"Ms. Odom, I can't wait to announce the winner of the iPhone. They gon' flip because Bryson never reads!" Ashanni said as she laughed.

"I know. These contests did exactly what they were supposed to do. These kids stepped up to the challenge, and I'm so proud of the two of you for making it happen," I said to Maui and Ashanni.

It had been nearly a week since I'd seen Jakari. I felt like I'd only been existing. Since I had to stay for the fucking pep rallies now, I couldn't even go to the diner today. I'd been trying to run into him 'unintentionally' without just going to his house, but I could see that I would have to just pop up. I missed him so much, and it was taking everything in me not to sink into depression.

I couldn't give up on him like he was giving up on me. He said I deserved better, but I deserved exactly what the fuck I wanted, and I wanted him! *Why couldn't he see that?* I knew what was best for me, and Jakari Bolton was the one. There wasn't another man out there that could handle me the way he did. I knew without a shadow of a doubt that he was it for me simply because I was acting so out of character.

I didn't take bullshit from no damn body. However, what Jakari did wasn't bullshit. What he was going through mentally wasn't bullshit. He had some real issues he needed to deal with instead of running from them. Until he dealt with them, nothing would change. He'd been this way for a long time, so I knew he needed time to break himself out of his regressive behaviors.

The more time it took, the more it was destroying me though. Tomorrow was Tyeis's baby shower. Although she'd had the babies two weeks ago, she still needed a lot for them. They were still in the hospital, but according to Uncle Jasper, they would possibly be going home in another two weeks if they kept progressing at the rate they were. They'd already gained twelve ounces. I called him Wednesday to catch up with the family and let him know that things between Jakari and I hadn't changed. He was still positive that they would with time.

He'd overplayed me calling him Uncle Jasper. I could hear the excitement in his voice, and he'd insisted that my desire to call him uncle meant that Jakari and I would work things out. I surely hoped he was right.

It seemed as if God was putting my words to the test when I told Jakari I would wait for him. Today made a week since he'd left me at the Toyota Center, and it seemed I'd been losing a piece of myself every day since. God intentionally buried him so deeply within my soul. I couldn't move on even if I wanted to. I knew Jakari didn't have malicious intent. He thought he was protecting me from him. *God, if only I could make him understand.*

The girls were looking for books. Their teachers had been gracious enough to give them to me for the entire period. We would be announcing the winners in about the next fifteen minutes. I went to my office and turned on my music. When Summer Walker's "Broken Promises" came on, it brought tears to my eyes.

"'Cause my heart is breaking. I've been mistaken. You're not the man I thought you were... Said you was ready..."

All of what she said didn't apply, but some of it was spot on. I went through a moment where I thought he wasn't the one, and that I was mistaken. I'd confided in Janay about what was going on, and she tried to warn me to protect my heart. Shit, at that point it was too late. My heart was already breaking. I needed Jakari to see that he was only hurting me more by staying away… by leaving me.

"Ms. Odom, you okay?"

I nodded quickly as I wiped my tears. I didn't realize Maui was even standing there. She came to my desk and gently rubbed my back. "Did my cousin do something?"

"No, baby. Let's get ready to announce the prizes. I'm tired of waiting."

She giggled and said, "Me too!" After backing away, she said, "You know, if Jakari did something, I'll punch him in his Adam's apple for hurting my favorite adult at HJ."

I smiled slightly and slid my arm around her shoulder. "Jakari didn't do a thing. Okay? Thank you for having my back though."

"Always. You know my party is coming up in three weeks! I can't wait! My daddy said he had the biggest surprise for me. When Storm Henderson says something like that, you know it's gonna be big. He doesn't sell wolf tickets… ever."

I laughed at this girl. She was too cute. She wasn't the typical fifteen-year-old. As Ashanni got their list together, I went to the intercom and announced that we would be giving away three prizes and what they all entailed. The third-place prize was a gift card for twenty-five dollars, second place was a kindle fire, and first place was an iPhone 15, donated by Mayor Storm Henderson. Since he'd donated two, we decided to do a wild card.

The wild card was the person who made the most improvement. Also, the grade with the most participating students won a pizza party sponsored by Jasper Henderson. The girls had gotten their parents to really come through for the prizes because had it been all up to me, some of those prizes would have been a hell naw.

As Maui and Ashanni excitedly read off the list of winners, I couldn't stop my mind from drifting back to Jakari. I bit my bottom lip as I thought about how I'd asked him if he wanted to help us with the program. Maybe I should've left well enough alone when he gave me his response, but my nasty ass needed to know more.

When the girls called out the wild card winner, they screamed as if they had won. I swore they sounded like some little chipmunks. The thought of that made me chuckle. Once they were done and the winners arrived in the library, we took pictures. Bryson was a football player, so he was the last to arrive. I assumed the players were in the gym or the fieldhouse already.

Ashanni blushed hard when he spoke to her. Before I could roll my eyes, I saw him grab her hand and kiss it. Was this her boyfriend? There was no way Uncle Jasper knew about this. After they took pictures, I watched them make googly eyes at each other, then she and Maui have a whole fit after he left.

"Wait a minute, now. Is he your boyfriend, Ashanni?"

"No, but I want him to be. He's been flirting since the first day of school. I've flirted back, but he hasn't even asked for my number yet. Ugh!"

I chuckled, remembering when things were so simple like that for me. When the bell rang, they made their way to the gym, and I locked up my office and made my way there too.

WHEN THE DOORBELL RANG, I WAS CAUGHT TOTALLY OFF GUARD. I quickly slid on a glue-less wig and straightened my clothes, although I knew Jakari couldn't care less about all of that. He was the only person that even knew where I lived. It had to be him, finally coming to his senses and realizing that he needed me as much as I needed him. I hurriedly applied some lip gloss on my lips then went to the door and opened it. My heart lept into my throat when I saw my mother standing there.

I frowned and asked, "How do you know where I live?"

"Hello, Yendi. Can I come in?"

My better sense was saying to tell her hell fucking no and slam the door in her face, but my heart was saying to allow her inside and not make a scene for the white folks I lived next to. Maybe she was here to try to make things right. They would never be like they were before as far as I was concerned, but I would sit here and listen, then nicely put her out of my place.

I stepped aside and allowed her to walk inside. She looked around as I closed the door, then followed me to the sitting area. I was sure to sit in the accent chair so she couldn't sit next to me. If she was that close to me, I could choke the shit out of her easily if she pissed me off. While my senses were telling me that she would indeed piss me off, I wanted to think positively.

She sat on the couch across from me. "You have a nice home. How did you find this place? The area is so small."

"I researched small school districts in Texas. I had an infatuation with Texas since it was where Daddy was originally from. Plus, the cost of living is less here."

She nodded and smiled. "Well, how are you doing?"

"Mama, why are you here?"

I was sick of the run around. I wasn't about to have casual conversation with her like nothing had happened. That was what she was used to. We'd bust her in her lies, and she'd never apologize or admit, for that matter, that there was ever a problem. We'd eventually get over it and move on. That wasn't going to happen this time. That was my daddy that she'd treated like shit for his last two months here.

"Yendi, we need to move past this. It was time for your dad to go, but I'm still here. I love you, and I want us to have a relationship."

"Before I left, I said that unless you were calling to, number one, apologize for the role you played in our severed relationship, number two, admit you have a lying problem, and number three, get help for said problem, we would have nothing to talk about. Are you here for that?"

"Yendi, your father wouldn't want things in disarray like this."

"You don't get to tell me what *my* daddy would want. He wanted his wife of forty-five years to be there for him. Instead, you were leaving him hungry all day, knowing he couldn't walk. When you *did* get home, you would barely talk to him. Then when you talked, you would pick arguments with him! You told him to get out and go live with one of his kids a week before he died!"

"That's not true! I would never tell your dad those things. I was there for your daddy!"

"You forgot I was there? I was there every damn day, bringing him food! Me and Janay! I would bring breakfast and snacks and she would bring dinner. So exactly what were you doing?"

"I brought him lunch on my breaks from work. I had to work."

"Whatever. You're doing just what you came here to do… get me all worked up, arguing with you. You are obviously miserable and lonely if you hopped a flight here just to argue with me. You made a blank trip, because I refuse to argue with your pathetic ass. My daddy died in an emotional turmoil because of *you!* He wanted to die because he didn't want to live without *you!* If you were so unhappy with y'all's relationship, you should have left a long time ago. You waited until he was sick and couldn't fend for himself to fuck with him. You got your revenge. Are you happy with yourself? You wanted him to die!"

I was crying so hard. Looking at her was disgusting me. I felt like either I was going to kill her, or I was gonna throw up. My emotions were going haywire, and I couldn't make them stop. "How could you think I wanted your dad to die? That hurts!"

"No! What hurts is that I think you killed him. Yeah, that's right. I think you killed my daddy. Whether it was physically or not, I don't know. You said you were getting him up to go sit in his chair the day he died. If you did, then you killed him. Every time he moved, trying to get up, his blood pressure would drop. If I knew that, then so did you. You picked with him until his blood pressure dropped, and you watched him die. Then you called the ambulance. Is that what happened?"

"No! Your dad was trying to get up. He wanted to take a bath and sit in his recliner!"

"If he did, it's because of you! He knew what would happen if he tried to get out of that bed! I'm not stupid by far! I peep shit! You wanna know what I peeped? You must wanna know since you flew all the way here for this. You are a lying sack of shit! You are my mother, and I'm grateful for all the things you taught me and the things you did for me. But what I realized was that none of that was for your love for me. It was all for your benefit."

I slowly shook my head as the painful truth spewed from my lips. "When I did good things or if I looked good, it was a reflection on you. It brought attention back to you, because you're my mom. You taught me everything I know. You'd tell people my love of reading came from you and that was why I wanted to be a librarian. You *never* read to me when I was growing up. You were always at work. So how exactly did I get my love of reading from you?"

She had the nerve to put her hand to her chest like I'd hurt her pitiful feelings. I kept going regardless. "Daddy's illnesses brought way too much attention to him and no attention to you. Everyone wanted to check on him so you kept his phone from him so he couldn't communicate with anyone. Then you told people that he didn't need a lot of visitors because he needed to rest, knowing how good it made him feel, knowing that people cared about him. You are a sick, evil, and cold bitch. You did all of that shit to him to benefit you. I will never forgive you for that. Period."

"You have to let the anger go, Yendi."

"What I have to do is get you the fuck out of my house before I kill you in here. Get out!"

She sat there staring at me like I she thought I was playing. I stood from my seat and started fucking counting. "Five, four, three, two, one…"

I crossed the room and yanked her up from my couch, causing her to fall to the floor. "Yendi! Oh my God!"

"I said get out of my house! I'm not playing with you. If I have to call the cops I will."

"I'm sorry if you feel that I had something to do with your daddy's death. I hate you feel that way."

I slowly shook my head and let out a chuckle. That let me know that I was teetering on the outskirts of insanity. I felt like I was about to snap, and she would be *my* victim after this. My siblings and I had been victims of mental and emotional abuse for years and didn't even realize it.

"That is not a fucking apology. An apology is accepting and admitting your fault in the situation. Get the fuck out, and this is the last time I'm gonna tell you. Next time, I'm gonna call the cops, and I'm gon' fuck you up in here. It's sad that you have gotten me to the point where I'm willing to hurt you. My respect for you is nonexistent. Anyone who believes your lies needs to reevaluate themselves. You tell all that shit to people who are easily manipulated, like Terrence and his mother. You can't manipulate me."

She stood from the floor, acting like she was hurting. Even if she was, I didn't give a fuck. She could limp her ass right out of here. After going to the couch and grabbing her purse, she made her way to the door as I followed her. When she got to it, she turned to me and smiled. That shit looked so evil. It was like the devil had fully embodied her. Just to think… she was once a minister. Let her tell it, she still was.

The last time I heard her preach was a total mess. It had no anointing. God was nowhere in the midst. She was stumbling all over her words, and she only "preached" for ten minutes. It was more like she was talking.

"Yendi, I wish you well, my darling. Despite how you feel about me, I still love you. You're my middle girl, and you will always be in my heart."

I rolled my eyes as the tears fell from them then opened the door for her to limp her ass out. She wasn't moving fast enough, so I gave her a gentle but firm push right out of the door. I slammed it shut, locked it, then leaned back against it for a moment. I turned and checked the peephole to see my cousin sitting in the car waiting for her. *Another stupid bitch.* I fell out with her years ago because of her jealousy.

I went to my room and got in bed. Before I realized it, I was screaming. "Daddy! Why did you leave me like this? Daddyyyy! I need you!"

I screamed and cried until I had to run to the bathroom to throw up. When I'd regurgitated everything in my stomach, I dry heaved for what seemed like forever. After cleaning myself up, I got in bed and pulled the covers to my neck, continuing to let the tears stream down my face and wondering why I had to even exist in this world without the love of my daddy. I was grieving my loss all over again… my loss of both of them.

CHAPTER 17
JAKARI

"Last time we talked about all the things he did that made you angry and that made you disgusted with him. This session, I want us to go back to your earliest memory of your father and how it made you feel."

I stared at Serita for a minute as I thought about what she was asking me to do. It had been two weeks since I'd seen Yendi, but my soul felt like it was trying to be at ease about my father. I hadn't seen him or heard from him since the game, and that alone gave me peace. I'd come to see Serita last week for my first session, and it was hard.

I ended up walking out on then going back in. I wanted to be better. I needed to be a better man, not for anyone else but for me. I was suffering inside because of shit I couldn't change. I couldn't change who Avery was, but I *could* change how what he did affected me. I couldn't allow that to dictate every decision I made in life. I lost my one because of this shit. I just hoped once I was in a better headspace that she was still available and was willing to give me another shot at her heart.

"My earliest memory is him teaching me to ride my bike without training wheels. I was scared, and I remember him telling me that he would be there to guide me along the way. That I could depend on him to be there for me. He said that would apply in life when I got older. I didn't understand what he meant back then, but now that I recall it, I understand now."

"How old were you?"

"Four. I told him that I couldn't start school the next year still on training wheels. That I was a big boy and big boys didn't have training wheels. After trying to convince me that I could take my time and that other kids would still be using training wheels and he saw I wasn't folding, he agreed to take them off. He said years later that he knew in that instance I would be a leader."

"Good. Now go back to four-year-old Jakari and tell me how it made you feel when your dad said he would be there for you."

"Like I could do anything. It made the fear rest for that moment, and it gave me courage to get on that bike. I felt safe…"

I lowered my head knowing that Aunt Syn and Nesha felt everything but safe. "Jakari, look at me. Don't do that. I can tell you went somewhere else in your mind. Don't think about how anyone else feels about him or how you feel about him now. I only want you in the headspace of the little boy who loved his dad and trusted him to keep him safe. That's it. I know it's hard, but you can do it."

"How do you stay so positive all the time though?"

"Practice. It took me a long time to make that a habit. I went through a lot in my life. I didn't truly get on the right track until all four of my children were grownups. My mindset affected them. A lot of times, we can get things right long before we actually do. I was depending on my ex-husband for happiness and to make me better. He did for a while, but when things went crazy and I made the horrible decision to leave him, I no longer had him as a crutch."

I could tell that decision still bothered her a little. She took a deep breath and continued. "I had to do the work for myself, and I crumbled under the pressure. I ended up on drugs and nearly killed myself a couple of times. My kids were young, but they remember every traumatic moment they were exposed to. Me putting off getting the mental help that I needed caused my kids to suffer. My relationship with them didn't improve until they were all finding the loves of their lives and getting married. That was when I chose to show them I was there for them."

"I hurt Yendi," I whispered.

It was my first time mentioning her in therapy. "Who's Yendi?"

"She was my girlfriend. We'd only been together officially a week or so. My issues with Avery caused me to neglect her. I knew I needed help a long time ago, but I was trying to be there for everyone else and neglected being there for myself."

"That's okay. You're here now. We're going to get you back on track. Now tell me another positive moment with your dad."

I smiled slightly. "My brother, Christian, had destroyed one of my wrestling men. He'd chewed that shit to death. I was pissed. I snatched it from him to go show my mother but ended up running into Avery…" I closed my eyes and took a deep breath then continued. "…running into my dad in the hallway."

We'd discussed when I first arrived that I would call Avery dad in this session because that was what I knew him as until my early twenties. The memories we would be speaking of would be those where he was Dad to me, not Avery.

"I told him what Christian had done and showed him how the Rock's hand and face were ate up. How was he gonna do the people's eyebrow if half his face was gone? I could tell he wanted to laugh, but he somehow restrained himself. He apologized about what Christian had done and said that he should have been keeping a closer eye on him. He also explained that Christian was a baby and didn't understand. Although he was three years old at the time, he didn't understand that he'd done something bad."

"How did you take that?"

"I felt bad for getting mad at Christian. I went back to the room as Dad scolded him for eating the Rock's face off. Once Dad left the room, I hugged Christian and told him it was okay. The next day, a new Rock figure was on my bed waiting for me when I got out of school."

Serita smiled and that caused me to smile slightly. "That obviously made you feel good, right?"

"Absolutely. There was nothing anyone could say bad about my dad back then. I supposed that's why I took his fall so hard and as my own. He taught me a lot. He wasn't a farmer and didn't really know about farm animals and ranching like the Henderson side of my family, but everything else, I learned from him. He taught me how to treat girls with respect. How could he teach me something he wasn't doing?"

"Easily. I taught my kids to tell the truth, yet I was living a lie, pretending to have it all together. He has an illness, no matter how sick what he did is to us. I'm a victim of rape myself. A grown man raped me when I was a kid. I was nine or ten when it happened. After a doctor's appointment and they discovered I had STDs, he shot himself in front of me. So I know what this journey looks like. It can get ugly if you don't get help. Even with all that history I have, I can see Avery as a man that has an illness."

I took a deep breath and nodded. *He has an illness. He has an illness. He sick as fuck… He has an illness. Something happened to him to cause him to do things like this.* I was at war in my head, trying to get my brain to accept what Serita was saying. That shit was hard.

"Jakari, his illness doesn't change who he was to you. It's okay to be angry, to be hurt, and to be disappointed, but those feelings should not have taken over your life's trajectory. Avery did right by you. I'm not saying that his offenses aren't serious. I'm saying that if he is truly wanting help with whatever he is going through, then you should let it go and start living your life. Don't base what he did as something you would be capable of. That wasn't even how he raised you to be."

"So you want me to establish a relationship with him?"

"No. I want you to stop harboring hatred and guilt in your soul for his actions. Those two things have taken over your life, and it's beyond time that you take that control back. You have to forgive him and yourself. Forgive yourself for hurting Yendi, because of how you chose to deal with the situation between you and your father. Life happens. We can either learn from it or fall victim to it."

Learn from it or fall victim to it. I'd fallen victim to it. I stared at her for a moment. "You're right. I fell victim and stayed there for twelve years. It's time to handle this like an adult and move on from it. That means I'll have to have a conversation with him?"

"Not unless you want to, although I think it will be healthy if you do. That doesn't have to be in person. You can email him if you want. Let him know what all you went through and how you are choosing to heal from it. Let him know what your boundaries are."

"I don't want a relationship with him, but I'm okay with him reaching out every now and then to see how I am, like he's been doing with my mom."

"Tell him that."

"Thank you, Serita."

"That's what I'm here for. We'll talk about how things went next week?"

"Yes, ma'am. See you then."

"Okay. I'm proud of you, Mr. Henderson."

"I'm proud of me too."

I gave her a smile as I left her office to schedule another appointment next week with the receptionist. Hearing her call me Mr. Henderson felt a little weird. I'd gotten my name changed. I didn't want to be associated with Avery. I did that the Monday after the game. While his blood was still running through me, I would no longer be advertising that shit by carrying his last name. I'd be getting back to the old me but a better version of him.

"He's dead."

"What?"

"You heard me. Seneca shot his ass. He said if y'all wanted to keep playing with him, it was just gonna give him time to recruit more muthafuckas y'all would have to worry about later. The ones working with him are backing out of this shit. You have nothing to worry about."

I'd gone to Watchful Eyes to talk to Ali. Our updates could no longer be done by phone, so I went to their business office to get them. "Well, damn. I guess so."

He chuckled. "We don't play around with bullshit. He was trying to destroy y'all shit. Why allow him time to get that shit more organized? Naw. Take his ass down now. Send a message to the ones thinking about continuing what he started. Ain't nobody gon' fuck with the Hendersons. Not on their best day."

"Are you a Henderson or me?" I asked Ali.

He chuckled as I shook his hand. I'd come here after running errands, checking on the local stores. There hadn't been any mishaps at any of them. While I was checking, I decided to come here. Since I was in Beaumont already, it wouldn't have made sense to make another trip tomorrow just for that.

"Your uncle stopped by yesterday. He seemed to be cool with us doing whatever we had to do to get rid of the problem."

I frowned. "Storm?"

Only his ass would do some shit like that. My eyebrows lifted even more as Ali said, "Naw. Storm is the tallest one, right?"

"Yeah. Who was it then?"

"Kenny. He and Philly came by. Philly is working with us this weekend to learn the ropes and how we operate."

"You know what? I can see that. Between me and you, he delivered the final blow that killed that nigga's uncle. He nearly destroyed Uncle Kenny's homelife."

"Makes sense then. Well, don't hesitate calling if y'all need us for anything else. Rondo loved being out there since he a country ass nigga."

I chuckled. "We appreciate y'all handling that bit of business for us. I'll be sure to keep y'all in mind. Keep my family in mind too for catering, wheels, haircuts... shit whatever y'all need that we can offer."

"Oh yeah. I've already been talking with Marcus about custom upholstery for my whip."

"That's what's up. Thanks again for handling that."

We shook hands, and I made my way back to my pickup. My SUV needed a break. I was running that shit in the ground. My pickup usually only got driven around Nome unless I had something to haul somewhere.

As I headed to Nome, I decided to take Highway 105 to get there since I was on the north side of Beaumont. When I did, I thought of Yendi. She hadn't called at all this week. She'd blown my phone up last week. Maybe she'd given up on me like I'd asked her to do. Although it was something I asked her to do, the reality of it had sunk in. She'd crossed my mind every day, but if I told her to let me go, I didn't think it was wise to call her.

Once in Sour Lake, I turned left on Highway 326, which would take me past her apartment and past the school. I missed her something fierce. Feeling her soft body against mine was priceless. I knew how much she meant to me, but I didn't fathom it would hurt this badly to let her go. I glanced at her complex then the school while heading home. Taking a deep breath, I turned up the radio trying to push thoughts of her out of my mind.

When I got to the office, I saw that Philly was still here, along with my mom. That was strange. She was hardly ever at the office. It was usually Aunt Tiff and Aunt Chas. I noticed Aunt Chas's car was still here as well though. I quickly got out of my truck to see what was going on, if anything.

After walking in, I wanted to turn around and walk out. Avery was standing there with my mama, Christian, and Rylan. I didn't see their vehicles. Maybe Mama had gone and picked them up. I swallowed hard then closed my eyes, trying to think about my counseling session the other day. *Positivity. Clue him in on my boundaries. Tell him where I stand.*

I opened my eyes and made my way to where they'd sat. When my mama saw me, she stood and came to me. "I'm sorry, baby. Philly called me when he got here. He said he wanted to talk to y'all and then he would leave."

I nodded then kissed her cheek and made my way to where they were now standing again. I couldn't believe Avery had driven out here, knowing how everyone felt about him, especially my uncles. As I got

HEALING FOR MY SOUL

to where they were, I shook Christian and Rylan's hands. I stared at him as he said, "Hello, Jakari."

I nodded then sat next to my brothers as Philly watched from the front desk. When my stepdad, LaKeith, walked in, I felt more at ease. I didn't want him trying to be tender or affectionate with my mother. With LaKeith here, I knew he wouldn't dare.

"Y'all are probably wondering why I'm here. I just wanted to see y'all and let you know how much I love y'all. I understand your position about a relationship with me and the predicament I left y'all and your mother in a little over twelve years ago, especially you, Jakari. I just wanted to ask for your forgiveness in person... beg your forgiveness. Knowing that all of you hate me is hard. I know your mom has forgiven me, but she is no longer mine... which I know is my fault. No disrespect LaKeith."

I glanced at LaKeith to see him lift his hand in a dismissive manner. Avery continued. "I'm so sorry for how I embarrassed and disappointed y'all. I can imagine you were angry, hurt, and torn. I was in therapy sessions the whole time I was locked up, and I'm in therapy sessions now."

He turned to me and stared for a few seconds, before saying, "I'm not seeing her anymore. We didn't know. I know it seems like I haven't become a changed man because of Shakari's age, but I'm striving to be just that. It's a struggle as with any addiction or mental illness. I'm sorry about what seeing me there did to you and your lady friend. Son, I just want you to know... all of you to know that I'm so proud of the men you've become. My only words of advice are that whenever you are feeling weak... get help. No matter what it is."

"What makes you think that I would accept any advice from you?" Christian asked. "Do you realize we've all changed our last names? Jakari and I are now Hendersons and Rylan's last name is Douglas."

"I realize that. Nevertheless, I know that all of you suffered mentally and emotionally because of what I did. My biggest downfall was not getting help when I knew something was wrong. Because I didn't, I hurt people I love. I deeply regret that. This destroyed my family. I know

175

Chrissy felt like I never loved her because of this, but that couldn't be further from the truth. Because I didn't seek help, I didn't have the tools to fight the urges. Please don't let hatred consume you. I know that all of you hate me. I get it, because I hate me too. I hate how I let this take over me."

"You're only saying that because you had to sit yo' ass in that cell for twelve years," Rylan said.

I'd been quiet and that was because I was trying to figure out what to say. I was trying to speak from a calm place and not one of rage. I could feel him staring at me, waiting for what I would offer. He knew my brothers respected me as the man of the house so to speak. I looked over at him and said, "I accept your advice. I just started counseling last week."

What I said stunned them all, because none of them new I was in counseling. "When I saw you at the game two weeks ago, I knew I had to do something. I chose to focus on how much I hated you and what you did instead of the love I had for the woman standing right next to me. I left her at the arena. What puzzles me is that she still wanted me after that, but because I don't know how to deal with my anger, hurt, and rage, I pushed her away, telling her she deserved better."

I took a deep breath then continued. "In my first counseling session, I talked about all the reasons why I hated you… all the reasons why I was the man I am today. My flaws because of what happened. The last counseling session I had the other day, she had me focus on all the good times and memories I shared with you. I looked up to you. I wanted to be just like you. You taught me so much. Honestly, I was hoping to get past my anger on my own. My last name was Bolton until I saw you in Houston. That was when I realized I needed help."

I slid my hands down my face as my mama stood from her seat and walked over to gently pat my back, consoling me. "She told me I had to call you dad when I referred to you. That session freed me from the anger. The disappointment and hurt are still there, because recalling all the good times made me miss them. In my eyes, you were a good man. You raised us in love and taught me how to be a man. What you did was heartbreaking, and I assumed a lot of the guilt for not asking questions or doing something when I recognized something was wrong with Nesha and Aunt Syn."

Avery held his hands in front of his face in a praying manner as the tears fell down his cheeks. I'd never seen him cry. "So I need to set boundaries. Pop ups like today can't happen. I can't handle a relationship with you. I'm just trying to get a handle on my life. You can text me from time to time to see how I'm doing, and I'll respond. If it becomes too frequent, I'll shut it down. Any progression toward a relationship happens in my time. I miss the father I once knew, but I know I will never have him back because of *what* I know. While I know you're the same man, my perception of who you are has changed."

"I understand, Jakari. Thank you. I love y'all so much."

The tears fell from my eyes as I said, "I love you too, man. I just hate the crime. I mean… you could have sold drugs, robbed a store at gunpoint, almost anything else, but rape, especially of helpless little girls, bothers me to my core. Just thinking about it makes me sick to my stomach. I'm trying to get over this now that I have help, but I know it will take time. All I ask is that you respect my boundaries and wishes."

"Son, I have the utmost respect for you and how you took care of my responsibilities after I fucked everything up. If you never speak to me again after today, you will still always have my love and respect."

He extended his hand to me. I stared at it for a moment then shook it and nodded at him. "I have to go. Guys, I love y'all," I said to my brothers. "Do what you feel deep down in your hearts is best for you."

As I walked out, I noticed LaKeith was behind me. When we got outside, he said, "I was proud of you before, but I'm even prouder of you now. The person I saw in there was a grown man, accepting his flaws, knowing his boundaries, and having an adult conversation without all the yelling, cursing, and disrespect. While Avery did despicable things, you still respected him as a man and as your father."

I nodded as he grabbed my arm and hugged me. I hugged him back briefly then got in my truck and wiped my face. This conversation was even more freeing than the therapy session. I was on my way to being a better man. The only thing missing was the love of my life: Yendi Odom.

Fuck all that shit. I picked up my phone and called her, but it went straight to voicemail. I looked at the time to see it was almost four. She was off work. I tried calling again, only to suffer the same fate. I had to accept that maybe I'd lost her. That was the only regret I had in life. I let go of a once in a lifetime love. I just hoped she was okay and doing well. I'd have to check on her with Maui and Ashanni. I just couldn't give up, not yet anyway.

CHAPTER 18
YENDI

It was a struggle trying to get myself out of the funk I allowed my mother to put me in. I didn't have a desire to do a thing, not even go to work, I missed an entire week. That wasn't like me one bit. After calling my job and taking off the entire week, I powered my phone down and sank my sorrows in alcohol nearly the whole week. Once I'd killed every bottle of alcohol in the house, it seemed my depression got worse. I couldn't lose myself in my inebriation.

I didn't leave the apartment once, not even to get more alcohol. Choosing to deal with how I felt head on, I started talking verbally to God and to my daddy, hoping that would make me feel better. It didn't. I'd gone back to work and thankfully, that had helped a little. I still wasn't back to who I was with Jakari, but I was making small steps daily. The girls had come to see me today, and Maui wanted to remind me of her party coming up. However, I knew they could see my lack of enthusiasm.

Today hadn't been any different. It had been another week, and I had to get ready for this stinking pep rally. Two weeks ago, my mama stunned me, and because I hadn't been talking to anyone, I still didn't know how she found me. The thought of that made me want to finally find out. I sent a group text to my siblings.

Hey, y'all. I hope you're having a great day. Umm... Mama showed up at my place two weeks ago and fucked my spirit all the way up. I'm curious to know how she knew where I lived, because I haven't spoken to her since before I moved.

I knew for sure Janay hadn't told her. To my knowledge, they still weren't speaking either. Her ex-husband allowed mama to see JaCory on his weekends, which my sister hated, but she had no desire to see or talk to Mama. So it was either Marie or Pete. I was willing to bet it was Marie though. She was the one that thought she knew what was best in situations like this and tried to force what she believed on others. Although she knew I was against even seeing Mama, she would allow me to be blindsided and then act like she didn't know what was going to happen.

Janay responded almost immediately. *You know I didn't tell her, because I have no desire to talk to her. Have a great day, Yen. I'm sorry that happened to you. Call me later.*

Just as I thought, she wasn't the one who spilled the beans on my whereabouts. Pete responded right after. That was surprising because he normally couldn't respond around this time while he was at work. Like Marie, it sometimes took him all day to respond. I knew his job kept him from responding most times, but Marie? I felt like sometimes she was avoiding certain things, confrontation was one of them. She was the type to throw a rock and then act like she didn't know it could do damage when it hit something. *Hmm. Somewhat like her mother.*

Hey, Yendi! Thanks, and you have a great day too. I haven't spoken to Mama in three weeks. She pissed me off yet again with the whole house situation, telling me if I wanted any of Daddy's things I'd better come now, because she was moving. I don't understand why she had to be so damn evil to everyone, especially Daddy. I'm having a rough day because I miss him so much.

I took a deep breath after reading his message. I missed Daddy too. I was sure we all did. Although he could get on our nerves at times, he was who we talked to the most. He always wanted to make sure we were good. Mama only called when she had lies to tell or she wanted to be messy about something. This bullshit with her only made things worse for us. Grief seemed to be lingering like a cloud over our heads. We were able to function, but the least little thing concerning him or the bullshit with Mama would knock us back a step.

Apparently, Pete was still having a hard time about her selling the house. Maybe he was just finding out. Janay found out from Terrence, and she told me. I thought she had told him and Marie as well. Since he and Marie were still communicating with her, Janay probably didn't feel a need to tell either of them.

Me: *I'm sorry, Pete. I blocked her a long time ago. So she sold the house?*

Pete: *It's been up for sale for at least a month now. She sent a message talking about it had already sold, but that was a lie. I passed by the other day and the sign was still there. Why would she want to sell a house that is paid for, to go rent somewhere else when she's complaining about not having any money?*

Janay: *She has money. Don't let her fool you. Daddy had life insurance, and he was a retired marine.*

Pete: *Oh, I know, but it still doesn't make sense, especially since she seems so unbothered about his death. How you cry watching a movie, but don't shed a tear when your husband of forty-five years dies? That's ass backwards to me. She can be sympathetic to everyone else, but not to us, knowing how close we were to Daddy. It makes me think she doesn't care.*

Me: *Maybe the guilt of how she treated him is suffocating her in there. If that isn't eating her alive then she's even colder and eviler than I thought. I'm about to go into the gym at work, so my signal is going to be worse. If I don't respond to further text messages, I'll talk to y'all when I leave to go home.*

Janay: *Okay. Have fun at the pep rally. LOL!*

I rolled my eyes and responded with a side-eye emoji and, *Yay.*

When I walked into the gym, kids were all over the place as usual. I made my way to the top corner and leaned against the wall, ready for it to all be over.

THE MINUTE I LEFT THE SCHOOL GROUNDS, MY TEXT MESSAGE ALERTS went crazy. I knew it was the group thread between my siblings. Thankfully, my apartment was only down the street from my job, so it only took me five minutes to get home, get inside, and get settled. I went to the messages and scrolled up to where I left off.

Pete: *Yendi, you got your pom poms? LOL!*

Janay: *She's gonna cuss you out when she comes back. LOL!*

I slowly shook my head with a slight smile on my face. The next message wiped the smile right off my face though. It was from Marie. *Call me when you can, Yendi.*

Janay: *Marie, you told Mama where Yendi lived? Why would you do that?*

Marie: *She said she wanted to talk to her and make things right between them. I know Yendi needed that.*

Janay: *And you know she's incapable of apologizing and very capable of lying. Even if you did, why wouldn't you tell Yendi? You would just let her be blindsided?*

Marie: *If I would have told Yendi, she wouldn't have even been home to talk to her.*

Janay: *And that should be her decision to make, not yours. You weren't around for most of the time we were dealing with her while Daddy was in the hospital. You came for four days and thought you'd seen it all. You pretended to be disgusted with her behavior, but you never stopped talking to her. It makes me think you enjoy her bullshit.*

Janay lit into her ass. That was unusual. Janay and Marie usually got along pretty well and talked more than Marie and I did. However, I felt like Janay was feeling defensive of me since I'd moved to get away, and I was grateful to have her in my corner... to have *somebody* in my corner. All conversation had ceased after Janay's last message. I knew it would. I was surprised Pete didn't interject with a message of his own. He must've gotten busy.

I took a deep breath and pulled up Marie's number to call her.

When it started ringing, my head started pounding. I felt like I was about to explode on her ass. When she answered, she said, "Hey, Yendi. I'm so sorry."

"Marie, no you aren't. You do what you feel is right or okay, and you don't consider anyone else in your decisions. I moved away to avoid her. Why would you think it was okay to give her my address?"

"I know. She just said she wanted to make things right between y'all and that you wouldn't allow her the opportunity."

"No, I wouldn't have, because you know as well as I do that nothing is going to change! She's a master manipulator, and you've allowed yourself to be manipulated. You know the truth, and you still fell for her bullshit! Quit dragging me into her shit! I don't want a thing to do with her. She disturbs my peace and my entire soul. Why would you want to put me through that all over again?"

She was crying, and it caused me to cry. However, it didn't make me regret a thing I was saying to her. I was crying because I was angry that she had the audacity to cry after the shit she'd created. "You're right, Yendi. I'm so sorry."

I rolled my eyes as more tears fell from them. She was going to make me distance myself from her too. It wasn't like we talked every day, but we at least texted each other once a week. She'd moved away from home when I was still in high school, so it was common to not talk to her as often. She created the distance by ignoring phone calls. If I called her and she didn't answer, I wouldn't call again. The ball was in her court to reach out. Sometimes that would take her weeks.

"I have to go, Marie. I can't talk to you right now, because I really want to cuss yo' ass out. To keep from doing that, I'd rather just get off the phone. I need to calm down."

I ended the call without giving her a chance to respond, grabbed my keys, and got in my car. I left the parking lot, heading to Sonic for a strawberry cheesecake shake. That always made me feel better. As I was driving, my phone rang and I just knew it was Janay, trying to see if I'd talked to Marie, but to my surprise, it was Jakari.

My heart rate picked up speed, and my body temperature rose. Why was he calling me when he told me to move on with my life? It had been three weeks since I'd seen or spoken to him. I missed him, but I was trying to honor his wishes. After blowing his fucking phone up that week after the game, I gave up. Maybe he wasn't the man I thought he was. Maybe God didn't destine us for each other at all. Maybe it was the devil disguised as a beautiful, fine, chocolate, country, thug looking nigga that he knew would make my knees weak and my pussy leak.

When he left a voice message, my eyebrows shot up. Jakari rarely left voice messages whenever he called, and I couldn't answer. He knew I would see the missed call and call him back. Going to my voicemail, I let it play through my Bluetooth.

"Hey, Yendi. I know I said for you to move on, but I just need to know that you're okay. I've been calling for the past couple of weeks, hoping to hear your voice and knowing you've been well."

He's been calling for the past couple of weeks? "I thought you'd blocked me, but since it rang several times before sending me to voicemail this time, I realized you'd probably had your phone off. I umm... I've been going to counseling. I'm finally handling my issues by facing them head on. I've been doing better. I've had three sessions so far. You don't have to call me back. You can send a text. Just let me know you're okay. Although we aren't together, I still care about you. I still love you, Yendi. Okay. That's it. Hope to hear from you soon."

He ended the message as I parked in a stall at Sonic. I just sat there in my feelings for a minute. His voice always commanded my attention. I missed Jakari like crazy, but before I could get lost in my thoughts, my phone rang again. This time it was Janay. "Hello?"

"Hey, Yendi. I wanted to call and check on you. Have you talked to Marie?"

"Hey. Yeah, I talked to her. She was apologizing me up a wall. I had to hang up on her though to keep from cussing her ass out."

"You should have cussed her out. That was wrong on so many levels. Not only did she tell her where you were at, she didn't bother to even warn you. That's messed up, and it pissed me off, so I know it pissed you off."

"It did."

"So what happened when Mama showed up?"

"She was on her normal bullshit about God was ready for Daddy, and she's sorry *if* I feel like she did something wrong… yada, yada, yada. I ended up yanking her ass to the floor."

"Oh shit! What led to that?"

"I told her to get out, and she was just sitting there like I was playing with her. I yanked her ass up, and she ended up falling on the floor. I counted her down like she was a kid, and she still just sat there."

"Well, she deserved everything she got plus some."

"Yep. I was way more emotional than I wanted to be the next time I saw her. I wanted her to see me doing well and not being fazed by her presence. I wasn't ready to be confronted by her. It doesn't help that Jakari broke up with me the week before, so I was already sensitive."

"What? Why?"

"He said he needed time to get his issues together. I mean… I told him I wanted to be with him to help him through them. So I kind of forced the issue about us being together when he wasn't ready. I pumped him up to think that he was. When he ran into his dad and left me at the basketball arena in Houston, he realized that he wasn't as ready as I made him believe he was."

"Oh my goodness! That was when you saw Nate again and Noah and TAZ, right?"

"Yeah."

"How did you get home?"

"His uncle came and got me. We actually bonded in that drive. Jakari cares about me. I know that. He made sure I got home, although it wasn't the same way I got there. He left during halftime, and Jasper was picking me up before the game was over. So it wasn't like I was waiting after people had left."

"Damn, Yendi. I'm sorry. Life just messed up all the way around, huh?"

"Yeah. Where's JaCory?"

"I'm on my way home. Terrence picked him up from daycare. It's his weekend."

"Oh okay. Well, let's finally get you a plane ticket to come see me in two weeks. I miss you."

"Yay! Okay. I'll look up flights when I get home."

"Okay. I can't wait to see you. I need friends. All of the people I've befriended are Jakari's family. It would be awkward for me being around them without being able to be around him. Although we aren't on bad terms, I'm hurt and trying to get over him."

"I understand. You know I don't have friends like that either. It's always just me and JaCory. I just got home, so I'll call you back in a little bit."

"Okay."

I ended the call and finally ordered my shake and headed home. My mind went back to Jakari, and I truly wanted to talk to him. I knew it wouldn't be good though. It would only make me long for him more. Grabbing my phone, I blocked his number. The tears fell freely from my eyes, because blocking him from my life and heart hurt like hell. Hearing his voice had me longing for him all over again.

When I walked into my apartment, I flopped on the couch and started looking for places to stay in Pearland. It was right outside of Houston, so it wasn't far from the action. Pearland wasn't nearly as small as where I was. It was about the size of Beaumont, maybe a little bigger. I could handle that though. It was still much smaller than D.C.

The cost of living wasn't much different from where I was, and the district had openings. While I loved being a librarian, I was a certified teacher as well. It wouldn't take too much to get certified in Texas. Plus, they'd allow me to work while I took the necessary classes and passed the state exam. There was always a need for teachers.

I didn't think I would be moving again, but this town was too small for me to be here, existing with Jakari. Although I hadn't seen him, I'd been holed up in my house for three weeks, not going anywhere but to work. I wanted to go to the diner just to see if he was really for real about not being with me, but I talked myself out of it. After my mama came and fucked my mental up, it was definitely out.

I needed to just focus on myself now, like he did. I thought we were better together but maybe that was one-sided. I was better because I wanted to be better for him. I should have wanted that for myself though. I'd considered him to be the healing for my soul, but that was too much pressure on him.

This time, when I started over, I would do it completely for me and not rely on anyone else to make me whole or happy. I was doing that slowly before I met Jakari, but falling for him fucked all that shit up. My soul thought it needed him… It still thought that. That was the reason I had to get away from here. He and his family were too close for me to ever forget him.

When I found an apartment to my liking, I clicked on the link to contact the property management to get a tour. They had an appointment available as soon as Monday evening. That was perfect. I'd leave work at one, get lunch, and be there by four. The place had two bedrooms, a spacious front room and kitchen, and a fireplace. It also had two bathrooms. It looked fairly new as well. This would be my last move if I could help it.

CHAPTER 19

JAKARI

"So you're saying they took it into their own hands to take Tyrese out?" Uncle Storm asked.

"Yes, sir. They didn't want to give the situation time to escalate," I responded.

He nodded repeatedly. "Keep them muthafuckas around in case we ever need them again. I like niggas that be about that action. Fuck talking and warning people. They needed to know the Hendersons ain't to be played with."

"Uncle Mayor, you have an important call from the council," Nesha said, interrupting our meeting.

He rolled his eyes. "If it's about that fucking game room somebody getting cussed the fuck out."

Aunt Jenahra chuckled, and it caused everyone else to laugh. Uncle Marcus stood and followed him out, I supposed in case he was needed. Uncle WJ stood as I sat, and said, "Thank you for bringing Watchful Eyes on board, Jakari Henderson."

Everyone chuckled as they passed a box around the table until it got to me. I frowned slightly, then opened it to see new business cards, nameplates for my door and desk, and a couple of company shirts with 'Jakari Henderson' embroidered in small letters on the front. I smiled and looked around the room at my aunts and uncles. "Thanks, y'all."

"I heard Avery came by the other day. I also heard that you handled it well. God was with him, because I don't know how I would have handled seeing him," Uncle WJ said. "Thankfully, Pop needed me. That caused me to be away from the office. Speaking of Pop," he said, then opened the side door.

When my grandfather walked in, we all stood. That was a surprise. We all applauded his presence, because it was rare that he left home ever since Grandma had died. He lifted his hand, gesturing for us to stop. "Y'all sit down."

We chuckled as the mayor and Uncle Marcus walked back in with frowns on their faces and flopped in their seats. I didn't know what the call was about, but clearly it wasn't on the up and up. "Mayor, do you wanna say something before I get started?"

He quickly popped up from his seat like a jack-in-the-box. "Yeah. These white people finna catch all this hurricane fury as soon as I leave from here. They pissed, because I got the 'black side' of Nome's drainage and shit fixed. They can suck my dick. Sorry, Pop. I'm about to fucking blow up on their asses then resign and tell them to fuck themselves. I paid for that shit out of my pocket. I'm about to let them see just how much the Hendersons boost Nome's finances. I ain't donating to another muthafucking cause unless it benefits us."

Everyone remained quiet for a moment, then Uncle WJ said to Philly, "Pull our resources from the volunteer fire department, the post office maintenance, the county maintenance, and the city. I don't give a fuck about none of that shit if they think they gon' railroad my brother."

Everyone stood and applauded again. "Storm when is the next meeting?" Aunt Tiffany asked.

"Tonight," Uncle Marcus said since Uncle Storm was in his phone.

"We all showing up. Y'all call everybody. Jasper get in touch with Red and tell him to spread the word on the 'black side' of Nome. Fuck those people. This shit gon' be war, and we coming with the big fucking guns. They think because we black, we gon' stand for their shit? They got another thing coming. We run this shit, and it's about time we start acting like it!" Aunt Tiff said.

Her face was red and so was Aunt Jen's. Everybody was so fired up we forgot about whatever Grandpa had to say until he stood. We quieted back down as he said, "I just wanted to let y'all know that I was back."

He laughed, causing us all to calm down and laugh along with him. "Welcome back, Grandpa," I said.

He nodded. "I can't grieve continuously like I've been doing. Thanks, Chrissy, for convincing me that I had more to live for. I miss Joan tremendously, but she lives on through my daughters. Hearing Tiffany go off just now reminded me of her fiery temperament. Having Chrissy and Jen at the house reminds me of her nurturing and caring side, along with her great cooking. I have her in all of you. Thank y'all for being patient with me and taking care of me, until I realized that. Storm, in the words of your mama, go show them who running the fucking show."

That did it. We all got cranked up all over again, until Lennox walked in with Baylor. That ended all thoughts of fucking people up. Everyone was cooing and being all sensitive. However, the minute Decaurey, Tyeis, and Angel walked in with Ellison and Essence, there wasn't an angry emotion in the room. I shook his hand after he gave Ellison to Uncle WJ.

"So they let them out, huh?"

"Yep. They were doing well. They've gained a pound and seven ounces, and their lungs are great."

"That's good. I'm happy for y'all. I know y'all are glad to have them home."

"Absolutely. No more running back and forth to that hospital."

"I feel you, bruh."

The door opened again and my baby brother, Rylan, and our cousin, KJ, walked in with frowns on their faces. "Why we wasn't invited to the party?" Rylan asked as his frown deepened.

Everybody chuckled and spoke to them. I noticed Angel walk over to Rylan and hug him. She was nineteen now, but Rylan was still too advanced for her, in my opinion. However, he hugged her and was being kind to her. That made me happy. "Yeah, you see it."

I frowned and turned back to Decaurey. "See what?"

"They've been talking on the phone."

I frowned. "No shit?"

"Mm hmm. She said she told him of her condition of down syndrome, and they talk about everything. It seems to be an honest friendship, but I know she likes him. I'm sure he knows it too."

"Hmm. That's interesting. What does Tyeis have to say about it?"

"Not much. Ellison and Essence have stolen all her attention."

"Did Angel ever talk to Creed?"

"Oh yeah! She did. He mentioned something about seeing her with me. They had him watching me. Once he saw her, that was a wrap. He found out that his dad knew who I was, so he stopped fucking with that nigga. He apologized to Angel, and he apologized to me. He said if we needed to know anything more, he would tell us. Since Tyrese been popped, ain't nobody moving. It was crazy that those niggas were related and didn't have a problem being with the same woman. Tyeis didn't have a clue about that shit. But this was all Tyrese's vendetta about Reggie and me wife-ing up Tyeis."

He flashed his wedding band, and I shook his hand again. They'd gotten married and didn't tell me. "Y'all muthafuckas! How y'all gon' get married and not say shit?"

"Man, everybody got they own shit going on. Mama, Daddy, Angel, and Jess were there. We'll celebrate another time."

I slapped his hand and hugged him. That shit only made me think about Yendi more. I pulled away from him and went to get a peek at the babies. They'd gotten a little darker, but they looked just like Decaurey, freckles and all. I slowly shook my head as I thought about how he was worried about them not being his.

Before leaving the office, I made my way to Rylan, KJ, and Angel. I spoke to all of them then turned to my brother. "Can I talk to you for a minute?"

"Yeah, what's up?"

I walked away from everyone, and he followed me. "What's up with you and Angel?"

"Nothing. Why?"

"I don't know. Y'all seem extra friendly."

"Yeah. We talk on the phone sometimes. We're just friends. I figured she needed one. All the girls in the family are younger than her, and I know she don't wanna befriend those rowdy ass twins."

I chuckled. "Naw, probably not. You know she feeling you, right?"

"Yeah. She knows I'm talking to somebody though. She's sweet, but I'm not feeling her like that. I call her my lil cousin."

I gave him the side-eye, because I didn't believe him. "You know I ain't tripping if you like her too, right? Just take it slow. She's much younger than you... like eight years. She ain't on your level sexually."

He rubbed the top of his head, indicating I was right. "She uhh mentioned sex and wanting me to be her first."

"What the fuck did you say?"

"That I didn't want to have to fight Decaurey and Tyeis. She said she was grown and could make her own decisions. I like her though. Her disability doesn't bother me. She's beautiful."

I lowered my head and slowly shook it. "What are you gonna do?"

"I don't know. I can't have sex with her without talking to Decaurey and Tyeis about dating her. They probably think I'm too old for her."

"Well, that and too experienced. But from what you told me, maybe not."

"Man, listen. She said some things that made my mouth drop open that night. She caught me way off guard. She nasty, but in an innocent sort of way. It's hard to describe."

"I get it. Just be careful with her."

"I will."

I shook his hand then headed to my truck. Grabbing my phone, I called Yendi. It had been three days since I left her a message and hadn't heard from her. This time it didn't ring several times like before. It sent me straight to voicemail. I knew that on iPhone, it allowed you to leave a message even if you were blocked. It just didn't notify her. I didn't leave another message. I ended the call and accepted that it was really over.

"Happy birthday, Maui!"

"Thanks," she said as she cut her eyes at me.

"Whoa! What did I do?"

"Ms. Odom isn't coming to my party. She hasn't been the same either. She's quiet and withdrawn like she's upset about something. She told me that she would be moving at the end of the semester. I hate that. Y'all aren't together anymore, so it must be something that you did."

I lowered my head as I thought about Yendi and how I had been calling her every day for the past two weeks. Today made a month since the game and since I'd last seen her at the viewing for the video that premiered yesterday. I glanced up at Maui to see the concern etched on her face. I walked away without responding to her and tried calling Yendi. She couldn't leave. I'd never see her again.

Damn. I still didn't feel I was one hundred percent ready, but counseling with Serita was helping tremendously. We would begin and end every session with something positive about Avery. This wasn't about his redemption, but about my freedom from guilt, anger, and hatred. I still had a long way to go, but I couldn't let her leave.

Her phone went straight to voicemail, and I knew I had to go to her place. There was no way I could let her leave here without knowing how much she meant to me. As I made my way to the back door, Uncle Storm asked, "Where you going?"

"See about Yendi."

"It's about time you stopped being a bitch ass nigga. Go get my niece. I miss her."

I rolled my eyes and kept walking. I didn't have time for his foolishness. Yendi was looking forward to Maui's party. Since I broke up with her, she'd been avoiding everyone. Uncle Jasper had asked about her on several occasions, along with Jess, Nesha, and my mama. Yendi was all alone again, and I knew that was taking a toll on her. She'd said that she loved having a sense of family here with my people. I took that from her.

When I got to my truck, my phone rang. It was Nate. We'd talked earlier in the week, and he was wanting to get me out there to Dallas for his next home game. It would take me about seven minutes to get to Yendi, so I could talk to him on the way. "Hello?"

"What's up, dude? What you up to?"

"Going try to get Yendi to talk to me."

"You finna pop up at her place? What if she got company?"

"Then I'm gon' tell her company that I need to talk to her. The fuck you mean?"

He chuckled. "I know that's right. Go get your woman. Jess messaged me, apologizing and letting me know that she could no longer give me permission to be wherever she was. If I showed up, it would be on me. Also, that she had to stop talking to me for the sake of her sanity and relationship with her fiancé. So, she's forcing me to let go."

"I'm sorry, bruh, but that's a good thing."

"Yeah, I know. Holding on to her definitely isn't healthy. I'm gon' still check with you to see how she's doing though. And you know I'm gon' stalk her page until someone else catches my attention."

He chuckled so I did too. "That I know. You gon' get past this eventually."

"I know. Well, I'll let you go so you can handle your business."

"Yeah. I'm almost there. I should be able to go to the game next weekend. I'll let you know how many tickets I need later today or tomorrow."

"A'ight. Good luck, man."

"Thanks. I'ma need it."

He chuckled as he ended the call. I was almost to Yendi's place, and my stomach was churning. I was nervous. I just hoped she would answer the door. After I turned in the lot and saw her car, I breathed out a sigh of relief. I was worried that she wouldn't be home. This woman completed me, and I needed her to know that. I would never get to being one hundred percent good without her. Her presence in my life made me better. It made me want to be better for her.

I got out of the truck and climbed the steps to her unit, feeling the tremble go through my legs. I'd never been this nervous about anything. I took a deep breath when I got to the landing and stood in front of her door. As I was about to knock, I heard the locks disengaging. I didn't know if she'd seen me or if she was about to leave. Since she wasn't taking my calls, she was probably leaving to go somewhere.

When the door opened, she jumped and nearly stumbled backwards at the sight of me. I put my hands at her waist to steady her. She looked into my eyes then pulled away. "Jakari, what are you doing here?"

"I was coming to see about you, Yendi. You haven't been taking my calls."

"Isn't that what you wanted? For me to leave you alone and move on with my life? That's what I'm trying to do. Why are you here, hindering my progress? I can't see and talk to you if you want me to move on."

"Can we talk, baby?" I asked as I grabbed her hand.

She swallowed hard as her hand trembled in mine. Gently pulling me inside, she closed the door, then set her purse on the countertop. We went to her couch and sat, her hand still in mine. I immediately tried to explain and be totally transparent with her as Serita had suggested at our last counseling session.

"I miss you, Yendi. I was a fool to push you away. I've been going to counseling. I've had four sessions so far, and they are helping me tremendously. I've even had a conversation with my father. So much has changed in the past month, but one thing I realized was that no matter how much help I got, no matter how much better I got mentally, I still need you. I love you, girl. I know I fucked up royally, but I need you to take me back."

She frowned slightly. "Take you back?"

"Yes. I need you, Yendi, and I know you need me."

"So in a month's time, you're saying you're able to handle a relationship?"

"I'm saying that after four successful counseling sessions, I'm ready to try again. I will still be going to talk to her weekly for the next two months. I don't want to be a fool and lose you. You're the only thing missing in my life. Tell me I'm missing in yours too."

She pulled her hand away from mine and lowered her head, allowing tears to escape her. I didn't know if that was a good thing or a bad thing, but I refused to leave from here without giving my all to get her back.

CHAPTER 20
YENDI

I was sitting on my couch, doing my best to hold in my feelings, but I was failing miserably. The tears were streaming down my cheeks. While this was what I wanted, I didn't know if I could trust Jakari with my heart again. This was so hard. Lifting my head, I stared into his hopeful eyes. "Jakari, I don't know. I don't know if I can take that risk again. The past month has been so hard for me."

"I'm so sorry, baby. I hate what I did to you."

"You don't understand," I said as I wiped my face dry. "I'm moving. My mother showed up here and as long as she knows where I live, I won't have peace. I was two seconds from beating the fuck out of her." I took a deep breath then stared up at him. "As much as I love you, I can't take you back."

He gently caressed my hand between his and lowered his gaze to them as he asked, "Why?"

"Unfortunately, I don't know if I can trust you with my heart again. I didn't just lose you. I lost a family. Uncle Jasper, Uncle Mayor, your mother, the girls… I didn't feel comfortable maintaining a relationship with them without having one with you. I told you to handle me gently, Jakari. That shit wasn't gentle. I crashed and burned. My mama showing up at my door sank me even further."

The tears started all over again, but the cries leaving my lips were ones of gut-wrenching pain. "I needed you! I needed your arms to fall into. I needed you to tell me that everything would be okay. I needed you!"

Jakari quickly pulled me to him and kissed my head. "You have me now, baby."

I fought against him, but he refused to let me go. "Jakari!"

"No. I can't let go. Let me prove to you that I can do this. You don't have to make a commitment to me, Yendi. Just let me come around. Answer when I call. Let me date you. I know I can prove to you how much progress I've made. Please, Yendi. I'm begging you, baby."

I stopped fighting and relaxed in his embrace and how good it felt to be in his arms. "I'm moving to Pearland. I went looked at an apartment Monday and put down a deposit. When the semester is over, I'm moving."

"Let me work hard to change your mind, baby. I'll never hang you out to dry like that again. You right. I didn't handle you gently. I fucked up. I can't say that enough. I thought keeping you around would be selfish. I couldn't see past that. Now I see that what I *did* was completely selfish. Leaving you alone when you'd given me your heart was cruel. I fucked your soul up. I fucked my own soul up, rejecting the one person that I want to be better for."

I lifted my head and stared into his eyes as he wiped my tears away with his thumb. I closed my eyes briefly. I still loved him. Did I want to take a chance on him again? I reopened them and said, "I don't know if you read my text message, but I wasn't angry about you leaving me. Even in your moment of turmoil, embarrassment, and anger, you made sure I got home. That was love, Jakari. I don't know if I would say safely since Uncle Jasper was high as hell."

He smiled slightly. "I read your message repeatedly. I let my therapist and Jessica read it too. For the record, they both thought I was a fool for distancing myself from you. I didn't know Unc was high... wait a minute. I'm lying. Unc is high more often than not. He's probably a safer driver when he's high."

HEALING FOR MY SOUL

I couldn't help but smile. "He said the same thing. Your uncle is crazy."

A soft giggle escaped me as I thought about our conversation that night. When I looked up at Jakari again, he laid his lips on mine. He pulled away, leaving me wanting more. "I'm sorry. I've wanted to do that since you opened the door. I want you to know that I will go at your pace. Whatever you want to do is what I'll do, except give up. I'll never stop trying to prove my love, devotion, and loyalty to you."

"Jakari."

"Yeah, baby?"

"Love me gently."

"I plan to. I'll never take you for granted—"

I pressed my fingers against his lips then slid two of my fingers in his mouth. "No, baby. Love me gently."

He pulled my fingers from his mouth slowly and bit his bottom lip then leaned in and kissed me, taking my fucking breath away like only he could. He pulled away from me and pulled my shirt over my head. He was quiet, but every move he made seemed intentional. There was purpose behind his actions. There always was. That purpose and intent was plain as day. It was one of intense pleasure and love.

He stood and pulled off his shirt then his pants. "I want to love you gently like you requested, but I didn't bring any rubbers. If you wanna wait, I'm cool with that, but I do want to please you."

He acted like this would be our first time without using a condom. I stood from my seat and slowly pulled his underwear down and over his erection, going to my knees in the process. I allowed his dick to slide all over my face until it reached my mouth, then slowly sucked it inside as I listened to Jakari's heavy breathing. My eyes rolled to the back of my head as I sucked his dick painfully slow with extreme suction. I swore my dimples would be more pronounced after this.

"Mmmm," he moaned.

That shit always got to me, and he knew it. His moans turned me on like no other. They were so sexy sounding. They didn't sound soft or feminine, but they sounded extremely passionate and filled with desire and enjoyment. I moaned right back as I took more of his dick into my mouth. He placed his hand on my head, gently guiding me. I knew what he desired though.

I released his dick, letting the saliva fall from my lips then took off my wig. He loved my natural state whenever we fucked or made love. A slow smile graced his lips. As I was about to take him in again, he said, "I'm supposed to be loving *you* gently, not the other way around. Let me take care of you, Yendi."

He helped me from the floor then took off my leggings and panties. When he sat on the couch, I frowned slightly. It still seemed like I would be the one working. Not that I had an issue with that, but he was supposed to be…"

"Come here. Stop thinking and just slide down this dick. I got the rest."

He stroked his dick as I made my way to him. After straddling him, he positioned his dick right where I needed it. He slid inside of me as I lowered on him. The moment I did, he slumped a bit more and gripped my ass cheeks, causing me to lean over to him, then began lifting and lowering me on his dick. "Oooh, Jakari. I missed you so much."

"I missed you too, Yendi," he said as he stroked me slowly but firmly.

My eyes rolled shut as my pussy twitched in excitement just that quickly. She was squeezing him, hoping he would never try to leave again. "Oooh, I'm about to cum, Jakari. Oh shiiiit!"

It felt like I'd dropped an entire glass of water on him down there, but he didn't seem to mind that at all. His pace quickened, and his stroke became a little rougher. He was so quiet. I lifted my head to stare at him. When I saw the glossiness of his eyes, it moved my soul.

"Yendi, I thought I lost you forever. To be in this position right now is so overwhelming. Fuck! I love you so much."

When the tear dropped from one of his eyes, I kissed where it had fallen then licked his face as mine fell as well. "I love you too… more than I've ever loved anyone."

"I believe you. I can feel it. It's the same for me. No woman knows what it means to be loved by me but you. I want it to always be that way. No more walking away. No more running from my problems. I'm going to face them head on, with you by my side."

My tears were free-falling and dropping to his face. I rested my forehead against his as he stroked me even more passionately, being sure to graze my G-spot with every stroke. His upward curve was perfect for that. As my legs trembled, I closed my eyes again. "Baby, oh shit. Jakariiii!"

I came hard. I could barely control the movements my body made. In one swift motion, Jakari released me, letting me fall sideways to the couch and hooked my leg in the crook of his arm, pushing it toward my shoulder as he entered me swiftly. "Can I fuck you, Yendi?"

"Please do," I said as a shiver went up my spine.

He laid his lips on mine and began fucking me like it would be the last time, knocking the damn wind out of me. "Oh fuck!" he yelled.

When he licked my ankle and the top of my foot, my body heated up, but the moment he licked my big toe and pulled it into his mouth, my body went up in flames. "Oh yeeeesss!" I screamed as I came for the third time.

"Mm hmm. Drown this dick, Yendi," he said in a low voice as he released my foot from his grasp.

I opened my eyes to stare into his, but he lowered his face to my breast and began sucking my nipple. As he did, his pace slowed a little. He pulled out of me completely, making my pussy want to cry a damn river. He said he needed me, but I needed him even more. My body, mind, nor heart knew how to function without him.

He stood from the couch and grabbed my hand, pulling me up as well. When he stooped, I knew he was about to lift me. What I didn't expect was for him to lower me on his dick. This nigga was strong as hell if he was going to lift and lower me on his dick without a wall to brace me up. Proving he was just that, he lifted me and lowered me repeatedly while he sucked my nipples, one at a time.

The lifts weren't dramatic, but it was enough to enjoy the moment. I pulled his head from my breasts and sloppily kissed him, sliding my tongue all over his fucking mouth. He enjoyed that thoroughly, because he stopped stroking me and walked to the nearest wall, slamming my back against it. When his fingers graced my asshole, he began stroking me with his dick again. "Ooooh, yeeeesss! Fuck me, baby."

No more words were spoken. Jakari fucked me hard against the wall, chipping away at my cervix like Andy did that wall in the movie *The Shawshank Redemption*. My screams were loud and hopefully, my neighbors weren't home. If they were, they were in for a porn they would never forget. Pulling out of me, he said, "Lean over the couch so I can see this ass jiggle on my shit."

I supposed I wasn't moving quite fast enough, because he shoved me over the back of it and entered me. I was moving slowly on purpose though, trying to unleash the savage beast in him. "Stop fucking teasing me, Yendi. Fuck!"

He slapped one ass cheek after the other then shoved them upward to watch the action. "This some beautiful shit, girl. I'm about to nut."

"Wait for me. I'm about to cum again tooooo," I responded.

"Come on then before I mess around and fill this pussy up."

His words ignited a fire in me and within seconds, my pussy was clenching him, begging him to stay. And he did…

"Yay! You made it!" Maui yelled.

I chuckled as Jakari placed his hand at the small of my back. After fucking me again in the shower, we somehow got dressed and made our way to Maui's party. I'd bought her a bridle for her horse, books, and a new Kindle Fire. She was excited about having another device to download her eBooks to. I hugged her tightly. "Happy birthday, sweetheart. So, what was the big surprise?"

"I got a new car! The exact car I wanted! My mayor daddy is the best!"

I laughed then said, "Congratulations! That's a great sweet sixteen gift."

"Better than great!"

She glanced at Jakari and winked then went to put her gifts with the others. I turned to Jakari and kissed his lips, happy that we were going to give us another shot. "Let me go and speak to everyone else."

Before I could walk away, I heard, "It's about time you brought my niece back."

I immediately knew it was the mayor. I turned around and smiled big. "Hey, Uncle Mayor!"

He smiled and leaned over so I could throw my arms around him. I could hear his chuckle in my ear. "Hey, niece. I'm glad you're back. That boy was lost without you with his stubborn self."

"Mm hmm. I wonder where I get that shit from," Jakari said.

"From your stubborn ass Uncle WJ."

Uncle WJ shoved him then hugged me as we all laughed. "I hear y'all had to put these folks out here on notice," I said to them.

"Hell yeah. They had to straighten up and fly right. They learned real quick that this was Hendersonville when WJ started pulling our money out of shit. Racist muthafuckas. I almost resigned on their asses, but Tiffany went off Joan Henderson style in that meeting, telling them I was the best thing that ever happened to Nome and that it was about time somebody looked out for the black folks around here that had been forgotten about for years. Shiiiid, after that, the county cut *me* a check to reimburse me for the work I had done with the drainage."

"I'm glad you didn't resign. They need someone with fire in them that can't be ran over. And who gon' run over a *Perfect Storm*?" I asked, quoting the title of the movie.

Uncle Mayor quickly caught on. "No fucking body. The ones that tried got done up and drowned. Don't fucking play wit' it. See… you, Jess, Tyeis, and Nesha gon' keep me gassed up. Gabriel… the Perfect Storm. I like that shit."

"Aww hell. Yendi, you done messed around and gave that nigga some ammunition?"

I turned to see Uncle Jasper heading my way. Throwing my arms around him, I hugged him tightly. While we hugged, he said, "I told you, didn't I? You ain't lost another family, baby girl. We here and gon' always be here."

I pulled away from him as the tears filled my eyes. When I did, he asked, "You still fucking with HJ?" He pulled a blunt from his shirt pocket and held it in the air. "I bet you could use a hit of this shit."

I laughed loudly as Uncle Mayor snatched the blunt from him and walked off. Uncle Jasper slowly shook his head and pulled out another one. I swore, he stayed stocked. "I could use a hit, but I'm still fucking around with HJ. I took a risk last time. I can't afford to chance it again."

"Damn. Oh well. You can't stand around me for too long though, or it won't matter if you smoke or not. You gon' fuck around and get a contact high. If they drug test you, it'll be like you had a spliff anyway."

I smiled and shook my head as he walked away. After greeting Aunt Tiff, Uncle Kenny, Uncle Marcus, and Aunt Jen, I found Mrs. Chrissy. She was seated with her sisters-in-law, Olivia, Aspen, Chasity, Syn, and Keisha. This family was huge, and I couldn't be happier being around all of them. It was a guaranteed good time when they were all together it seemed.

When she saw me, she stood from her seat on the couch as I waved at everyone else. She approached me with her arms outstretched. I went right to them and nearly cried. Her embrace was so warm and inviting, something I never felt from my own mother. It made me realize that the affectionate moments with my mother were nonexistent my entire life. She never really showed me affection. This was clearly something I needed by the way it affected me.

As she pulled away, she kissed my cheek then wiped the lipstick off. I smiled at her and said, "I'm so glad to be back."

"And I'm beyond ecstatic to have you back. That means that my son has gotten better mentally and realized that he can't live happily without you. You are an important piece in his puzzle, and I truly believe that he will be blessed abundantly simply because of you."

The tears I was so desperately trying to hold back fell down my cheeks. *Jesus Christ.* This was definitely where I was supposed to be. My doubts about Jakari had dissipated in a matter of minutes and now his mother was giving me the confirmation that I'd made the right decision by accepting him back into my life.

"Don't cry, baby." She put her hands to my cheeks. "Jakari doesn't enter into anything without strong conviction. That includes relationships. I haven't seen him with a girlfriend in a long time, but I am absolutely sure that you will be his last. God has ordained this, and I feel like you need him just as much as he needs you."

"Thank you, Mama Chrissy."

She smiled as her eyes watered and kissed my forehead. "Chrissy, why you got my niece over here crying and shit? Niece Yen, she hurt yo' feelings? Does the Perfect Storm need to make an appearance?"

I smiled and chuckled. It was obvious it was Uncle Mayor without me even turning to see him. He was just the distraction I needed. "No. She was speaking life into me and confirming some things for me. She don't need or deserve that kind of action, Mayor."

He smirked and slid his arm around me then pulled me away from her, bringing me off to the side away from everyone. "I'm glad Jakari came to his senses. He clowns around a lot, but I could tell he wasn't happy. He made seeing after Chrissy and his brothers his responsibility, but he put his life on hold. He needed to be free, and you were the one to free him. Real shit."

"Thank you. He's been that for me too."

Jakari walked up and grabbed me by the hand, pulling me away from Storm. I laughed as he frowned. "Jakari don't get fucked up. I'll set Gabriel to the side real quick and become an angel of war on your ass."

"I'm Michael, so back the hell up," Uncle Jasper said.

I wasn't sure what the whole angel references were about, but they started going at each other as Jakari pulled me away from them. "You sure you want to be a part of this bullshit all the time?"

I chuckled as I slid my hands over his beard and pulled his face to mine, kissing his lips. "Absolutely. I love them already."

"I can tell. They love you too. But the real kicker... I love you more."

I smiled big. "I love you too, Jakari."

"I need more time with you tonight. Are you really serious about moving? That's like two months away."

"I am, unless you can convince me to stay. Then me losing my deposit will be worth it."

"I might as well give you that deposit money back then. You ain't going no fucking where. The only place you moving to is my house in Henderson Village. So either you can call them now or later, but the outcome will remain the same. No point in stalling. It's inevitable. Besides, after you forced me to fill you with love, you might be pregnant."

"Forced you?" I chuckled as my eyebrows lifted. "How in God's name did I force you?"

"Girl, that wasn't in God's name. Don't be putting that shit on Him. That was that satanic suction... them Lucifer lips... that demonic depth... that devilish drip..."

"Jakari!" I yelled with laughter. "I get the point, nigga! That damned demon dick played a huge role too!"

I covered my mouth, realizing how loud I was. My face heated up as he laughed. "Don't be embarrassed now. Let everybody know how I fuck up them insides up, girl."

I slapped his chest as he pulled me to him, glancing at Uncle Mayor as he stared at us with his lip turned up. "I'm so happy you're back in my life, Yendi. Call and get your deposit back. Tell them you found a better opportunity in Big City Nome, Texas that you can't fucking pass up on your best day."

"Is that right? Cocky ass."

"I might be cocky, but ain't that shit true?"

I bit my bottom lip, then gently sucked his bottom lip between mine. "Hell yeah," I said after releasing him. "I'll call Monday, but what about my mama knowing where I live?"

"See, you ain't listening to me. You live in Sour Lake right now. I said to tell them you found a better opportunity in Big City Nome, Texas. Yo' mama don't know shit about Hendersonville. Even if she did, she gon' have to go through an army of muthafuckas before she can get to you. Yendi, at the end of the semester, move in with me. For real. You can move now, but I know you'll be more comfortable with that by the end of the semester."

"My lease is up then."

"Fuck that lease. You know who I am, girl? I help run a nationally known company, supplying these people with rice, roux, rice dressing mix, grass, and rodeo steers. Who gon' check me, girl? My grandpa own the company. My uncle is the CEO. My other uncle is the fucking mayor. They betta act they know who they dealing with. You saying you'll move in now?"

"I'm saying I hope you don't make me regret this."

"You know how many people would whup my ass if I hurt you again? Na, what moving company you wanna use?"

EPILOGUE
JAKARI

TWO MONTHS LATER...

"Rope that shit, Rylan!" Uncle Jasper yelled.

Aunt Tiff wanted to put on her annual Christmas rodeo behind Grandpa's house again, but it was too damn cold. So she decided to wait a couple of months and have it in February when the kids were on their winter break. I wish they had that shit when I was in school. They had mid-winter break for Christmas, winter break in February, and spring break in April.

It was still cold but not as cold as it was Christmas day. The family was putting on a show, and Yendi was in awe. She'd never been to a rodeo, so watching me drive the tractor, move hay bales, and tend to the animals was interesting as hell to her. She asked so many questions, and I was willing to answer every one of them.

Rylan had roped a steer and flipped him to tie him down. He was competing in tie-down roping at the rodeos now. My family was amazing as hell when it came to this rodeo shit. Aunt Tiff had all our family friends here, and I had a feeling this shit was going to get bigger and bigger every year. This was the second one, but I was more than sure it would be a family tradition now. Once Aunt Tiff got tired of it, her daughter Milana or Uncle Kenny's daughter, Karima, would surely take it over.

Yendi and her sister Janay were talking amongst themselves for a while, watching the show... particularly Christian. I wasn't sure how old Janay was, but Christian had just turned thirty-one. I knew Janay was younger than Yendi, and my baby was thirty-three. They couldn't be that far apart in age.

We'd been living together for the past two months and getting along better than ever. I'd had my last counseling session with Serita three days ago, and the better man I'd become was the best present I could have given myself. Yendi had been doing better as well. She hadn't heard from her mother, nor had she talked to her sister, Marie, again. She said she would in time, but that time wasn't now. I assured her I would be there for her whenever that time came.

Yendi turned to me and snuggled against me. "I have a late birthday gift for you in my pocket."

I frowned slightly. "Girl, my birthday was a month ago. What'chu talkin' 'bout?"

"Well, I didn't have it then, because it took a little while to get shipped."

My frown deepened. She had me all kinds of confused. She pulled out a rectangular box as her sister stared on, along with my mama, who was on the other side of me. I pulled the wrapping paper off to reveal a plain white box. "I hope you didn't buy me nothing expensive, girl."

I'd bought her a diamond earring, necklace, and bracelet set that she nearly came on herself about for Christmas, and she kept saying that she had to buy me gifts to equal up to that. She just didn't know. She'd go broke trying to keep up with me.

She giggled. "It's expensive... very expensive. Just open it!"

I pulled the lid off the box and saw a fucking pregnancy test sitting in white tissue paper. The screen on it read, PREGNANT. My head snapped up as I stared at her. We hadn't used a condom in months, and my shit was firing off at her cervix like it was dart practice every chance it got. I looked back at the test, at a loss for words.

"Damn, baby," I finally got out. "I'm gon' be a father."

I closed my eyes for a moment then opened them and pulled her in my arms and kissed her lips. She placed her hands on my face and said, "Yes, you are. A wonderful one."

"Congratulations, son! I'm gon' be a MiMi!"

I chuckled and hugged my mama as Aunt Tiff said in the mic, "We have another Henderson on the way! Congratulations Jakari and Yendi!"

I frowned. "Don't frown, baby. She was the only one who knew before you. I wanted her to make the announcement to the family. And more good news... Uncle WJ offered me a job in public relations with the business to help Aunt Aspen. What do you think?"

"I think you should do whatever makes you happy. I can't think about that right now though," I said as everybody was congratulating me. "All I can think about is how you carrying my baby."

I kissed her lips again as Rylan approached. "Congratulations, bruh! I'm gon' be an Uncle Ry Ry."

"You know the baby won't be able to pronounce the letter R for a while. You'll be Uncle Y Y."

He chuckled. "That's cool too. I'm wit' it."

Angel appeared at his side, and he hugged her as she said, "You did so good!"

"Thank you, baby girl."

She stared at him for a moment, then smiled and walked away. That was obviously some kind of silent communication. He watched her walk away then turned back to me. "I'm almost twenty-eight now. She won't be twenty until October. What am I doing?"

"She's grown. Y'all haven't slept together yet, have you?"

"No. She's pressuring me though. Staring at me all the time, saying nasty shit on the phone, and discreetly touching me. I still ain't talked to Decaurey and Tyeis."

"Well, sounds like you need to talk to them soon."

"Yeah," he said as he slid his hand over his waves.

"You did good out there. You thinking of a career doing that?"

"I don't know. Probably just a lil side hustle."

I nodded as I pulled Yendi closer to me. "Congratulations, sister-in-

HEALING FOR MY SOUL

law," Rylan said then hugged her. He turned back to me. "I'll get at'chu later, bruh."

I nodded as I chuckled. Christian had made his way over and was talking to Janay. I didn't know how that developed. Maybe they'd talked the last time she came to town. She had her son with her this time, and they were leaving tomorrow. Giving my attention to my baby as Uncle Storm and Uncle Jasper fought over who would be the baby's godfather, I pulled her to me and coaxed her to sit on my lap.

"I'm so happy, baby. We've come a long way in a short amount of time. I wanna marry you before the baby gets here. I'm gonna ask the right way, but I ain't up for surprises. I want you to know exactly what my plans are regarding us. We can get married at the barn when it warms up a bit more."

She kissed my lips and took it further by sliding her tongue to mine. I gripped her ass as she gave me the business right here in front of everybody. She was gon' fuck around and find out that I didn't give a shit about public displays of affection when it came to her. Fuck this rodeo. We'd be putting on a bedroom rodeo in a hot ass minute.

When she pulled away, she said, "Whenever you're ready to celebrate, so am I."

I stood, forcing her to stand and told everybody bye. They all chuckled, knowing what was about to take place. She told her sister something as I pulled her away. "Jakari, for real?"

"You said whenever I was ready. I'm past that, baby. I need to feel that hot pussy sliding all over my face."

I stopped walking and slid my hand between her legs. Her knees buckled as slid my arm around her waist. "Mm. See, you ready too. Got you cumming on yourself, wasting my shit."

"Ooooh shit. Take me to the truck and fuck me there."

"Keep playing and you gon' get fucked right here," I said, then stooped and picked her up.

I continued to the truck, gently nibbling on her neck. Once inside, I slid my seat back and reclined it. I pulled out my dick and stroked him fiercely. "Come on, Yendi. Quit playing."

She pulled off her leggings, straddled me, and slid down my dick, letting me feel that hot wet shit. My eyes closed, and I bit my bottom lip as she fucked my shit up. When the horn blared, it broke my concentration, and I fired off. "Fuck, girl. That shit got too good. Let's get home so I can get at you right. You got me anxious as fuck."

She giggled and slid to the passenger seat. "I'm happier than I've ever been Jakari. Thank you for doing just what you said you would do. You proved I could trust you. You helped heal my soul, baby. As long as you are in my life, no one else matters, except our baby."

"I love you, Yendi. I'm happy as hell too. I didn't know how bad I needed the love of a woman until you came along. Thank you for making me want to be better. You healed my soul too. Now let's get home so I can destroy that pussy."

The End

If you did not read the author's note at the beginning, please go back and do so before leaving a review. 😊

FROM THE AUTHOR...

This story was hard as hell for me. For those of you that follow me, you are aware of my father's death. I lost my dad on September 30, 2023, the day after I released Don't Walk Away, book 17 of this series. The last two months of his life were a struggle for him; physically, mentally, and emotionally. Those two months and the months after were difficult for me as well.

I was extremely close to my dad. I talked to him every day and saw him every other day. He was one of my biggest cheerleaders, although he wasn't a reader. He said he could never read my books, knowing that I write those nasty sex scenes. Not his daughter. LOL! However, he always passed out my business cards and kept up with my releases, wanting to know their debut ranking.

I started writing this book two weeks after his death, and it proved to be more difficult than I thought it would be. I purged myself through Yendi. Everything she was dealing with are things I have been dealing with for the past four, almost five months (since August 3, 2023). I changed names and altered situations a little to protect identities, but it's my story to tell. The final scene with Yendi and her mother is the only scene that doesn't have any truth aspects, but it's how I imagined that would go down if it happened.

FROM THE AUTHOR...

Now to the story! Ugh!

Jakari's issues were so understandable. I couldn't imagine dealing with knowing my father was a pedophile. It would be extremely hard for me to accept and to have a relationship with my dad after that. The way it affected his life, especially after the situation in the prologue, was sad, but his reactions were so realistic to me.

The way Yendi blew into his life like a fresh breeze was beautiful despite his initial conversation with her. LOL! The way she felt for him was so spiritual. Her willingness to be there for him before she even knew what he was dealing with was powerful. A lot of times, we as women do this, but we do it for the wrong men. She knew that Jakari was worth it, and eventually, he proved that he was.

Per usual, the mayor came through with the bullshit. Jasper was hilarious, and I was glad he was there to offer advice and wise words through his high-ass thoughts. LOL! The twins didn't have much to say in this book, surprisingly. Maui and Ashanni said it was their time to shine. They were so sweet. I totally enjoyed writing them.

There are *so* many stories that could come from this book! So we have Nate and his obsession with Jess, then there's Rylan and Decaurey's bonus daughter, Angel, and finally, Christian and Yendi's sister, Janay. I can also see Ashanni and Bryson possibly being down the line as well. However, I do believe Nate will be next. Be looking for that story early next year. Then we'll get back to Hendersonville.

I truly hope that you enjoyed this drama-filled ride that probably had your feelings all over the place. As always, I gave it my all. Whether you liked it or not, please take the time to leave a review on Amazon and/or Goodreads and wherever else this book is sold.

There's also an amazing playlist on Apple Music and Spotify for this book, under the same title that includes some great R&B tracks to tickle your fancy.

Please keep up with me on Facebook, Instagram, and TikTok (@authormonicawalters), Twitter (@monlwalters), and Clubhouse (@monicawalters). You can also visit my Amazon author page at www.amazon.com/author/monica.walters to view my releases.

FROM THE AUTHOR...

Please subscribe to my webpage for updates and sneak peeks of upcoming releases! https://authormonicawalters.com.

For live discussions, giveaways, and inside information on upcoming releases, join my Facebook group, Monica's Romantic Sweet Spot at https://bit.ly/2P2l06X.

OTHER TITLES BY MONICA WALTERS

Standalones

Love Like a Nightmare

Forbidden Fruit (An Erotic Novella)

Say He's the One

Only If You Let Me (a spin-off of Say He's the One)

On My Way to You (An Urban Romance) (a spin-off of The Revelations of Ryan, Jr.)

Any and Everything for Love

Savage Heart (A KeyWalt Crossover Novel with Shawty You for Me by T. Key)

I'm In Love with a Savage (A KeyWalt Crossover Novel with Trade It All by T. Key) (a spin-off of Savage Heart)

Don't Tell Me No (An Erotic Novella)

To Say, I Love You: A Short Story Anthology with the Authors of BLP

Drive Me to Ecstasy

Whatever It Takes: An Erotic Novella

When You Touch Me

When's the Last Time?

Best You Ever Had

Deep As It Goes (A KeyWalt Crossover Novel with Perfect Timing by T. Key)

The Shorts: A BLP Anthology with the Authors of BLP (Made to Love You- Collab with Kay Shanee)

All I Need is You (A KeyWalt Crossover Novel with Divine Love by T. Key)

This Love Hit Different (A KeyWalt Crossover Novel with Something New by T. Key) (a spin-off of All I Need is You)

Until I Met You

Marry Me Twice

Last First Kiss (a spin-off of Marry Me Twice)

Nobody Else Gon' Get My Love (A KeyWalt Crossover Novel with Better Than Before by T. Key)

Love Long Overdue (A KeyWalt Crossover Novel with Distant Lover by T. Key) (a spin-off of Nobody Else Gon' Get My Love)

Next Lifetime

Fall Knee-Deep In It

Unwrapping Your Love: The Gift

Who Can I Run To

You're Always on My Mind (a spin-off of Who Can I Run To)

Stuck On You

Full Figured 18 with Treasure Hernandez (Love Won't Let Me Wait)

It's Just a Date: A Billionaire Baby Romance (stand-alone series with C. Monet, Iesha Bree, Kimberly Brown, and Kay Shanee)

You Make Me Feel (a spin-off of Stuck On You) (coming soon!)

The Sweet Series

Bitter Sweet

Sweet and Sour

Sweeter Than Before

Sweet Revenge

Sweet Surrender

Sweet Temptation

Sweet Misery

Sweet Exhale

Never Enough (A Sweet Series Update)

Sweet Series: Next Generation

Can't Run From Love

Access Denied: Luxury Love

Still: Your Best

Sweet Series: Kai's Reemergence

Beautiful Mistake

Favorite Mistake

Motives and Betrayal Series

Ulterior Motives

Ultimate Betrayal

Ultimatum: #lovemeorleaveme, Part 1

Ultimatum: #lovemeorleaveme, Part 2

Written Between the Pages Series

The Devil Goes to Church Too

The Book of Noah (A KeyWalt Crossover Novel with The Flow of Jah's Heart by T. Key)

The Revelations of Ryan, Jr. (A KeyWalt Crossover Novel with All That Jazz by T. Key)

The Rebirth of Noah

Behind Closed Doors Series

Be Careful What You Wish For

You Just Might Get It

Show Me You Still Want It

The Country Hood Love Stories

8 Seconds to Love

Breaking Barriers to Your Heart

Training My Heart to Love You

The Country Hood Love Stories: The Hendersons

Blindsided by Love

Ignite My Soul

Come and Get Me

In Way Too Deep

You Belong to Me

Found Love in a Rider

Damaged Intentions: The Soul of a Thug

Let Me Ride

Better the Second Time Around

I Wish I Could Be The One

I Wish I Could Be The One 2

Put That on Everything: A Henderson Family Novella

What's It Gonna Be?

Someone Like You (2nd Generation story)

A Country Hood Christmas with the Hendersons (Novella)

Where Is the Love (2nd Generation story)

Don't Walk Away (2nd Generation story)

The Berotte Family Series

Love On Replay

Deeper Than Love

Something You Won't Forget

I'm The Remedy

Love Me Senseless

I Want You Here

Don't Fight The Feeling

When You Dance

I'm All In

Give Me Permission

Force of Nature

Say You Love Me

Where You Should Be

Hard To Love

Made in the USA
Coppell, TX
20 February 2025

46195488R00128